D0884769

A FORTNIGHT BEFORE THE FROST

Sigurd Hoel

The poet André Bjerke said at the death of SIGURD HOEL (1890-1960): 'If he had written in English, he would have had a world reputation'. Hoel's novels certainly transcend their local settings, as the narrative turns into a deep-probing psychological quest.

A key to Hoel's major novels, as exemplified by *A Fortnight Before the Frost*, is his use of the insights offered by psychoanalysis. As the novel's action proceeds, layer upon layer of hidden motives are unveiled, resulting in what Hoel himself called a 'figurative representation of an analysis'. Significantly, the book was written at a time when Hoel was in analysis with Wilhelm Reich, and on one level it portrays, through the Holmen-Ramstad antagonism, the love-hate relationship between Hoel and Reich.

But chiefly the novel enacts a search for the forces which determine people's lives. Holmen's behaviour is repeatedly traced back to a childhood trauma. The inevitable return of the repressed is accompanied by scenes of violence. The countervailing Reich-inspired theme of redemption through eros offers a welcome relief from these dark forces of fate.

SVERRE LYNGSTAD has published several volumes of criticism, including *Sigurd Hoel's Fiction* (1984) and *Knut Hamsun, Novelist* (2005). Among his numerous translations are Sigurd Hoel's *The Troll Circle* (1991) and *Meeting at the Milestone* (2002), Kjell Askildsen's *A Sudden Liberating Thought* (Norvik Press, 1994), Arne Garborg's *Weary Men* (1999), Dag Solstad's *Shyness and Dignity* (2006), and Knut Hamsun's *Growth of the Soil* (2007). Dr. Lyngstad is the recipient of several prizes and awards, and has been honoured by the King of Norway with the St Olav Medal and the Knight's Cross, First Class, of the Royal Norwegian Order of Merit.

Some other books from Norvik Press

Kjell Askildsen: *A Sudden Liberating Thought* (translated by Sverre Lyngstad)

Victoria Benedictsson: *Money* (translated by Sarah Death)

Hjalmar Bergman: *Memoirs of a Dead Man* (translated by Neil Smith)

Jens Bjørneboe: *Moment of Freedom* (translated by Esther Greenleaf Mürer)

Jens Bjørneboe: *Powderhouse* (translated by Esther Greenleaf Mürer)

Jens Bjørneboe: *The Silence* (translated by Esther Greenleaf Mürer)

Johan Borgen: *The Scapegoat* (translated by Elizabeth Rokkan)

Fredrika Bremer: *The Colonel's Family* (translated by Sarah Death)

Camilla Collett: *The District Governor's Daughters* (translated by Kirsten Seaver)

Kerstin Ekman: *Witches' Rings* (translated by Linda Schenck)

Kerstin Ekman: *The Spring* (translated by Linda Schenck)

Kerstin Ekman: *The Angel House* (translated by Sarah Death)

Kerstin Ekman: *City of Light* (translated by Linda Schenck)

Arne Garborg: *The Making of Daniel Braut* (translated by Marie Wells)

Knut Hamsun: *Selected Letters* (2 vols.) (edited and translated by James McFarlane and Harald Næss)

Jonas Lie: *The Family at Gilje* (translated by Marie Wells) (2011)

Runar Schildt: *The Meat-Grinder and Other Stories* (translated by Anna-Liisa and Martin Murrell)

Amalie Skram: *Lucie* (translated by Katherine Hanson and Judith Messick)

Amalie and Erik Skram: *Caught in the Enchanter's Net: Selected Letters* (edited and translated by Janet Garton)

August Strindberg: *The People of Hemsö* (translated by Peter Graves) (2011)

August Strindberg: *The Red Room* (translated by Peter Graves)

August Strindberg: *Tschandala* (translated by Peter Graves)

Hanne Marie Svendsen: *Under the Sun* (translated by Marina Allemano)

Hjalmar Söderberg: *Martin Birck's Youth* (translated by Tom Ellett)

Hjalmar Söderberg: *Selected Stories* (translated by Carl Lofmark)

Anton Tammsaare: *The Misadventures of the New Satan*

Elin Wägner: *Penwoman* (translated by Sarah Death)

A FORTNIGHT BEFORE THE FROST

by

Sigurd Hoel

Translated from the Norwegian
by

Sverre Lyngstad

Norvik Press
2010

Originally published in Norwegian by Gyldendal Norsk Forlag as
Fjorten dager før frostnettene (1935).

Translation © Sverre Lyngstad 2010.

Norvik Press Series B: English Translations of Scandinavian
Literature, no. 48.

No. 2 in the series: Classics of Norwegian Literature.

*A catalogue record for this book is available from the British
Library.*
ISBN: 978-1-870041-88-1
First published in 2010 by Norvik Press.

This translation has been published with the financial support of
NORLA (Norwegian Literature Abroad) and Institutionen Fritt Ord.

Norvik Press
Department of Scandinavian Studies
University College London
Gower Street
London WC1E 6BT
England

Managing editors: Helena Forsås-Scott, Janet Garton, Neil Smith,
C. Claire Thomson.

Website: www.norvikpress.com
E-mail address: norvik.press@ucl.ac.uk

Layout: Neil Smith
Cover design: Richard Johnson

Printed in the UK by Page Bros. (Norwich) Ltd, Norwich, UK

CONTENTS

Forty Years is Life's Midsummer

Dr. Knut Holmen, ear, nose and throat, was pleased to hear the door to his office snap shut behind him.

Through for today.

A good day. The office hours had been pleasant, and it was pleasant to be through with them.

He swung his left elbow out and looked at his wristwatch.

Five to five. Righto. He felt quite hungry, everything in order. He had skipped lunch today to give an edge to his appetite. Such things were part of the art of living.

He stopped on the stone step outside the entrance and peered at the sun.

Life and the solar system are going swimmingly, he thought.

It was a quotation. He used it on and off. It was from a poet, he couldn't remember who. A good poet.

Fine summer weather! The broiling hot sun felt like a friendly weight. The sky lay sparklingly blue above the house tops. Slightly more blue than a few days ago, the white July heat haze was gone. All the better.

A breath of wind swept along the street from St Olav's Place, gaily ruffling the forelocks of the maple to the left of the entrance door and gently brushing his cheek.

The first breath of autumn?

Far from it. August 3rd – still the middle of summer.

August 3rd.

He took a deep breath, relishing the sensation that his lungs were filling up.

Forty years old.

Forty is life's midsummer.

The man who had said that to him today was eighty, so he ought to know.

He gave himself an appraising look. He liked the fine light-grey summer suit, which hung so loosely and comfortably on one's body, the trousers with their knife-edge creases, the brightly-coloured tie with its broad blue diagonal stripe, the new light-grey shoes.

It felt good to be well dressed. It was part of the art of living.

Well. And now the question of dinner. Where would he dine today? He had postponed the decision on purpose. There were several places to choose from, good places, an agreeable choice he had postponed. It was his birthday today, he would have all the pleasures, one after another.

Bristol? Speilen? Continental? Skansen? Kongen? He mustered them all in his head as he strolled down Universitetsgaten. Some late office workers were rushing past on their way home. He doubly enjoyed his own well-dressed composure at the sight of their shabby haste.

Crossing Pilestredet, he sensed a warm whiff of newly baked bread. The smell of newly baked bread was the best smell in the world, and now he was hungry, really hungry.

The Bristol grill? You dined well there. Long baguettes, red wine silhouetted against those pale-green tablecloths, a cheerful flame in the grill – good, but you sat imprisoned behind mat windowpanes, it was a place for the winter. Speilen? Certainly – but to sit inside now in the middle of summer!

Take the car and drive up to Frognerseteren? But the car was in the garage. And the city was so fine today. The veranda at the Continental? To sit looking at the backs of Bjørnson and Ibsen, at the tram stop and the theatre, and with people moving back and forth across the square... Fresh air, summertime and sunshine...

All of it excellent; but that veranda faced north – funny how everything in this wintry town faced north. It was something of an architectural feat, because the city was actually located on a south-facing slope, but if there was a street with only one row of houses, you could bet it stood like a wall on the south side – Drammensveien, Akersgaten, Ullevålsveien. Ah, what a street! Our Saviour's Cemetery, Our Lady's Hospital, the Catholic Church. The Spa, the German Church, Trinity Church, the Swedish Church – and the police station and prison. And on the south side, wreath shops and coffins and funeral homes.

And always shade. And always north wind. And there, in the shade and the north wind, alongside the wreaths, the coffins, the churches, the cemetery and the prison, shades of people ran about, guilt-ridden office souls in thrall to duty – remorsefulness itself hawking and wiping its nose was running there in the shade and the north wind. A street for puritans, for Norwegians... No, today he refused to think about this.

It would have to be the Continental.

He crossed Kristian IVs gate and, walking past Café Minerva, he remembered his student days – coffee from white pots and thick slices of white bread with goat's cheese. That's where Dancke's Bookstore was located in the old days. Old days? It was yesterday. It was ten years ago.

On the other side of the street the birches were fluttering in the light wind, the leaves glittering like ocean waves – ah, to go swimming tomorrow, a sweet thought. And in there, in the middle of the garden, as the Bible says, stood that old academic privy – was it still in operation? he wondered. Did a hoary old woman still sit there selling tickets through a hatch to needy students whose stomachs had been ruined by cheap boarding houses, and who squatted on top of the seat for fear of catching syphilis? Ah, idyllic youth!

He stopped at the corner of Karl Johans gate, in front of the ice cream parlour. He stood there for a moment, intending to drop by the newsstand.

A young girl went by, dressed in summery white and her own skin. Brown, golden, a blend of copper and gold – her muscles glided under the skin as if under silk. She was heading up the street. Alas yes! He sighed and went in the opposite direction.

Passing Myhre's, he suddenly tapped both breast pockets, though he already knew – he'd forgotten his cigar. Forgotten to open the box, to tell the truth. What the... He checked himself, wasn't going to get vexed today; on the contrary, it was lucky that it came back to him here, right outside Myhre's. He turned into the store, picked up the fine, rich scent of many varieties of tobacco and soon found himself bent over a newly opened box of long Parthagas, exactly like the box he'd been given by Agnete this morning. She knew what he smoked on red-letter days. Long supple cigars, with a faint suggestion of green in the midst of the warm brown – what did they remind him of? Why did they always make him feel such longing, such a desire to travel?

They lay there like twelve slim, supple, sun-tanned girls in a row.

He carefully selected one. The remaining eleven could lie there for the time being. Strong stuff. For each such cigar you smoked, you became a bit older, a bit less fit for a real sun-tanned girl. An average man could make love to a woman three thousand times, then it was over – arteriosclerosis, internal death. Tobacco promoted the calcification. Three thousand large Parthagas, three thousand supple brown cigars, no more nut-brown girls. No more... Nonsense.

He had the brown girl nicely wrapped and left. The sun beat down. The street was nearly deserted. He crossed in the direction of the kiosk, looked up at Freia's clock on Egertorvet Square – ten past five. He bought *Dagbladet* and *Politiken*, skimmed the front pages at once and stuck the papers under his arm – for later, everything in due course.

He walked on the south side, under the trees, casting a cursory glance along the row of benches. Barely a vacant seat. Mostly men. Of all ages. Strange – otherwise wherever people foregathered in their leisure hours, women were a decided majority, in hotels and boarding houses, at concerts and in the theatre. But these orchestra seats seemed to be reserved for men. All at once he saw it – most of these men were out of work. He ran his eyes along the row – there was no mistaking it, something in their postures gave it away, something limp, melancholy, hopeless. No, this he refused to look at today!

He turned his head away.

'Good afternoon, Holmen!'

He started.

'Oh, good afternoon, Mrs Gunnerus. So, you are in town? Goodness, how marvellous you look!'

He always told ladies, on principle, that they looked marvellous – that is, if they didn't look too dreadful. Mrs Gunnerus was not outright bad-looking, at any rate, and when she smiled gratefully, like now, she became almost passable.

'Well, actually I'm staying at Hankø, as you know,' Mrs Gunnerus said, smiling, 'but my husband had to go to town on some business that couldn't wait, and so I simply made a trip of it, too, and came in – when I've been away from the city a couple of weeks I really miss it, you know. But how come you didn't travel down today?'

'Work,' he said. 'Work that couldn't wait.'

Mrs Gunnerus' eyes darted back and forth, up and down the street, brushing the windows of Handelsbygningen and following the cars that shot by. But her mouth ran on.

'I have greetings from your wife – and both children – they're having a great time. And how are you? Ah, delighted to hear it! But imagine having to spend the whole lovely summer in the city and not being able to come down even for weekends – oh well, you probably have fun here too, no doubt you do, oh, you men, we know you, all right.' She made a threatening gesture with her finger, exuberantly roguish, while her eyes darted here and there.

'Next week my husband has to go on a trip and stay away – I believe for a fortnight – and then I plan to come here and live it up in earnest, so see you then, ha-ha-ha!'

She floated on down the street. He shot a glance after her.

Good-looking, all in all. Nice figure, all in all. And good-humoured, and...

He always felt a bit sorry for Mrs Gunnerus, without knowing why. But he preferred to feel that way at a distance. Her proximity was disturbing.

So, Agnete would be alone down there this Sunday. Then, perhaps, it was too bad he hadn't gone down. Maybe he ought to, he could still...

No.

He crossed Universitsgaten right in front of the row of taxis waiting for Blom Restaurant clients. Two or three of the drivers were busy with some game or other at the edge of the lawn. The point seemed to be to throw one another off balance. Poor devils, hanging around here waiting for a job – oh well, weren't most people doing just that? What else was he doing? The only difference was that he sat in an office and that there were more than enough jobs – good times, war was brewing, people breathed a sigh of relief and could afford to have adenoids.

How much had he earned today? Well, including social security, ninety kroner besides the two operations – not bad in the middle of the summer. And in addition those shares at the broker's, which were going up every single day – the war, of course, and Holland which would soon have to give up the gold standard – he'd made two hundred and a bit more on them today. Even though, on principle, he didn't count those earnings, as they could be gone again tomorrow, he could at any rate afford a first-class dinner. He passed between the two poets in their flower beds and went briskly past the tram stop.

'Hello, Holmen!'

'Hello!' He touched the brim of his hat and at the same time increased his speed; he had no desire to get stuck with that actor. A city was full of dangers. All of life was full of dangers. And the art of living – the art of living pleasantly – consisted, up to ninety per cent of it, in avoiding unpleasantness. The remaining ten percent consisted in providing pleasures for yourself.

Hm. That wasn't really a heroic philosophy, was it? Not really heroic, no. Was this the way you had thought things would turn out, long ago? Oh, nonsense – heroism, that belonged to youth, to his salad days, greenhorn that he was. A certain judge had a saying: Life consists of trifles!

There was something in that, something...

He went quickly through the door of the Continental, nodded to the doorman, greeted the hall porter who stood behind his counter and bowed politely. He had stayed here for a couple of days on and off.

Pleasant to be able to walk calmly past doormen and hall porters, waiters and maîtres d's. That was one of the last things you learnt in life. It presupposed many things – a quiet conscience, good clothes, money in your pocket, and confidence in figuring your bill, neither too large nor too small tips – oh, those painful, thin-skinned student years, pride and humiliations, poverty and lack of manners, pimples and shyness and impudence and fear, every waiter a secret enemy, and every maître d' a combination of the devil and God himself who saw through you and made you blush to the roots of your hair! What was it that Swede said? It's good to grow old, being young was just too hellish.

Old? Old? Forty. Only forty. He took the stairs three steps at a time. I'm not old as long as I can take the stairs three steps at a time, the man said.

He checked his hat, took a turn over to the parapet and looked down at the bar. Empty. A couple of people were hanging about down there, sitting in a depressing and hazy semi-darkness and looking as though they'd been forgotten. Why did all bars have to look so infinitely depressing? Oh well, that was one of the riddles of existence, the solution of which could conveniently be postponed.

It was now half-past five. The dining room appeared quite deserted. A man sat alone at the little table beside the front column, a fairly large party sat at one of the sofa tables to the extreme right, out by Røde Mølle. Big, broad, loud fellows. They were discussing timber prices. Three waiters were distributed over the floor area, resembling statues in tails. One of them turned his head when he came in, as though a button inside him had been pushed, but he checked himself and was again a statue facing the timber proprietors from the Østerdal Valley.

He crossed the soundless carpet and walked through the narrow door out to the veranda.

A man was sitting out there, at the middle table by the wall – well, if it wasn't Jens Gunnerus!

Holmen said hello and was about to walk over and utter a few pleasantries – that he had greetings from his wife and how was he doing – when he noticed a hint of embarrassment in Gunnerus' eyes, oh, he had company, the table was set for two, and a summer coat was draped over the chair back, ho-ho! The lady had just gone out for a moment. And outside, in the street, Mrs Gunnerus was walking about, her glances flying in every direction...

He found himself a table at the parapet.

*

The waiter brought the bill of fare and the wine list. He became absorbed in a conversation about the menu. This was important, this was one of the joys of the day, he'd looked forward to this moment with pleasure from early in the morning. This had to be done thoroughly. And he did it thoroughly, while at the same time keeping an eye on Gunnerus.

The waiter gave quiet, guarded advice. The waiters here were very good, people who knew their trade. It was always pleasant to talk with people who knew their trade, it inspired confidence. All things considered, wasn't that the chief purpose of civilization – giving confidence? Confidence and well-being. Such a restaurant was a very civilized place. And such a waiter, who could recommend a dish without finding fault with the others, who could make you understand almost without words that you ought to choose a slightly less expensive wine because, in fact, it was better than the more expensive one – and who recognized you if that was appropriate, but had never seen you before if the situation required that – such a waiter was one of the greatest benefits of civilization. Yes indeed. Life was good. Over there Gunnerus was writhing in his chair.

He discussed the food and the wine exhaustively with the waiter; enjoying things in advance, he forgot about Gunnerus for a moment – until something or other made him lift his eyes.

Gunnerus had got up to leave. Strangely, the lady had not come back – ah, there she stood waiting by the door, she'd been given a hint. Actually, Gunnerus had not yet finished his meal, he hadn't had coffee or enjoyed his cigar – that wasn't at all like Gunnerus.

Holmen cast a glance at the lady. Fair-haired, lightly and brightly dressed, tanned and bare-armed. Gunnerus took her coat on his arm and left. He forgot to turn and say goodbye. The lady turned around and went ahead of him. Tall and slim, her back young and bronzed by the summer sun. Then they were out of sight. On their way out.

Well, it would have to be a fillet of flounder tout Paris to begin with. And a half Rhine wine to go with it. And...

And down there came Mrs Gunnerus. As if she had scented her prey. Came walking up on the south side of Stortingsgaten, was just now passing Høyres Hus. She walked slowly, having a good look around. If one hadn't been above thinking that way, one might be tempted to think that she had walked down Karl Johans gate looking for her husband, had dropped by, say, the Bristol bar and grill, the Grand Hotel bar, and Speilen – but no Gunnerus – and the Cecil, second floor, perhaps, or the Metropol, but no Gunnerus, and now she was coming up Stortingsgaten on the lookout for, oh well, something or other, Gunnerus, say, and Gunnerus would come strutting out of the door down there in five or six seconds, exactly in time to run straight into the arms of his wife. What was written in Holy

Scripture? 'There is a lion in the way; a lion is in the street.' You could've said hello, dear Gunnerus, my excellent friend, you could've shown some politeness for once, bighead that you are, and exchanged a few words with an old fellow sinner, instead of being superior and caught fornicating, then you'd have had a chance of seeing what I'm seeing now and what you will see in a moment... There she disappeared around the corner, behind the narrow pavement café.

It was not nice, absolutely not nice, but he did go over to the parapet and peered, stretched and peered – even if he were to be called a cad for the rest of his life, this he had to see. Even if he never again would be considered a gentleman.

Mrs Gunnerus walked slowly along the pavement. She peered past the myrtles, into the restaurant – just in passing, that is – but no Gunnerus! She walked on, very slowly, as if thinking hard – no no, fine ladies probably walked rapidly when thinking – nonsense, fine ladies never thought, they were always taken by surprise – there she reached the entrance to the Continental, there – no, she walked on, slowly, extremely slowly, but kept moving. And nobody came out. And she walked on. Now she was up at the corner, where she cut across, now she was on the National Theatre side. Nobody came out, and she walked on, towards Drammensveien – now she turned around and looked back, but no, nothing, no Gunnerus, no lady. There the good wife turned onto Drammensveien. There she disappeared. What had become of Gunnerus? He had been swallowed up by the great darkness – or was it by the bar? Or was it – oh, you dunce, you could've spared yourself all this excitement: in my Father's hotel there are many mansions...

Ugh! No, it really was good that it turned out as it did. Oh, you hypocrite! Certainly it was good – good for Mrs Gunnerus.

He felt sorry for Mrs Gunnerus. Poor thing!

He noticed he was in excellent spirits.

At other times running into Gunnerus unexpectedly would put him in a bad mood. God knows why. Oh yes. A stuck-up fellow. Proud of his so-called family. Of the fact that his forefathers had stood behind a counter and short-weighted customers for several hundred years. Proud of his decorative cranium, with nothing inside it.

Well. You can't always choose your circle of acquaintances.

'The soup is served, if you please!'

He gave a start and turned around. The waiter's face betrayed what looked like a faint shadow of a hint of a smile. Then it was gone. Utterly serious, utterly deferential, he stood there and adjusted his chair.

Delicious soup!

He sat on the veranda as on the bridge of a large ship and looked out across the city. The west side of the cupola of the National Theatre was in bright sun, the east side in deep shade. The trees in the Students' Promenade stood there like a massive green wall. Now and then flocks of pigeons appeared in a swift arc over the treetops; having taken off and left their grain behind, for reasons unknown they made a short flight around the square and down again – perhaps a preacher at the foot of the Wergeland statue had frightened them with eternal bliss.

And down there the traffic went on; women in white or in butterfly colours and men in indifferent grey emerged from the shadows, appearing and then disappearing into the shadows again. The trams were clanging, he felt nice and warm, it was a good place to be.

Skål, Knut! Many happy returns! He emptied his glass of sherry with lingering delight, put it slowly down again and felt: Now he was enjoying life!

As far as he could see from up here, those white and flowery ladies strolling about or standing down there were not exactly exciting. No, indeed – it was vacation time, the exciting ones must be elsewhere.

No doubt he should have been elsewhere.

Where? Down at Hankø?

No.

He didn't have a bad conscience because he had lied a bit to

Agnete. She could manage by herself for once. Anyway, they had long ago agreed on a month's marital holiday every year, a simple spiritual hygiene – that it had so far not been carried out was another matter.

A man needed to be alone occasionally. And your fortieth birthday was, after all, quite a milestone.

It was a long time now since he had celebrated his birthday alone. He probably hadn't done it since – well, since he was thirty-three. You got married and suchlike, of course, older and such...

He could remember how seriously he took his birthdays in his youth, in his salad days. Then he held a reckoning: what have I accomplished this year?

That was when he was still comparing himself to the greatest of men. Nothing less would do. Napoleon, Caesar, Alexander, even Jesus – good Lord! And he always thought, sure, they had accomplished a great deal. But then, of course, they were so much older than him! Just you wait!

From the moment he reached thirty-three, that sort of thing stopped of itself. Thank God, you did grow up eventually.

The soup was delicious. The sherry was marvellous. And then came the fillet of flounder. The waiter poured the Rhine wine with a motion of his hand as if pouring nectar for a king. The wine was cold, the glass became misted immediately.

Such a slender misted glass filled with golden wine – how beautiful!

He came to think of the old parson and his words of wisdom: 'And let us eat slowly – remember, food is after all the best thing we have.'

He ate slowly, drank slowly, looking out over the parapet, over the trees and the roof ridges onto the square below, where the two hollow-eyed poets stood like two empty tin cans, each on his own lump of cheese and in his own herring salad.

He recalled something a friend of his had told him. One of the first days he was in Oslo as a student, he had lost his way and ended at Grefsen. Looking out at what lay before him as he stood there, he had thought, this city shall one day be *mine*.

Well, this friend was from Bergen and may have had a penchant for rhetoric. But the feeling, what out-of-town student wasn't familiar with it! He himself had thought the same, only a bit more in East Norwegian style, half concealed. Just you wait! he'd thought – not once, but ten times, maybe a hundred times.

Yes, and now?

He could've done worse.

The city hadn't become *his*, oh no. It wasn't his name that filled the papers, not to him that the journalists came running every time the same people popped up in the newspaper columns and made fools of themselves. Well, to be fair, it wasn't such cheap exploits he'd been dreaming of. And the things he had dreamed of? Well, he had accomplished something, anyway.

Well, accomplished...

Oh, yes. *Something*, anyway.

He had known many farm boys who had come to this city with the thought of conquering it. Most of them had been driven back in defeat – had fled back home again, broken or full of hatred. A few, those who refused to flee, had to choose between two possibilities.

Either to acquire all the externals here in enemy country – the manners, the repartee, the style, the flirtation, the jargon – and thus risk becoming nothing but an empty shell: defeat, that is.

Or go about picking up the externals with a deliberate calm defiance, become an authentic city man little by little, taking the turns a bit more slowly perhaps than those born in the city, so that you had to put up with being defeated by inferiors in the first round, but knowing that in the next round we shall see, and in the next, and the next.

Ah, what a sweet sensation – to sit at one's ease watching the city slickers and know that one can afford to wait, being a master of two milieus, two worlds. What did they really know, these natives? They sat up to their necks in their own little nests, unaware that anything else existed, and consequently saw neither one thing nor the other. He who knew one milieu knew none, he who knew two knew them all.

Slowly and steadily – he knew he had chosen the better portion.

He had become warm – and the fillet of flounder had become cold. In sheer distraction he'd finished almost all the Rhine wine, hadn't even noticed how it tasted. Was that the way to treat God's gifts?

For that matter, God knows if what he'd thought held water. Slowly and steadily? Calm defiance? At any rate, the city had turned him into a sartorial snob. So perhaps it had conned him into defeat all the same...

You ought to enjoy such a wine, not gulp it down. Enjoy the wine? What was it he'd said, that damned – what was his name again – Ramstad – that evening in Røde Mølle, how long ago now? Almost a fortnight ago? *Are you enjoying the wine?*

'You sit there enjoying the wine, Dr. Holmen, and I ask myself, are you enjoying it? And I sit here enjoying my highball. And I ask myself, am I enjoying it? Tell me, have you ever tried to figure out how much of our pleasures is merely a dull repetition of ourselves, and how much is a slavish imitation of others?'

A queer fellow, that Ramstad.

'I'm testing my values at the moment – have you ever done that, Holmen? Have you tested your values? One ought to do so now and then – test them, devalue them, depreciate them, those that are ripe for it, I mean, for it's possible, of course, that a few actually measure up to the gold standard.'

Did he enjoy the wine?

He tasted it.

Certainly. Of course he enjoyed it. Absolutely.

That fresh, effervescent taste – you felt fresh and as it were newly bathed all the way through. That beer could be just as good was another matter.

'No thanks, no more flounder.'

On the other hand, whether he truly – truly – liked fillet of flounder, of that he was less certain.

Test one's values – so, in a way, it was Ramstad, perhaps, who was the primary reason why he sat here celebrating his birthday in solitude.

'You've made good – a respected physician, a good practice, nice income, a lovely wife, beg pardon – and children, two children? But do you dare sit down by yourself and work out – mercilessly, I mean – how much genuine joy, I said joy, you get from it all? And how much is simply imitation, self-assertion, competition? Beg pardon, now I'm drunk.'

Ramstad was a fool.

There came the chicken.

That was something he felt sure about. It was a delight, of that he was absolutely sure. He recalled his home as a child, in the days when they ran a poultry farm and were poorer than anyone could imagine, how crates of chickens were dispatched to the city, while at home they could never afford anything but old salt pork – yes, he certainly enjoyed chicken.

The waiter handled two forks with one hand, like tongs, picked up the chicken with it and placed it on his plate. As deft as a surgeon.

The Chambertin gleamed ruby-red in the glass.

A beautiful wine... Wait, first a bite of chicken.

The roasted parsley was the best part.

Now!

He took a deep draft.

That wine was really rather good. Even though, as he drank it and found it to be good, he could possibly be said to imitate millions of people who had done the same before. Dear Ramstad, you're a queer fellow, possibly very clever, but you are a bit of a fool. You walk four times around the house to find the door, which stands there open right in front of your nose. I take it a little more easy – skål!

Real joy – competition? Hm – no. But this chicken was really very good. Even if he didn't get it as a child, so that there was a kind of self-assertion and revenge in it.

And the parsley, that certainly was good.

Revenge? How?

'Remember one thing, Dr. Holmen, you're a peasant boy like me – from the same hamlet even – and you hate these city people. Yes, you do! These stuck-up good-for-nothings are going to pay for all those years we walked around here, penniless and lonely – am I not right? What? Am I not right?'

Strange. Ramstad's chatter must've made a certain impression on him, since it had taken such a firm hold.

The glass had become full again. The waiter must have come up and filled it.

He drank.

Hate?

No.

Revenge?

No.

He had given some thought to these things before. He did not hate these well-fed, well-dressed, well-satisfied fellow students from well-situated Oslo families. They had irritated him a bit, sure. Reared from birth for good positions, pretty girls, secure careers, and all the advantages. How lightly and indifferently they went about their studies, most of them. Those who weren't marked out to be professors after their fathers, that is, those who were had to make an effort, of course. He and the other students from out of town had to work doubly hard – the professors didn't associate with *their* parents, didn't play cards in *their* homes. And it was not *their* uncles who occupied leading positions and could smooth the way for them.

Never did it occur to any of these daddy boys to invite any of the out-of-town students into their homes. Oh, those student eating places! No, because there, at home, were sisters. And they were reserved for their friends, cousins, second cousins...

Inbreeding? In the so-called better quarters of Oslo it was worse than in the most restricted rural parish. There they made soup from the same pig bones generation after generation – pure breeding, all right – pretty, stupid, narrow-hipped girls who burst at the first child. But the strangers had to be kept out.

It cost me ten years of my youth! he suddenly thought, feeling hot and hateful. It was as though he'd said it aloud, he started and looked about him. He was alone.

Ten years. Toil, toil, with hardly ever any joy. The ten best years of his youth – that's what they were called, wasn't it?

They're owed to me! he thought angrily.

Another thought occurred to him the same moment, so quickly it seemed to have been lying in ambush: So, I'm really only thirty years old!

He thought quickly of something else, refusing to look more closely at that thought.

Oh, damn it! Now the chicken had also gone cold.

There was a puff of wind, the white tablecloth fluttered.

It was actually a bit chilly here. Yes, the veranda faced north. Those puritans! They couldn't even build a decent veranda, they appointed architects who thought the sun was sinful.

Ouch, what a draft!

These damned city people.

Maybe he should move inside.

But those accursed farmers in there were so noisy; they made an outcry as if each was standing in his own forest, calling to the others. But now they were breaking up. It must've been the bill they had been shouting about, with everyone wanting to pay – it wasn't until tomorrow, when they examined their wallets, that they would change their tune. They were in a good mood now – the broadest of them slapped the one city dweller resoundingly on the shoulder; and *he* smiled, quietly and shyly, making it impossible to tell whether he was a slavish soul who thought it was great, even if a bit troublesome, to rub shoulders with the deepest core of the people, or a con man who had pulled the wool over their eyes. But now there was peace in the restaurant, at any rate.

He walked inside, leaving the glasses and the newspapers for the waiter. Only two tables were occupied in the entire dining room now; a young couple were having a very important conversation, and a man, a slightly slumped-over older man, sat behind a bottle of wine.

He chose one of the tables facing Stortingsgaten. The waiter brought the wine bottles, the glasses and the newspapers.

There they came with the raspberries. Time to drink up the Chambertin and switch to the sherry.

Skål, all you men of forty, except that damn Jens Gunnerus, if *he* should happen to be among them, something I strongly, *very* strongly doubt, by the way; it would be just like him to be either more or less, more or less – oh well, a little more or less, what difference does it make? None at all.

He could tell he'd been drinking, his thoughts were all over the place. But when he exerted his will on them, they sorted themselves out. Good Lord, you didn't have a birthday more than once a year. At most. In reality, only once every seventh year, once in a blue moon. Skål again, Knut!

He began reading *Politiken*. Reading newspapers cleared one's head. He put it aside and picked up *Dagbladet*. Put it aside, picked up *Politiken* once more.

Well, well. There was something he had made up his mind to get to the bottom of some day – and another thing.

Nothing had come of it.

There had always been so much else to do.

It was the old thing. Life got in the way.

You had so much to do that you didn't get anything done.

Like what happened with his scientific work. His doctoral thesis. The daily work of the practice and – well, one thing and another got in the way.

You had so much to think about that there was no time left to think.

The prophylactic methods he'd touched on, which would render half the doctors superfluous. The same thing there. People suffered so much from sore throats that there was no time to prevent sore throats.

Hang it, who could find time for everything, anyway!

The great achievements would have to wait.

Yes.

If Napoleon and Alexander and Caesar and Jesus had their hands as full as he, maybe their achievements would've had to wait a while, too.

Which would have done them a lot of good.

The great achievements.

Yes.

And Napoleon and Alexander too. And Caesar. Not to speak of –

Yes.

Then they might not have produced so much damn nonsense.

No.

He didn't play second fiddle to anybody. He would like to see the forty-year-old who, all things considered...

What had those others had to deal with? Nothing at all!

No, stop! Now he could really tell he'd been drinking. That he wouldn't stand for – he didn't want to get drunk on his own birthday. No, he didn't.

He stood up, felt a floating sensation in his body, walked more stiffly and elegantly than was his wont through the door, through the anteroom, down the little staircase into the men's room, fixed his tie and washed his face thoroughly in cold water – ah, it did him good, his head cleared, oh, how it cleared and straightened itself out; it was as though a superior had appeared and started to give orders, everything settled back into place again, he felt it with satisfaction.

The boy in there received a krone.

He felt nearly sober again. In excellent condition.

He returned calmly to the dining room.

The young couple had left. Another couple had replaced them and were sitting at another table. They had something important to talk about – she was hitting his face with a flower time and again. The elderly gentleman behind his bottle of wine sat there still, slightly more slumped.

Oh dear!

He rubbed his hands.

He was in a glorious mood.

Glorious.

Birthdays were glorious days.

And there came the coffee. And the cigar. Glorious. That was really what he'd been looking forward to all along. What pleasure could be greater than the pleasure of a good coffee and a first-class cigar? And both were harmful, both taxed one's vitality, as the most exquisite pleasures unavoidably do.

He lighted the long, greenish-brown, supple cigar. Ah! How good!

He sucked in smoke and aroma, puffed out, sniffed at the cigar, ah! – as he had seen people do before he himself could afford –

Oh, nonsense!

It was as fine as it could be.

Right now he was friends with the whole world.

He would definitely send a note to Agnete, who had remembered him with these cigars. Gorgeous cigars. He waved to the waiter and asked for paper and an envelope.

A fountain pen – oh, he had his fountain pen on him.

My friend, I have a fountain pen, a fountain pen, my friend – so now!

He wrote:

'Dearest Agnete!

On this, my so-called big day, I'm sitting here having dinner in splendid isolation at the Continental – besides me, there are only three in the entire dining room; it's the dead hour, work kept me busy very late today. And so, you see, I can't help sending an ever so little thought down to Hankø, to you and the two little brats. A weekend down there today and tomorrow together with the three of you could've been perfection – but it won't work, in a moment I have to be in the swing of things again. But just to let you know the direct reason that I'm writing to you here and now: I'm right now enjoying the first of your cigars. It's excellent. As you obviously know, by dint of mind-reading or other magic, it is my secret favourite brand you've found. The best cigar in the world – which, unfortunately, out of respect for my tobacco heart, I only dare grant myself on red-letter days. So – I'm smoking your cigar and thinking of you, and feel marvellous, except that I miss you.

Remember me to the small fry.

Your Knut'

He read it through. Oh well, it would pass, he didn't have the time to conjure up any grand passion. He handed over the letter and took a deep puff at the cigar. It was really true – it *was* an excellent cigar. Agnete had a knack for that sort of thing.

He took a deep swallow of the sherry.

All at once he felt profoundly moved by Agnete.

Sitting all alone down there, while he –

Bloody hell, what a thoroughly dishonest letter!

Bloody hell? What was that supposed to mean? It was written to please her – solely to please her. Was anything wrong with that?

He would say it again: Was anything wrong with that? Wanting to please his wife, who...

A harmonious marriage.

The most harmonious marriage he knew.

He straightened up.

I love my wife! he thought.

He sat a moment.

I love my wife! he thought once more, with a start.

He took a mighty swallow of the sherry.

Hm. He could feel he'd been drinking.

He smoked for a while.

A glass of cognac would do him good now. It would clear the brain.

He beckoned to the waiter. 'Hm – listen!'

But the waiter was politely unreceptive; he shrugged his shoulders and gestured regretfully with his hand – small restrained movements which could've served as models for an actor.

'I'm sorry. Saturday...'

His perfect politeness made discussion hopeless.

No, of course not. Unless you were an actor. Otherwise it was no use.

If only he had been an actor.

Or, at a pinch, an author.

But when you weren't an actor – and not even an author...

Well. Then he would damn well have to be content with the sherry!

Skål, Knut.

Knut, yeah. Author, yeah.

Why in the world hadn't he become an author – he who was Norwegian and peasant-born and was even called Knut, and whose birthday fell on the day before Hamsun's. It was that sort of thing which usually determined one's destiny. Most of those who became authors certainly had less reason to do so.

Talent?

Every Norwegian was talented.

Moreover, talent was, in all probability, a highly overrated affair. Early concentration of interest on a certain kind of achievement...

Wait! He had considered it, after all.

Considered it?

Nonsense. Pull yourself together!

Certainly. He remembered – he ought to remember that.

He had dreamed about becoming an author. Of course he

had. All Norwegians dreamed about it. And when he wrote the usual love poems in senior school, and they turned out a bit better than most such poems, and one of the girls actually fell a little in love with him for that reason – it was that red-haired one, whatever her name was – well, then he was so much in love with himself for a while that he decided to become an author.

Later, when he was a university student and really fell in love, he wrote something again, that he remembered – it was still lying somewhere – that was the year he was in Ålesund as a journalist, in the aftermath of that scene with the landlady – yes, damn it, a whole year as a journalist. He recalled little from that period – it was a mistake to hire him, a country bumpkin, as journalist in a fishing town; he was probably a bit down at the time and consoled himself now and then by the fact that his name was Knut and he had his birthday the day before Hamsun's – the number next to the winning one.

Actually he was writing something that year – a novel, that's right, he even half finished it – and when he felt any doubts, he thought he was probably no more stupid than others who wrote.

Why did he quit? He couldn't remember... Oh, yes. He began to read Söderberg. That was it. And suddenly he realized that here was something he couldn't learn. Something that could never be learned. Something behind the sentences and the pages.

Fancy having forgotten all that!

But how come he began to read Söderberg?

Söderberg in Ålesund? But, of course, it was that customs officer. Who owned all Söderberg's works and spoke Swedish when he was drunk. But how did he get involved with – oh yes, it was that time down at the quayside, when he'd been on board that Icelandic ship and the customs officer came around the corner just then, thought he meant to do a bit of smuggling and cried out, '*Hey, there!*'

A weird chance, eh? If he'd turned left at the quay that time instead of right, he wouldn't have met that customs officer. Some crossroads that was!

'Hey, there!' the officer cried, and so there was no novel and no author either, oh no.

Though very possibly he had talent. If you just looked at all those who... And the very fact that he understood he had no talent, that showed a certain *judgment*, damn it! And you don't have such a judgment if you don't ... it presupposes a sense of ... it's really decisive proof of talent. Indeed, yes. So he could've become an author, if only he hadn't...

'Hey, there!' the customs officer cried. And with that it was over.

And then he fell in love with that sixth former who planned to study medicine, and just then his father was a little better off and soon upped and died, tactful as ever. And his infatuation with the sixth former wore off – she was a shrew anyway; but by then he was a medical student.

And so he didn't become another Hamsun.

Hamsun...

How did it feel, he wondered, to be famous and seventy-six years old?

About the same as being seventy-six years old.

How strange – we never envy people who are substantially older than we are.

So we must value youth higher than anything else.

And so here he was. A decent doctor, a decent practice.

No, he was not dissatisfied, that was not it.

But he should've been something else. Author? Far from it. Whose idea was it to be an author? Nonsense. But – for example – why hadn't he become a scientist?

Chance. Chance again. The crossroads once more.

He had often thought of this.

If he hadn't let himself be tricked into going on a spree that one evening in the midst of the exams for the third level, then... If he had stayed home and read the chapter he had decided to read, then he would've got ten, perhaps eleven, instead of seven. And would've beaten Blich by precisely those points and would've been ahead of him for the award of that fellowship – ought to have beaten him anyway. That would have changed a lot.

And this was all decided at such a confounded crossroads. He remembered it as though it were yesterday – he was standing down below Riket, at the corner of Pilestredet and Nordahl Bruns gate – it was raining too, or wasn't it? He couldn't remember if it was raining or not. Of course it was raining!

No, wait...

He couldn't remember if it was raining.

What the hell was the difference whether it was raining or not!

He stood there, trying to decide if he should walk up Pilestredet and go home and read that chapter, or walk down Pilestredet and allow himself a turn on Karl Johans gate. How stupid – it was even raining! Or wasn't it? Nonsense! What difference did it...

But then he thought, what the hell! He even thought, what's the harm in a couple of raindrops?

So it *was* raining! He had known all along! It was raining.

And so he walked down the street, but already on the next corner he ran into Halvorsen with the two girls.

Oh, he recalled so clearly that he thought, what the hell, I'll take that turn.

Some turn that was!

For all the rest of his life.

That's how it was with everything.

With everything.

Why, for example, was he married?

And why exactly to Agnete?

Oh, stop it!

What? Why?

Stop it?

Never!

And the thing with Agnete –

There again was a crossroads, he knew that – he knew as soon as he stopped to think. Oh, let it be, there were crossroads everywhere. Nothing but crossroads. His life behind him – cross upon cross of crossroads, and he'd always taken only one road, and what the other would've given him, that... Unused possibilities. Unlived life. Unlived, unlived, unlived life. He had never given it any thought. Not in this way. But soon time would be getting – short. Getting short, yeah. Getting short. Soon time would be... What nonsense. A human being cannot achieve anything without giving something up. Not win anything without losing something.

And he had achieved something.

An excellent practice. An excellent income. An excellent marriage. Excellent – well, friends, for example.

But if you were to die now, who would you call on?

Call on? If I were to...

Yes, who would you call on?

Who? Of my friends? If I were to...

That damned Ramstad!

No. He wouldn't sit here any longer, hanging out by himself. He would go out and call up – a couple of friends. He would have company, in his home. A couple of friends, pleasant company, it was his birthday, he would have pleasant company. Yes, he would have company!

He was already on his way out, ran through the anteroom, down the little staircase, got into the telephone booth, fumbled for ten øre coins, found them, stopped to think a moment all aquiver: Berntsen, sure! He called, it rang, no one answered. Oh, come to think, Berntsen was staying down by Ny Hellesund, he knew that; but what about Sunde, yes, Sunde! What was his number now? Where was the telephone book? His hands shook a little. He found the number and called, it rang and rang, no answer. He called again. No answer. But he just *had* to get an answer from Sunde. Sunde was not on vacation, Sunde was a brilliant man, good-humoured, nice wife, and he was not on vacation, good Lord, he talked with him yesterday, after all, and now he *had* to get hold of him, so...

He called and called, more and more angry. Even if he had to stand here until tomorrow!

But no one answered. He had to give up.

But what about Solheim, for God's sake! Solheim, the surgeon, who always took his vacation in the hunting season and shot animals when he couldn't cut into people.

No one answered.

Spending the weekend out of town, with his wife, of course.

But Gunnerus, perhaps Gunnerus...

He was about to grab the telephone book. Then it was as though someone said, he could almost hear it, 'Now you're drunk! You're drunk now!'

The effect was instantaneous. Things became clearer. He felt himself become calm again.

Well, well. That didn't work. Anyway, how could he expect to find anyone at home on Saturday evening. But he could have a good time alone too. In his own place, for example. With one of the books he'd bought today. *Life Begins at Forty*. It might be fun to see what was in it.

He walked quietly in again, as if after a well-executed errand.

'May I have the bill, please.'

He paid and gave the correct percentage of extra tip, neither too much nor too little. Then he quietly got up and left. The young couple had gone. The solitary man sat deeply hunched over behind his bottle. Some other people had entered, two or three couples, he didn't look closely at them.

A strange attack, out of the blue. Luckily it passed as quickly as it came. He'd had quite a bit to drink – half a Rhine wine, a whole Chambertin, half a sherry. He felt it, the light flickered slightly, he had that floating sensation, and his distance from the carpet wasn't quite as usual. Otherwise everything was in order.

Should he drop by the bar?

No. There was never anyone in the bar Saturday night.

In the anteroom he lighted a cigarette. His hand didn't shake. In the cloakroom, the boy handed him his hat. The attendant himself wasn't there – a man who, when handing over a hat, made you feel you were party to an official act. This young man was all right, but he simply gave him his hat.

The sun had set, twilight was on the way. He looked at his watch. Goodness – twenty to nine. He'd been sitting up there for nearly three hours. Oh well. Birthdays were birthdays.

Actually, it was pleasant to have a bit of a – of a floating feeling. A sensitive, impressionable, very receptive condition. Open to the world. Pleasant. Very pleasant. He walked slowly up toward Drammensveien. Past the new buildings where the tram tracks were forever being relaid. Strange how quickly one forgot. How did that house look which had sat on the corner all those years? Oh yes, at the upper corner there was a display of the world's ugliest lampshades, and at the lower corner there was a laundry. That he recalled because he'd once seen Otto Sverdrup, the North Pole skipper, come out from there, broad as a barn door and with a forked beard, a slim packet tucked under his arm. It contained a starched shirt, only one, that was easy to tell. It was the day before Roald Amundsen returned from a polar flight.

Now they were both dead.

They were dead.

And what had they got out of their lives? he wondered.

What have you got out of your life?

Ramstad again. How strange.

What have you got out of...

Pure nonsense!

He turned on to Drammensveien. The lawn on the left displayed strong colours, red and green. The Palace Park on the other side was a dark-green wall built on poles, with a world of receding shadows at the basement level.

Above the trees, the sky was bluish-green, as in April.

Sky high up, light high up. Twilight down here.

Daylight and twilight met and produced shadows in the air.

The bats were flying.

The light flickered slightly.

The street was like a gulf. The bottom of a riverbed.

A stream of people. Strangers. Pale faces floating freely, as if by themselves, slightly above their bodies. It probably was due to the evening light they had at their backs.

Where were they going, all of them? A regular migration.

I come from nowhere and am going no one knows where.

At the bottom of the river of oblivion.

Now he was going home to have a good time.

He didn't feel like it.

Sooner anything else.

All right. Who said he had to go home? There were a thousand other things. Cinemas, excursion spots...

He didn't feel like it.

He felt a bit confused. Finally he found a sentence he could walk in time with, Don't feel like anything – without a wish and well-contented.

A couple of people greeted him. He returned their greeting.

People he knew, not strangers at all.

He could call up Fanny, find out if she was home. She was always glad and cheerful, Fanny was.

He didn't feel like it.

He could go to Røde Mølle.

The devil take Ramstad.

He passed Handelsbygningen. A great many people were wandering about here too. A great many people everywhere. A lady was coming toward him, she looked at him as she passed by. He returned her look, he'd seen her before but couldn't remember where – she was pale, with dark eyes, dressed in white with a silver fox around her neck in spite of the warm weather. She had a peculiarly rocking walk – where had he met her? He turned to look once more, she turned the same moment. Should he turn around? And ask her where he knew her from? He couldn't decide and wandered on, until he reached Lapsetorvet.

Should he go on? And in that case – Bygdøy Allé or

Drammensveien? Crossroads once more, crossroads forever and a day. But now he was going to cheat destiny, now he would let both roads just lie there, now he would turn around and go back again. Where had he seen her? Where had he...

All at once it came! It was her, of course – it was *her*.

Tomorrow and for always!

And the landlady in the doorway...

Oh, what an evening!

When he took off her coat. And her dress. And then garment after garment. And shyness made her blush. And love made her blush even more. Until the last trace of shyness vanished with the last garment and only love was left, like a jubilation.

And they gave themselves to each other, and she – nineteen and had never been with a man before and hadn't told him – moaned and gave herself, moaned and gave herself, until rapture won out over all else and she rose like a bird...

Tomorrow and for always!

And then the landlady stood in the door. Wild, foaming at the mouth. Yelling, screaming: 'Slut, whore! In *my* bed. And you're sick too! Dirtying *my* sheets! And sick too. Swine!'

Why didn't he kill her – why in the hottest hell...

How she cried afterwards. That a human being could cry like that.

'Oh, oh, oh. Knut! Help me!'

This one and only woman in his life who had given herself to him wholly and absolutely, without an ulterior motive.

In youth. Before calculation entered the world.

Tomorrow and for always! Tomorrow and for always!

And he'd never seen her since.

The telegram the next day – mother very ill –

Never seen her since.

The only one – the one and only...

He had turned and was rushing along Drammensveien.

Twenty years old.

Twenty years ago.

He had held life itself in the hollow of his hand. What had he done with it?

What have you made of your life?

He rushed by the lighted windows of Handelsbygningen. A man greeted him, he returned the greeting; he didn't see who it was, not that it mattered. Tacking your way ahead, falling into line and wangling your way ahead, smiling and sweet-talking your way ahead, being greeted and greeting in return – oh, how charming. A pitiful status seeker's existence, calculating, anxious, cautious. Good God, how modest. Without any self-confidence. *Moderate*, he called himself. Cultivated, sensitive, considerate, prudent – nothing but cowardice, cowardice, cowardice, cowardice – easily scared and afraid, covering yourself here, securing yourself there – securing, insuring – insuring? Of course! *Who* was insured? He was, that was clear – forty thousand kroner – what? *Forty* – now it was becoming a joke – anxious, polite, don't step on anyone's toes and in return you're allowed, most graciously, to exist – but *fear*, had he inspired any of the swine with fear? Not a bit, and the result? He was regarded with contempt, treated with amiable condescension; even in his own wretched world all this craftiness, cowardice, caution, and prudence had paid off poorly. *Prudence!* He stuck out his tongue as he ran along, staring people directly in the face.

But *why*, in God's name, *why* had he been so cautious, so completely needlessly cautious, so deadly afraid? Oh, if one only knew! He knew it well, of course: he was afraid of her abandon, it was too great for him, it frightened him. It wasn't simply that telegram, not at all, it wasn't simply that landlady – that mean, damned, eternally accursed landlady – it wasn't only her at all, oh no! Cowardice, anxiety, fear – fear of a love as weighty as the starry sky. Fear of the starry sky. Of its grandeur, its solitude.

Oh, deny it if you dare, you're *afraid* of it, old man! Do you think I haven't noticed, when you are in the mountains with those surgeons of yours, supposedly to go hunting – you who aren't even a proper huntsman, not even a proper killer, which those surgeons *are* at least. As little as possible out in the open in the evening, at any rate in clear weather, you take refuge by the fireplace, suck on your pipe, keeping safe and comfortable and snug – yes, *snug*, bah! Not to mention when you're alone in the mountains! Bolt the door! Lock the door to the stars. Why, I wonder. Answer me, will you, eh?

Even if you well know there are no longer any dangerous animals in the mountains, none except snakes, which don't take shelter at night-time – afraid of the starry sky and of snakes! Hah! But do you know what you're forgetting, dullard that you are? That the flame in the hearth is just as tremendous a thing as the whole of the starry sky, that the distance inward, into matter, into molecules, atoms, and electrons, is just as deep and dizzying as the distance to the most remote star. That you have forgotten. You lack imagination, don't even *dare* to have imagination. And you ran away from, forgot and betrayed the only girl in your life who came to you unconditionally, and...

You put blinkers before your eyes and fingers in your ears, became a good, diligent student, a hard-working fellow – hard-working, well, a regular status-seeker perpetually on the make, with the door bolted, cowardice upon cowardice, emptiness upon emptiness – toadying to the big shots, avoiding the dangerous ones – career, hope of a career – making a marriage of convenience, more than half on calculation – it was not your fault that Agnete – er, well – turned out to be a little better than you deserved. Oh, shabby, shabby, shabby.

Having passed along the fence in front of Sofies Minde, he walked past Quist's bookstore and some flower shops and furniture displays. He stared at all he met, all he passed, stared intently, noticing that people stared back, some nudging one another, some whispering and turning around – he saw all this quite clearly, he even knew what they were thinking, it was as though he could *see* their thoughts, as though there no longer were a separation between his brain and those of the others, no wall, no barrier; they thought he was tipsy, some believed he was slightly crazy, some knew him by sight from before, some knew who he was, which gave an extra edge to their pleasure – just think, that well-known person was tipsy, slightly crazy! He thought as he trotted along, why do you stare at *all* the women? She was in white and had a silver fox around her neck, which wasn't like her at all, by the way, so you need only stare at women in white, with a silver fox around their necks... It isn't very smart for one of Oslo's well-known physicians to run like that, not the least bit smart. What? Not a bit smart! You clever rogue! You coward! You sly fox! Tacking your way ahead, swinging your way ahead, sneaking ahead, cautiously, cautiously, cautiously, looking out for an advantage, advantage, advantage, your own wee little dirty advantage, shutting your eyes to everything else, everything that was a thousand times greater and more important – oh, you chicken! What has become of your courage, daring, the romanticism that you actually had a little of once upon a time – when you knew that you were only one of the many, and knew you were to be part of the struggle for others, without any kind of payment, because the poor, the despairing, helpless and oppressed are simply unable to pay? You have run away, that's it. Deserter! Runaway! Have you forgotten all this? Did you think you'd never meet up with these thoughts? Did you think you were safe, hiding in the corner with your face against the wall? No way!

He stuck out his tongue at himself again, while staring at everybody and running on down the street – with short, hurried, tripping steps, as if the pavement burned his feet. Swarms of thoughts and pictures raced through his head, like what happens when you fire a shot in the mountains and the whole landscape suddenly comes alive with flapping birds – a multitude of thoughts and pictures all mixed up, intertwined, with everything floating as in a dream – oh, wait, now he remembered what he dreamed last night – wait a moment, now he *almo*st remembered, it was – no, now it was gone again.

On passing the Glitne Building, he met a couple who greeted him, a greeting he returned mechanically, as if in a puppet theatre – he was running with long steps now, there were fewer people here and nobody to stare at. Now he passed the lawn again, now the tramlines, now he reached the point where

Stortingsgaten turned off – crossroads, crossroads – but nearly everyone went down Stortingsgaten and precisely for that reason it would be just like her to go down Karl Johans gate – no, no, don't stop and start doubting now, no doubting now! He followed the main stream down, rushed past Scala, and, thinking she could've gone to a movie, dropped by Saga.

But there weren't any people in front of Saga. He discovered that the show didn't begin until half-past nine – with the appearance of vaudeville performers, the whole excellent summer programme. Come and see – indeed! So, Casino, Circus, Eldorado, one of the downtown cafés, ten thousand other places – it was hopeless. He was grazed by a total discouragement, like the shadow of a big black bird; but he pulled himself out of the shadow. It was *not* hopeless if only he was dead set on it; and why couldn't chance work in his favour for once – it *must* work in his favour this one time – he was already on his way up Roald Amundsens gate, ran past the compact row of parked cars along the premises of Continental, recognized Gunnerus' licence number en passant – hah! What if Mrs Gunnerus had taken a peep down here! Oh, drop the gloating! He rounded the corner travel agency with the globe over the door and maps and ships in the window, and ran on – she was going to Casino, sure she was, no doubt about it, and he instinctively felt that, if he was lucky, he would catch her as she stood at the ticket window buying her ticket, that kind of instinct never deceived you. He passed the entrance to the Continental without even looking inside, passed the long, narrow sidewalk restaurant without looking inside, ran at top speed across the street in front of the Theatre Café – a man tipped his hat, he tipped his hat back without looking, a car honked ferociously directly into his ear, he felt a wheel brush his trouser leg, heard a furious voice but didn't turn, just rushed on.

A crowd was standing in front of Casino, the usual moviegoers; they were stretching their necks for their beloveds, who played hard to get and turned up at the very last moment, the customary business trick they had learned from their mothers or possessed by instinct – or was it just their bird brains which didn't manage to keep track of everything? Just think, both handkerchief and mirror and comb and lipstick and God knows what, so the lovely one forgot to powder her nose and had to go back upstairs, and then was late! Maybe that was it, he didn't know, and what did it matter anyway – he saw at a glance that she wasn't there at any rate. He made his way toward the ticket window.

She wasn't there. No, she had already bought her ticket and stood downstairs, or had already gone in... He walked down the stairs. No. He went toward the middle aisle and, sweeping the usher aside, said, 'I'm Dr. Holmen, I'm looking for someone, it's important!' He stuck his head in – eight or ten people were sitting in there, scattered about – no. Wait! No, she wasn't there.

The bird cast its shadow upon him again, but in a moment he had escaped from under it – well, he'd been mistaken there, he'd fooled himself, that happened, but just wait, here you had to proceed systematically, taking your chance with Circus or Eldorado – what time was it? He raised his arm: Five to nine! Too late to catch her there. But in that case she would not be out until a quarter to eleven! And meanwhile he could search the cafés, she was dressed to go out, oh, he would find her again, no doubt about it, once he got out of here – he threw himself against the stream of people pressing forward down the stairs, cut his way like a knife through butter and found himself in the street again. There was a light breeze, the evening air wrapped itself around him like a cool, fresh bath, and he stopped a moment, wiped his forehead and sucked up a big gulp of air, delicious – his disappointment was forgotten, he made a fresh start, *now*, streaking toward the Theatre Café, to take care of that first. A strange sensation – as he hurried along the street he wasn't aware of touching the ground, he didn't walk, he flew. He looked sharply at everyone he met but, allowing nothing to alter his course, flew on – he lay low, leaning forward on the air, cleaving it, flying backward – back through time – back – to her –

'Hi, Holmen!'

About to pass through the corner entrance of the Theatre

41

Café, he turned around sharply, as if he'd heard a shot.

It was Sunde, with his wife and a man he didn't know. They came bustling around the corner by the pavement restaurant, Sunde at the head. They were in high spirits, flushed and laughing.

'You are the man!' Sunde talked a mile a minute, eager and loud, introducing the stranger, a lawyer this or that, obviously from the provinces, a husky guy with a red face, wispy red hair, and an excessively self-confident manner.

Well, this was the story – the Sundes were going to use the weekend to look at some forests up in Åsnes, had packed a basket of provisions and everything and were already sitting in the car with drinks and goodies, and the moment they turned onto Drammensveien, a reckless brute of a driver came from the left, forcing Sunde to jump on the brakes and – crash! He could feel something go, and sure enough, the rear axle was broken! And Saturday at noon, and...

Mrs Sunde burst into laughter: 'Oh, you should've seen Einar when it dawned on him that we would have to turn round!'

She laughed till the tears came.

Sunde continued to fuss. 'The driver? Oh, *he* drove on, just like that. But I managed to take down the pig's licence anyway, so...'

He talked, brandishing his stick and pointing, as if it were all taking place here and now.

And so the Saturday outing went up in smoke. They would have to make a Sunday outing instead. They could set out early. The repairman had promised. But the rear axle... Here came a detailed description of the damage. Sunde talked himself into a sweat. Tiny little drops of sweat collected on that broad nose of his. His eyes glittered with eagerness. What Sunde was interested in was always the most important thing in the world. Right now the brakes on his car were the most important thing in the world, and it was unthinkable that anyone could be of the opinion that anything else was more important in this world.

'And so we made calls here and there for you, for we had

heard you'd been seen in town – '

Mrs Sunde interrupted: 'Yes, because we came across Mrs Gunnerus – oh, God, how funny she was, dying to hear if we'd seen Mr Gunnerus! But she didn't dare say so straight out, not for the world – oh, hold on to me, will you!' Mrs Sunde was dying with laughter. She bubbled and simmered when she laughed, like a pot boiling over. A pot full of potatoes. The unknown lawyer wanted to be in on it, too, and laughed in deep blasts, 'Haw-haw-haw!'

'But you were nowhere to be found. Not at home and not in the office, and – '

'Well, you see, here we were, a party of three with the evening ahead of us, and with you we would be four, and a game of bridge – '

' – and so we ended up in the bar here at the Continental, and there we've sat – oh, I don't know for how long, and on and off we've sent a delegation out to the telephone – '

'We wondered if we should've gone up to the dining room, but that is empty as the desert now in the summertime, so...'

They all spoke at the same time, laughing uproariously and trying with a good deal of noise to hide from themselves and others that they had been bored, that they were still bored, that they were empty and confused and looking for help at any price against the emptiness and the boredom.

As he stood there listening to them, he was in a painful way in two places at once.

He was far away, rushing along a road, and he had to hurry, it was a matter of life and death – but suddenly people were forcing their company on him, latching on to him, joking and jabbering that life consists of trifles, trifles, trifles.

And at the same time he stood here hemming and hawing, hearing and seeing, and all his sense impressions were importunately sharp.

The coarse pores on the tip of Mrs Sunde's nose, the small, anxious eyes of Sunde. The affectation in Mrs Sunde's perpetual cheerfulness, the hollowness of Sunde's happy eagerness – so, the two of them were bored with each other, peevish with each other when they were alone. Had he been deaf and blind, not to notice any of this until now? He had associated with these people, they had been his friends – wasn't that what they were called, people towards whom one felt totally indifferent?

Totally indifferent – except that he could, with total indifference, picture himself murdering them.

He said something or other about a rendezvous, stammering out his words and bringing a protest from Sunde, while Mrs Sunde grabbed his arm. Tearing himself angrily away, he glimpsed the embarrassed, astonished, offended faces behind him from the corner of his eye – then he got through the door.

It had all taken scarcely more than five minutes, but it sufficed; he had come down to earth again, the present had reared its head in the shape of three people and barred his way. She had been almost within reach in the invisible medium before him, and now she had stolen a march on him again, got lost, sunk into the ground, sucked in by the darkness, by the past, vanished at one of the ten thousand crossroads that lay ahead of him – no, behind him – and here he was tramping blindly along...

Suddenly he felt completely disheartened. It was no use. After all, she could be in any number of possible places; on his way down he had passed cafés, cinemas, hotels, numerous side streets, countless entrance doors – she could be in a hundred thousand places now, so why not just as well give up!

No! Not give up! He forced himself: quiet now, no panic now! He walked slowly through the café, looking around carefully, first the left side all the way in, then back to the starting point, and then the other side. The room was filled with the usual Saturday evening summer clientele. A man greeted him, visibly embarrassed, a patient who hadn't paid his bill and now felt he'd been caught cheating. He returned the greeting, discovered he had the hat on his head and removed it.

She wasn't there.

He walked out, into the pavement restaurant, peering right

and left.

No.

He walked across the street, passed the tram stop, crossed the square before the theatre and reached Karl Johans gate. People were strolling up and down, women's white dresses provided spots of light along dark rows of benches, there were whispers and murmurs, a woman's shrill laughter.

Which way? No stopping now, not for the world, no stopping now. First, the Grand Café, Palmen, Speilen. He walked more briskly.

The doorman bowed politely as he passed. He had stayed here a couple of times.

Palmen was empty, sad, desolate as a desert. A couple of lone clients were separated by endless stretches of empty chairs.

He walked past the doorman's loge, along the corridor, straight through Speilen.

No.

Onward! Up to Bristol!

Slowly, some of his hunting mood returned, but the going was heavier now, it had acquired a bitter, indignant and spiteful quality – don't give up, never give up, even if the devil and all his angels... He had lost something, his faith, the certainty – he couldn't help recalling something: you're asleep, in the middle of a lovely dream, you're flying, blissfully happy, then you're awakened, but you refuse to wake up and drop into sleep again on purpose, wanting to fly on; you fall asleep in a way, fly in a way, but your flight is not the same, you hit bumps on the ground, thud, thud, and awake a little each time... He cursed and swore inwardly as he ran up the street, groaning.

Hat in hand, he walked through the Moorish Hall, on the lookout. A young man sitting with a young lady in the sofa by the wall bowed respectfully.

He had grown sufficiently old for people he didn't know to bow respectfully. She wasn't there.

He looked in on the rotisserie and the grill.

No.

Suddenly he felt very tired, the disappointment affected his knees, and he let himself sink into a chair at the newspaper table. A gentleman on the other side of the table looked up fleetingly from his paper – a white-haired gentleman with black eyebrows, horn-rimmed glasses, swarthy, with firm inter-national features which gave the impression of being burned in clay – why did he notice all that? Didn't know. He sank down into himself, didn't know where he was, floating again.

Tomorrow and for always!

Then, abruptly, he felt something like a jolt in his consciousness: What if she calls you at home!

He jumped out of his chair.

Had he become a complete dunce? Totally obtuse? Chasing after her at Speilen and Bristol, as if *she* could possibly hang around there – he had to laugh. He did indeed laugh, heard himself give a brief burst of laughter, then noticed a pair of inquiring eyes on the other side of the table; he had already grabbed his hat and was heading for the door.

Telephone... He had forgotten, but now he remembered: *she, too, turned around* – she turned and looked at him – she recognized him – and he did have a telephone –

'Taxi, please!'

A taxi was right there. He jumped in. 'Drive as fast as you can!'

The taxi buzzed off down Kristian IVs gate, along the row of parked cars, across Universitetsgaten, along fresh rows of parked cars, Tullinløkken, Frederiks gate, Wergelandsveien – the car, growling like a dog, devoured the streets, fast, but not fast enough! He bent forward to increase the speed.

How dumb he had been, dumb, he ought to have rushed home at once, to the telephone and the telephone book – in a pinch he could call Håkenrud, find out about her through him – it was there he'd first met her, after all.

If only she wasn't calling now, while he was on his way.

'Oh, drive a bit faster, can you!'

The chauffeur made a screeching turn at Parkveien. Faster ! Faster!

They rolled past Palace Park; he glimpsed a couple on a bench in the semi-darkness in there, and a man wandering about by himself, stoop-shouldered, lonely, old. The taxi flung him into the corner as it turned onto Uranienborgveien – one, two, three – another turn, Oscars gate. The taxi stopped. He tumbled out, slightly dizzy, fumbled a bit with the money. There! He took the stairs three steps at a time. As long as I can take the stairs three at a time... The first flight. The second flight. The third flight. If only she wasn't calling right now.

He stood in front of the entrance, fumbling for the key in his pocket – what the hell, he had it in his hand as he fumbled for the money. Ah, there...

Then he heard it.

The telephone was ringing in there. Far away, faintly, like a pulse: a ring, silence, ring, silence, ring –

His hand trembled so badly the keys fell on the floor. Of all the devilish... He got hold of them, heard the telephone go on ringing, the key in the lock, the wrong key, damn damn, a fresh key, the telephone still ringing, the right key this time, no, yes, no – are you being stubborn, you – ! In a fit of ungovernable rage, he felt like breaking the window, but then the door suddenly opened without difficulty; with the telephone still ringing, he left the key in the door and ran through the hallway and across the living room, with only a few steps to go – . Then it stopped, the last brief click was like a full stop.

Too late.

He lifted the receiver anyway and heard only the dialing tone. That empty, remote, lonely dialing tone, the ether, cosmic space, a sound like that of a cold wind across endless desolate distances. Faraway times and places...

He stood there with the receiver close to his ear. Something had to emerge from this sound, a voice, something or other.

Wind. Cold. Solitude.

Slowly he put down the receiver, with a numb feeling of utter impotence.

If only he had... But it was no use reasoning. No use. No use. But maybe she was at Håkenrud's. Call Håkenrud. Ask for

Helga – Helga – what was she called beside Helga? He had forgotten! But that didn't matter. Helga was enough, there was only one.

His hands benumbed, he fiddled with the telephone book.

No Håkenrud. There was no Håkenrud in the book. He just needed one name, and that was not in the telephone book.

He flopped down into the nearest chair. He couldn't be bothered to stir any more. Wouldn't ever bother to stir any more. He sat there utterly listless. It was all the same anyway. Maybe she would ring again. No matter. It was all the same. Sit still and wait. Maybe she would call again. Still and ... all the same...

Had he slept? He jumped up, a sound buzzing in his ear. Had someone called him?

It was only the wall clock over in the corner, it always coughed twice every quarter of an hour, like an old man full of dignity before he takes the floor. What time was it? A quarter to ten.

He had left the door open.

And now he remembered: when he ran down the hallway he had glimpsed something white on the floor, just inside the crack in the door. Mail! A letter! Had she dropped by?

He rushed out and turned on the light. Yes. Some mail was lying on the floor. A note from Sunde – he had been in a cheerful mood already then. A couple of subscription invitations. A letter with unfamiliar handwriting. He tore it open. Something heavy fell out, two Yale keys wrapped in paper. What...!

The letter was from Ramstad.

He tossed it aside with a disappointment that resembled hatred. He walked to the entrance door, took out the key and closed the door.

Then he picked up the letter again.

*

'Dear Dr. Holmen,

Do you remember our excellent evening at the Røde Mølle a fortnight ago?

We talked about all kinds of things. But among other things I said that I intended to go away for a fortnight or so, and that I was looking for someone who could keep an eye on my apartment; it's old-fashioned and needs looking after, and the caretaker on the premises is a bit lax that way. You said you were available, you remember? True, it was late – I don't recall exactly the number of our highballs.

Do you stand by your offer? The trip came up a bit sooner than expected. I wasn't able to get hold of you on the telephone this morning, and time is too short to make it home now. I enclose the keys, hoping that you can at least drop by and turn off the electric power to the bathroom and the hot water in the kitchen, if nothing else – it would be impractical if the whole works should blow up.

One more thing. You're staying in town, right? If you should wish to change residence for a couple of weeks – you know, variety is the spice of life, at least as far as I'm concerned – just help yourself. Clean sheets have been put on, that I know, the morning help sees to it every Saturday.

Frankly speaking, I had the impression that something of the sort might amuse you.

I myself am taking to the woods, will be away for a fortnight and have no address.

Regards,
A. Ramstad'

There was a postscript with some practical information – the name of the caretaker and the morning help, explanation of the switches for the hot water, beside the address, a number in a small side street off Wergelandsveien.

He didn't even read it through properly.

He was thinking of something else.

Ramstad.

Ramstad, who was constantly popping up today. But he was thinking about something beside that. This offer took care of everything. It was like working on an inextricable knot and suddenly getting hold of the end of a thread that unravels everything.

It was as though a weight was lifted off him.

He had made his decision.

He? Made? It had been made for him. He remembered what he'd been thinking an hour ago. Why cannot chance for once be on my side? Here chance had been on his side. A fortnight on holiday in the past. Wander along old trails. Stop for a moment at old crossroads. Go about things calmly and systematically. Track down Håkenrud. Find *her*. Clear up many things. Test one's values. Afterwards – afterwards he would see.

He would grant himself these fourteen days. He went through his practice in his head. No, there were no difficult matters at the moment. Nothing he couldn't leave to Strand. He went over to the telephone at once, called, and heard the calm, slightly drowsy voice of Strand.

Could he refer his patients to him for a couple of weeks?

Strand wasn't even surprised, he was too phlegmatic for that.

Certainly. As long as it didn't interrupt the hunting season. And if there were any special instructions...

Fine. He would receive what was necessary in writing. That was that.

It remained only to write a note to the secretary, asking her to take care of whatever else was required – a sign on the door, a phone call to some of the patients.

He took a cab down to the office right away and wrote out detailed information for her.

So. Through with that.

He felt really through, completely through, as though he would never be there again. That probably ought to upset him, but it did not. On the contrary, he felt an enormous relief, as if he were about to allow himself a fabulous holiday. A holiday without equal in – hell, why be modest! – world history. He felt as if he'd stolen a fortnight from eternity. Fourteen long days of extra life free of charge. Whee!

All that remained to do was to inform the maid, write to Agnete, see to –

See to what? He was only going to move into another apartment a few blocks away.

He discovered it didn't feel like that. He was going on a long journey with an unknown destination.

He had begun to walk up towards Ramstad's apartment. These first steps – there was something solemn about them. His chest expanded. He looked up. A dark, clear starry sky. He took a couple of deep breaths. So this had turned into a red-letter day after all.

*

He passed one of the houses farthest down in Wergelandsveien. A telephone was ringing in there. Only now did he remember that he'd gone away from his. What if she'd called again, while he was gone!

The uneasiness got to him only for a moment. He knew it was by no means certain that it was she who had called. In fact, it was almost unthinkable, after twenty years, shy as she was.

He looked at the time. A quarter past ten. He could still easily make the cinemas, if he wanted to. But he wasn't sure he wanted to. That was just *too* haphazard. No, the whole situation had to be tackled in an entirely different way now. He was mildly surprised by how calm he'd become, just mildly surprised; it was as though he didn't have any strong feelings at his disposal just now, as chaos was gradually replaced by a slow-paced working order.

Not being familiar with the little side street, he couldn't find the correct number right away. As so often in such side streets, there was something wrong with the numbers, few as they were, one house sitting behind another and a couple fronting altogether different streets – the entire street was reminiscent of those elderly ladies who lead an extremely simple and withdrawn life, but nonetheless manage, with small means, to create a certain confusion suggestive of a former time of greatness, with both husband and lover and the lover's mistress and the latter's friend, who is a friend of the wife's husband...

The street lighting was poor as well.

He was looking around for quite a while. In the end he'd managed to find all the wrong numbers, with only one house to go, as far as he could see. So that ought to be the correct one; but it had no number, once again as far as he could see. It was sitting behind one of the others, and the lighting was exceptionally poor. It was a grey, quite handsome house of four stories, with a small garden in front. He retraced his steps to see if the low garden fence might have a number on it. At that moment a woman walked out of the door. She walked straight toward him on the coarse gravel, which crunched drily, like empty egg shells, under her shoes. She gave a little start the moment she noticed him.

He tipped his hat and asked if this was number five.

Yes.

She remained standing for a moment, with an expression as if she knew him. Giving her a second quick look, he knew he'd met her, but couldn't remember where.

She noticed his glance. 'Aren't you Dr. Holmen?'

'Yes.'

'I'm Vera Boye.'

'Oh.'

She laughed.

'I can't expect you to recognize me. I was a patient at Ullevål Hospital once – four years ago.'

At that moment he remembered her. A stream of memories emerged.

A young girl had been found unconscious in the street and was brought in for emergency aid: ear inflammation, most likely after a blow – he remembered the surgery very well. And afterward, her slightly dissipated father on a visit, sitting there with tears of pure alcohol in his eyes. Others came too. Many others. He remembered well her strange charm and visited her

52

more often than necessary; it could have developed into almost anything, she was half in love with him, his memory wasn't deceiving him there. And that wasn't surprising, the nurses had filled her with stories about the fine operation. She had a mysterious side to her, he couldn't make out her background. Her father was simple and straightforward and a drunkard, but an aunt was completely different, and some friends – no, he just couldn't figure her out.

Why didn't it develop into anything? She disappeared, he couldn't quite remember...

'Yes, I remember you very well,' he said. 'Hm, what a strange coincidence!'

'Yes.' She was looking at the ground, digging the gravel with the toe of her shoe.

Yes, now he remembered – he fell ill himself that time, and when he got on his feet again she was gone. And afterwards – well, afterwards... Several things got in the way. A hundred things, a hundred tiny little things.

Something always got in the way.

How stupid he ran into her just now.

'Anyway, it was nice meeting you again!' he said.

She didn't say a word.

'You know, I'm here on a curious errand,' he went on (one had to say something, after all). 'A friend of mine, or rather a casual acquaintance of mine – quite casual actually' (why did he have to say that?) – 'has written and asked me to keep an eye on his apartment while he's away.'

Now she looked up. 'And he lives here – in number five?'

'Yes. It should be here. His name is Ramstad.'

She thought it over for a little while. 'Yes, there is a Ramstad here,' she said.

Pause. She was looking at the ground again. He was trying to understand something which in reality might be quite simple, but he couldn't do it – he had a feeling that thoughts from two different levels were intermingling and producing a tangle. He had come here chasing a girl who stood at a crossroads in his past calling him. And on the way he stumbled on a girl who stood at a crossroads in his past, and – how did it all hang together? A curious coincidence. But, after all, life consisted of coincidences, blind coincidences, or was there another law of life?

'Well, I'm just going up to take a look at the apartment,' he said.

'But why don't you come up with me? Since chance, or fate, or whatever it's called, has let us meet here? It must've meant something by it? That much at least?'

Why was he standing here proposing this? It was just a piece of foolishness.

'Hm – fate,' she said hesitantly. 'It's late, so I really ought to go home. Okay, I'm coming with you,' she decided quickly.

'You've been visiting here?' he asked, as he was fiddling with the keys. (Idiotic question.)

'Yes.'

She answered so briefly that a pause ensued. He unlocked the entrance door and let her in. They mounted the stairs in silence.

The staircase was nice, wide and old-fashioned. The house was old and slightly modernized – the light in the staircase came from narrow cylinders and cones of mat glass, the latest fashion, fake modernism, but the entrance doors boasted old coloured glass, imitation of stained-glass windows, an earlier fashion, fake romanticism. There were two tenants on each floor. Altogether it made a good impression, bourgeois and respectable; he had really pictured Ramstad's staircase differently. At the top there was only one door. It was dark. He bent down and read the name:

> *A. Ramstad*
> Engineer

He unlocked the door and let her in first.

The hallway was old-fashioned, with breast-high brown oak panelling. A large mirror hung on the wall to the left, with a small red table in front of it. There was a brown door straight ahead, and one to the right. The one to the right led to the bathroom, as it turned out, a large modern bathroom with a partly sunken tub and light-green tiles on the walls. At the far end of the bathroom was another door. Peering in, he saw a small bedroom.

A bed, a table, a clothes closet with a mirror. All right.

The door straight ahead led to a large room; it was dark, but through the two windows there came a pale reflection of light from a lamp outside. A couple of tree tops stood out like shadows against the windowpanes. He fumbled at the wall near the door frame, found the switch and turned on the light.

It was a plain, average man's room, with a semi-circular fireplace in one corner and a broad couch in the other. A couple of chairs and a low table stood before the fireplace, and between the windows there was a table. A combined living and dining room. It had a phonograph and a radio and a few bookcases. Nothing was particularly modern, the chairs were quite ordinary, good chairs to sit in, and the dining-room table was an ordinary table to eat at.

There were two doors. The one on the left led to a small kitchenette, with a big hotplate and a tiny little icebox. On the right was the study – books from floor to ceiling along two walls, and a large writing table before the window. A door led to the bedroom.

That was the apartment. It suited him perfectly.

She had followed him from room to room. He turned toward her. 'Well, what do you think?'

'About what?'

'The apartment, of course.'

'Oh. Well, the apartment seems to be all right.'

'All right? It's perfect. I couldn't have made it better myself!'

He wandered back and forth through the two rooms for a few moments. He liked the study best – the large bookshelves and the solid heavy writing table inspired him with a zest for work; in fact, he could fetch the started dissertation, his card files and notes, and take a look at things now and then. The two weeks seemed like a little eternity. Oh, he would do wonders.

A large globe stood beside the writing table. There he could undertake strange journeys when he had nothing else to do. At one time such journeys were the most interesting thing he knew – he had lived in a furnished room where a globe had been left behind by an old teacher. It was long ago, a little eternity. To him it seemed like yesterday.

Against the third wall stood a low, wide cabinet. A long row of shell cases of different sizes had been placed on top of it; higher up, on the wall, hung several rifles, some revolvers, and a pair of automatic pistols. An entire arms collection. Of course, explosives were Ramstad's specialty.

He took a turn to the living room again, sniffing about like a dog in the woods. Above the wide couch hung a huge sword and a broad axe, and between them an old print, the picture of an execution – scaffold and stake and wheel. So. One played at being a sadist, while indulging in daydreams on the couch.

She had remained in the study. She didn't seem to be greatly interested in this apartment. So little interested, in fact, that he felt his own eagerness as a discourtesy which had to be explained: 'You see, I'll be living here.'

'You'll be living here?'

She sounded astonished.

'Yes. For a couple of weeks. I want to be by myself for a while. To meditate a little. Test my values. There are several things I have to figure out – myself, for one.' (Had he taken leave of his senses, chattering like this to a strange lady?) 'In short' (now stop it, and watch your mouth), 'we must drink to this. If Ramstad has such a thing as liquor in his place.'

The low cabinet with the shells on top contained everything they could wish for – a couple of dark bottles of port and madeira, and a couple of decanters with something in them. He sniffed: Whisky. Sherry.

Furthest back on the shelf stood a broad bottle of cognac.

He rummaged in the cabinet with guilty delight, much the same as when he made illegal forays to the pantry in his childhood days.

She wanted a cognac. He wanted a whisky. They sat down in the chimney corner. He went into the kitchen, found some soda in the icebox, but no bottle opener. He felt he'd seen one somewhere; wasn't there one lying on the writing table? He went into the study.

No.

But he had seen it, all right – or was it something else he'd seen there? Something he couldn't see now?

Again this sense of floating which he had experienced several times today, without knowing what it meant – whether it was something he'd forgotten, which he ought to remember, or something he'd seen which he missed.

She called to him, 'Is it the bottle opener you're looking for? Here it is.' She was holding it in her hand.

She sat looking into the black, dead fireplace.

'Do you know this Ramstad very well, since you're going to stay in his apartment – or rather slightly, since you haven't been here before? Pardon me for asking.'

'Actually, I don't know him at all.'

She looked at him. He laughed.

'It's true. But it's quite a story. He's a funny guy, this Ramstad. You should see him – I guess there isn't a picture of him here? No, you don't hang photographs of yourself in your own home. Well, he's tall and thin and dark, with curly hair, looks slightly Negroid, yes, in fact, he makes you think of a white Zulu; but he's Norwegian enough, we are from the same hamlet, by the way, so in a way I know him. He's a few years younger than I. Thirty-three, he said. A critical age. He was a mere boy when I became a student, and since then I've barely been home; we've never had anything to do with each other, so in a way I don't know him. We aren't even on a first-name basis, which on reflection is rather strange; after all, people from the same hamlet are usually on an informal footing, even if they've never exchanged a word, so to speak, but we addressed each other formally from the very first moment. I had a fleeting contact with him a few years ago, in connection with some business matters, I met him at a broker's – but that's neither here nor there. He's a chemist, consultant to an explosives factory; however, he seems to have various interests – he's no doubt a gifted person. You should hear him talk, he never shuts up, and what he says is not *all* nonsense. Like testing one's values, an expression he's simply managed to foist on me. A cold fellow. A bit of an eccentric, maybe. Well, this summer I ran across him again – but here I am talking and talking. Skål!'

They drank.

She turned her face towards him when they drank their toast. Otherwise she was looking into the fireplace all the time, so he saw her in profile.

A lovely profile. A lovely girl all around. But she looked a bit tired. Very tired.

That time, four years ago, the doctors just called her Tut's mother-in-law among themselves. Nefertiti, wasn't that the name of that lovely young Egyptian girl who was featured on the cover of every book at the time? Vera Boye looked like her. The same pure, pale profile, the same high, arched brows – they were genuine, that he could see. Strangely, though, she looked thoroughly Norwegian at the same time, as if she'd come straight down from one of the mountain valleys, the daughter of a local king. But she was an authentic Oslo girl, born at Kampen, the daughter of a planing mill worker. Oh yes, they had certainly talked about her. He was rather sweet on her at the time. She radiated a mysterious charm, he remembered it well.

Now he was protected, immune, injected with that great love of twenty years ago.

She half turned her head towards him. 'Well, so you met him...'

'Yes. Ramstad, you mean. It was pure chance. It happened about a fortnight ago. Let's see... I'd been at the National – the National Hospital, you know – and was standing at the corner of Pilestredet and Nordahl Bruns gate. I still remember it was raining... . No, nonsense, the sun was shining...'

How strange. How curious.

He sat for a moment, lost in thought.

'And so you became bewitched?'

'No. Excuse me. I just happened to recall an old incident. No, I ran across some friends in the street. And that led to a so-called first-class dinner, with a *nachspiel* at Røde Mølle. And there we came across Ramstad. He knew one of the others, and me too in a way, and the upshot was that he moved over to us. But – and this is really funny – I had the impression that it was *me* he was talking to all along, although it was one of the others he actually knew. Nothing but nonsense, of course.

'Anyway, I noticed him before he came over – well, I knew him, after all – yes, I *noticed him*. He was staring at me whenever he thought I wasn't looking. You notice that sort of thing. And when he did come over, I quite definitely had the impression that it was *me* he was interested in.

'And today I received this letter.' (Why on earth was he sitting here saying all this?)

Irritated, he got up and looked about him for cigarettes.

'Excuse me for sitting here talking nonsense about this chap Ramstad,' he said, to round it off. 'After all, he's of no interest to you.'

'Oh, he is!' she said politely. But it was all too clear that she was very tired.

'No. But, you see, he concerns me – well, for several reasons. Among other things because – well, because there's something about him. If you knew him you would understand. The fellow is not altogether ordinary. And – there is something in it all which I don't understand. And I prefer to understand things, it's a bad habit of mine.' (Stop now. Stop.)

Pause.

'Skål!' he said.

They drank.

Another pause. She was staring into the fireplace, as if she saw something or other in there. He glanced over – nothing but soot and a bit of ash.

It had been a mistake to ask her to come up. Poor girl, she looked tired and depressed. And he couldn't think about anything to talk to her about either, now that the topic of Ramstad was completely exhausted.

An awkward pause – wasn't that what they called it?

But he sat here feeling fine.

Free as a bird! Fourteen days!

An eternity of time! He had a sense of happiness and buoyancy, it felt as though his whole ribcage were rising, like an aeroplane just before it becomes airborne.

It was this same feeling of buoyancy, and a desire to help someone who was depressed, that made him say, 'Frankly, I was quite keen on you that time, four years ago.'

She looked at him. And smiled – a pale smile; but she did smile. 'Yes? Well – just as frankly, I was rather keen on you too. But then you disappeared. That was just before I was to be discharged. You became ill, I think?'

'Yes, I became ill. It was something – '

He couldn't remember what it was.

'It was my throat. And when I came back you were gone. I remember trying to track you down. I dropped by the bookstore, where I knew you worked. But you were gone.'

'I wasn't there any longer,' she said. 'I went away to train as a beautician.'

'And so...'

He noticed he became slightly disappointed and embarrassed.

She laughed. 'I can see you were disappointed. Yes, I'm working in a beauty parlour now. It probably isn't quite as refined as working in a bookstore – I don't know. But it's a good deal better paid. Because – books are a luxury. But beauty is a necessity of life.'

'Disappointed? Far from it!' he said.

Far from it. He was not disappointed.

The pause had been punctured. They talked about this and that. The conversation wandered hither and thither.

Weren't they, in fact, flirting a little?

Her eyes had acquired a semblance of life. Something

60

mirthful? No. Something bewildered and helpless? He didn't know.

He thought, Who is she really?

And here he sat carrying on a tentative flirt with a young lady – though an hour ago –

Who are we really?

Oh well, you must be allowed to play a little, he thought.

She looked at the time and jumped up.

It was past twelve-thirty.

She lived on Parkveien.

He took her arm as they went into the street. He noticed again that she was tired, walking slowly and leaning against him without saying a word.

He looked down at her. 'You're so quiet.'

She looked up. 'Am I? *Everything* is quiet now. Not a soul anywhere.'

The side streets they were walking were deserted.

Shortly afterwards he noticed that she was trembling against his arm.

'Are you cold?'

'Oh no.'

He put his finger under her chin and looked at her.

She closed her eyes. She had been crying. She was still crying. The tears flowed quietly down her cheeks.

'I'm so tired,' she whispered. 'That's all. I worked overtime today.'

It was that same feeling of buoyancy that made him, in an attempt somehow to comfort her, pull her close and kiss her.

He could afford that. And he felt sorry for her. And, when all was said and done, she too was one of his crossroads.

She stood still, completely passive. It was as though she were asleep. But the next moment he noticed that she was responding. A fragrance rose from her lips, fresh and sourish. It reminded him of woodland bogs in autumn, with early morning fog and a clear sky, and tallyho. He noticed, despite the warmth that surged up in him, that he himself was very tired now, his thoughts took off in different directions and ran ahead on their own.

Those fourteen days, he thought, don't really start until Monday – what if I steal one more day?

'Will you spend tomorrow with me?' he said. 'We can go swimming at Ingierstrand Beach.'

Pooh. He could afford that.

She smiled. 'Thank you. I'd like that.'

'All right. So I'll pick you up. At?'

'Half-past ten?'

'Half-past ten.'

Lying in bed at home afterwards, he tried to think coherently about what had happened this day.

But it only came to glimpses and pictures. He thought of Helga – well, not Helga, but *her*, the one he'd met this evening, for the first time in twenty years. He felt restlessness and anxiety beginning to peal inside him again. There was no time to lose. No time to lose!

He escaped into his thoughts of the coming fortnight.

On holiday in the past! He saw in his mind's eye many crossroads from bygone days, thought about all those untrodden paths and knew: in these fourteen days he would wander on some of them. He sensed a new power within himself that filled him with delight. Oh, he had plenty of time. A world of time. He would do wonders.

With this sense of strength, triumph and peace he fell asleep.

That was how it began.

A Sunday Outside of Time

He woke up fresh and rested, with a feeling that yesterday evening was far away. It belonged in a nocturnal world, on the other side of the moon.

Was it he who had rushed down Drammensveien beside himself, in a state of ecstacy? *He* in ecstasy!

Come, come. Not too supercilious, thank you, just because it was daylight. Yesterday had ended with certain decisions, if he remembered correctly.

He began to think back.

Gradually the day before became less and less remote, his decisions less and less strange. If he lay a little longer, perhaps...

But why loll in bed like this!

He got up.

It was Sunday. Today he was on vacation from everything, even from vacation itself. A holiday outside of time.

The weather was of a summer greyness, with a silvery lustre to it; the sun was just waiting behind the clouds. He decided there would be sunshine. Then he stepped into the bathroom.

Afterwards, newly shaven and bathed, he padded about in slippers, dawdling a bit. There was nothing more agreeable than dawdling like this – playing a record or pondering long and deeply over a shirt and tie. Ah, life could at a pinch be quite livable.

He was alone in the apartment, both maids being at Hankø with Agnete and the children, and the morning help they had taken on in the meantime was religious, thank God, and didn't come Sundays. He walked back and forth between the kitchen and the dining room, made breakfast and set the table.

Indeed, life could be quite livable.

He was hungry. Bacon and eggs, red tomatoes, honey, cheese – and with milk from the icebox and piping hot, fragrant coffee.

One pipe.

Then he finished dressing and gave a nod of recognition to himself in the mirror. This was him. Or, from yesterday on, perhaps he had better say: this was also him – a clean-shaven, well-kempt gentleman, not yet definitely old, although he had turned forty, in a light-grey suit with sharp creases in his trousers, light-grey suede shoes, grey gloves – no, what the hell, bah! He tossed the gloves aside.

But, on the other hand, swimming trunks, beach shoes, bathrobe, sombrero and sunglasses.

Then he went down to the garage.

A nice glossy car was highly apt to increase a man's self-confidence.

A nice glossy girl too. Though – at first you were uncertain and in love, afterwards you were certain and out of love, both bad, in part for your self-confidence, in part for the girl.

A car, on the other hand... There was never any trouble with a car. And if there was trouble with it, you let someone else take care of it for the present.

A car was a sweet girl, all right, glossy and pretty and obedient; if you said 'toot,' it tooted, 'run,' it ran.

It ran.

And now the sun peeked out. It had just been on watch, waiting.

And Vera seemed to have done the same. She came through the front door the moment he pulled up.

She was a morning person. He was glad about that. He could belong to that type himself, but only provided he was encouraged. Agnete was – well – a bit phlegmatic in the morning.

He stepped out to help her get in.

64

'Up so early and no tears?'

She nodded. 'Yeah. It's mainly in the evening that I cry.'

She looked at him and then the car. 'Oh, how nice, and spruced up.'

'Yes, it's not bad.'

'No, I meant you, Dr. Holmen.'

'Ah.'

She had addressed him formally. All right.

'Obviously in fine condition.'

'Oh, thank you!'

'No, now I meant the car.'

'Get in!' he said. 'And don't stand there talking nonsense. We have no time to lose. My body is thirsty.'

Yes, the sun would come out. If they were lucky – and they were.

Down by the railway station there was a long line of people in front of the busses to Ingierstrand. It was ten thirty-five.

The car was in a good mood, went easily and briskly along the harbour, down Bispegaten, through the Old Town and along Ljabruveien.

Out there young married couples were taking their Sunday stroll, pram and all, a pleasant sight in itself; but when would the young wives learn that *they* were the ones who should wheel the pram? Every third husband who was charged with wheeling a pram in public was collecting material for a divorce.

There were long rows of cyclists with bathrobes strapped on the back and pedestrians with swimming togs thrown over their arms. The pedestrians were on their way to the Katten beach. As for the cyclists, their destination was uncertain.

They didn't talk much. He was kept busy with the driving, making a point of sneaking past as many as possible. He slipped in and out among cars and bikes, like a shuttle. She was looking out through the open window.

'Feeling fine?'

'Feeling fine.'

The water looked very green.

'How green the water is!' she said.

'Yes, very.'

There were often algae in the water at this time of year.

There was already a long row of cars in the park below the restaurant. He paid his ticket and put the car nicely into the row. They went to the changing rooms and parted outside the door.

'See you here?'

'See you here.'

He got his hanger and bag for twenty-five øre and entered one of the stalls. There were two men in there from before. One of them had to be a sailor, he had a blue tattoo on his chest – the torso of a woman with the caption *Auf Ewig Dein*. How many had looked at that tattoo since?

A silly question.

She was waiting outside, modestly wrapped in a blue-striped bathrobe.

They walked down to the beach. The paths swarmed with people wandering about, but one could still see glimpses of bare rocks and sand in between. Two men in swimming trunks came walking up towards the changing rooms.

'How green the water is!' one of them said.

'Yes, very.'

They walked past an ice-cream counter, up a flight of stairs and down another, and reached the rocky slopes near the water. They were densely occupied, but not yet overcrowded. Chiefly young people. Shapely figures. Uncomfortably shapely. Powerful shoulders, no belly, absolutely none. You couldn't possibly figure out where they had put their breakfast.

Involuntarily he pulled his stomach in a bit, sort of quietly behind his bathrobe. He had no belly, not a trace of belly, but he pulled it in a bit.

Anyway, he was going to start his early morning exercises again. He had been neglecting them for some time. One mustn't neglect such things.

To which social class did all these people belong? You couldn't possibly tell. The conventional class markings were left behind in the changing room. Out here there were different rules.

They slipped in and out among people who lay, sat and stood in groups or singly; lots of young ones, some older. A couple of women had come down there fully dressed and had pulled down their dresses to get a bit of sun on their shoulders; they looked strangely indecent.

A middle-aged, somewhat stout gentleman greeted him. Holmen returned the greeting, but noticed that he felt embarrassed. He had never seen Managing Director de Wahl without clothes before. He was wearing pale-blue swimming trunks that swelled tightly over his belly. Fully dressed he appeared powerful and commanding, as if he owned the whole planet and intended to keep it; now he looked as if he had swallowed a globe and couldn't get rid of it. There was something wrong with him, as if he'd been in the changing room but forgotten to straighten out his body.

She walked ahead of him. Perfectly at ease, with a peculiarly free-swinging gait. He noticed it put him in a good mood to see her walk.

Handsome people were handsome.

They passed the first rocks and came to a steel-wire fence. Down below was a dock where the Nesodden boats put in. They went up a flight of stairs, along a small platform with the fence underneath them, and down a flight to a different rocky slope.

A couple of middle-aged men greeted him – prominent men whose throats he'd swabbed. Oh, how poorly most of our leading men held up over the years. All too many good dinners, all too many highballs and cigars and parties, all of which, combined, added up to responsible positions. Now the holders sat there like ugly grease spots in the beautiful landscape. Ugly people was one of the ugliest...

Ugh!

His contempt for those who were in poorer condition than himself could almost suggest that he envied certain others.

He had to say something. 'Out here, there's a different kind of class distinction. Who is a managing director here, and who is the junior office clerk? The managing director whose title gives him punch is reduced to a comical elderly gentleman with a paunch. And the most junior office clerk, if he's trained and all right, gets all the stolen glances – he's the managing director.'

She cast a momentary glance over her shoulder. 'And if the comical elderly gentleman notices, the junior office clerk will certainly notice in the office tomorrow who is managing director.'

'You're caustic before twelve, are you? That's really something!'

There was more and more room as they moved away from the restaurant, the ice cream, the slide, the diving platform, and the other sensations. They found a good place for themselves near the sea, with the right southward slope, without too much of a crush.

She slipped out of her bathrobe. He experienced something of a shock. He had known she was all right, but...

Pretty girls were really pretty.

She was very pretty. Everything that should be there was there, and it was where it should be. She had a green swimsuit which consisted of as little as possible, but fitted her like a snakeskin. There was no doubt that here she was the managing director. He couldn't avoid feeling that he was the most senior office clerk.

What made it easier to endure was that she was so natural. She knew she was attractive and enjoyed it, and that made her feel at ease.

She had a head of hair that was quite extraordinary – dark-brown with a copper lustre. And it didn't appear coloured.

She had a side parting, and the fringe tended to fall into her eyes. Then she would toss her head and fling it back. The next moment it hung down into her eyes again.

'That hair of yours isn't bad at all. It's one of the nicest things you have.'

'I love my hair,' she said.

'It looks electric.'

'It is. I can make it give out sparks in the dark when I comb it. It's such fun!'

'You don't use anything artificial on your face, do you? That's strange. You who – '

'Work in a beauty parlour? Oh yes, I have to apply a little makeup and such at work, for business reasons. But I rub it off afterwards.'

The nearest neighbours were a young married couple with a little son. About four years old or so, he was running around without a stitch. He was in excellent spirits. Fear seemed utterly alien to him. He had a tiny felt dog, a terrier, which he was deeply absorbed by, but he was interested in all sorts of things besides. He had the curiosity of a puppy. The faces of all who looked at him became a little friendlier. His parents looked at each other and at him and at each other. If they hadn't had the boy, you would take them for newlyweds.

He couldn't help thinking of something.

Per was also four. Agnete had insisted on getting him a swimsuit this summer. He had grown big enough now for anything else to look odd. Everyone else did likewise, and her parents had always made a point of it. Children were to be brought up to be bashful.

They hadn't agreed, but he had given in. Cowardly of him...

Stop. Today is vacation.

The boy had discovered Vera. He looked at her once, looked after his dog a bit, and looked at her once more. Then he came over and looked closely at her.

'You are pretty!' he said.

Vera laughed. The boy looked at Holmen. 'She's pretty!' he said.

It was a statement from one man to another.

'You're right, son!'

'I'm not your son. I'm Jens's son. And when I grow up, I'll be even bigger than him.'

With that, his thoughts had found a new direction; he ran up to his father.

'Isn't that so, Jens?' He pulled his father's hair.

'Oh sure!' his father said, laughing. 'Much bigger.'

He called his father by his first name. A good idea.

'And this will be much bigger than yours?'

'Oh sure. Much bigger.'

Satisfied, he busied himself with his felt dog again, playing with it.

The parents looked at him for a while. Then they looked at each other again. They were in love – so much in love that they could afford to let the boy be happy.

Holmen watched this little family picture for a while. He became lost in thought. He didn't know what he was thinking of.

Vera gently brushed his arm. 'Let the thoughts rest. Today the sun is shining.'

What a hand she had. It was as though she brushed something away.

He lay down obediently. A few little breaths of air came along. It felt as if the sun brushed his skin warmly, like a friend.

They were lying side by side on their bathrobes. There were a few clouds in the sky, but the sun slipped cleverly between them and shone all along.

'The sun is kind today.'

'It certainly is.'

'Silly to have these trunks over one's belly, isn't it?'

She sighed. 'You're complaining? You men are lucky, having everything in one place, so all you need is a pair of shorts.'

He felt so nice and warm that he merely grunted.

They dozed from time to time. Now and then they turned slightly, so that no side of their bodies would feel left out. On and off they conducted long conversations, approximately like this:

'This is nice, eh?'

'It's nice.'

To the north, above the Oslo valley, there hovered a dark-blue cloud, with greyish-blue stripes running slantways down the sky.

He nudged her. 'It's raining in Oslo.'

'But not here.'

Pause.

'The nice weather won't last, I think.'

'No?' She was drowsy.

'No. There are clouds everywhere.'

'Not before the sun.'

True enough. He hadn't thought of that. He settled down again.

But a while later they both woke up feeling something unfriendly. Now there really was a cloud before the sun. Quite a large one, which would last a while. They might as well go into the water in the meantime.

She put on her swimming cap, which suddenly gave her a striking likeness to that Egyptian queen.

They went down to one of the small stairs that led into the water.

She dived as though she'd never done anything else. Yes, of course. These young women were proficient in everything that related to sex, however remotely. *He* dived badly, and knew it. The water struck him as dangerous until he was well in it, and God knows if it didn't seem dangerous until he was safely out of it again.

They swam side by side out to the nearest float. In the meantime the sun had come back, and the water was in a laughing mood. There was an entire popular assembly on the float, letting themselves be baked. They climbed up, wiped off most of the water, and baked themselves with the rest. To the north, in the direction of the airport, someone was going down the slide on his belly and plunged into the water with a big splash. From the top platform of the diving tower someone jumped out, described a slow arc in the air and drilled his way down into the water like an arrow. To the south, one of the Nesodden boats was putting in at the dock, disembarking a load of people. The boat was broad-bellied and heavy, spewed smoke and tooted wretchedly, and looked as if it belonged to the previous generation. In the area beyond the float a whole squadron of kayakers were romping about. Rowing in ranks and in snowplough formation, they whirled around in Eskimo style as they sat in their kayaks showing off.

Great ideals were shattered. Only one white man, he'd been taught, had been able to pick up that trick from the Eskimos – Fridtjof Nansen. Now every snotty kid could repeat the trick after him. God knows whether such things shouldn't really be considered destructive. Here quite ordinary people were diving and swimming as if they had done nothing else all their lives. What if the Norwegian people's other great superterrestrial hero, Olav Tryggvason himself, suddenly turned up out here and began to behave like a master swimmer, but was hopelessly outdistanced by Hans Johansen, a journeyman painter from Vålerengen, a quite ordinary fellow, but with powerful arms from swinging his paint brush?

'Come, let's swim ashore again!' she said.

She dived in and popped up again, overjoyed and laughing – Queen Nefertiti from a backyard in Kampen.

They basked in the sun again.

He noticed that something was starting up inside his head – scattered thoughts, which had often occurred to him out here, arranged themselves lazily in groups, very lazily, for the sun was scorching.

Something was happening on these beaches. Not only here, by the way. In the stadiums too, and on ski trips, when young girls and boys went off together. But now, here... He noticed the difference from one year to the next, from spring to autumn, too, or most of all. People grew handsomer in the course of the summer. With firmer bodies, calmer faces, freer, more natural.

It was a refreshing sight. These young people were getting something out of life.

He recalled himself and his friends when they were twenty. It was at the time of transition for sport. Saturday night often meant a binge – tobacco smoke as dense as the November fog, cheap liquor and cheap bragging, impotent dreams of great deeds at some future time – and Sunday morning: nausea, sleep, the morning after.

As dense as fog – he recalled something still farther back: the servants' quarters, where he took refuge as a child. That acrid blue tobacco smoke, so dense you could write with your finger in it. Men on chairs and in the beds. Cotters, working men, farmhands and folks who had dropped by. What was it they talked about? Politics, the class struggle? Nonsense. Well, it was about that too, in a way. But most of all it was dirty talk about women. Whee, what fantasy, real talk, indeed.

Respectable people called it *filth*. 'Disgusting filth!' his mother said. And maybe it was. But – was it called filth because it was filthy, or was it filthy because it was called filth?

Phew – much too warm for that problem just now.

Lolling in the beds, they puffed on their pipes till the air was as thick as a stuffed sack, while they talked and bragged, whinnying with laughter or letting rip with a crashing fart.

The one who talked the dirtiest and bragged the most was the winner.

What were they bragging about? *So and so many times* – in one night or one hour.

'I took her eight times, you bet! She cried and begged for mercy in the end. But I kept at it!'

They slapped their thighs and bragged, and listened to the others. And bid up. Oh, there was no end to their feats.

At home their wives were waiting. They didn't seem to be in a great hurry to get home to them.

He recalled one evening – one man was boasting that he'd once pulled out his sheath knife and cut open a girl because she was too small for him.

There was a brief moment of silence then, before they began to guffaw in the beds round about.

He remembered so vividly the face of the one who sat there bragging – big and red, a broad grinning mouth and small eyes glancing quickly here and there. Afterwards, when the others were roaring with laughter, he shot a large blob of spit far out on the floor.

He himself, a tiny tot of seven or eight, sat on the pile of firewood by the stove, all ears and wide-eyed as he listened and watched. No one paid any attention to him. He sat there with a guilty conscience. He was really forbidden to be in the servants' quarters. That is to say, Mother forbade it, Father didn't think it mattered that much. And so he went there, but with a bad conscience. He should've been somewhere else...

Later that evening he slipped across the yard and into the house. It was an autumn evening, and the stars were staring at him, large and stern. He was afraid of the dark, there was always danger behind him.

When he grew up, he would have to do things like that. He felt small and afraid.

Now, of course, he could see that the men sitting in the servants' quarters were a flock of children; afraid of the dark, they bragged themselves big and strong. Sure – but what help was there in that? The fear remained.

And yet the servants' quarters were a refuge. It was more cheerful there, despite everything, than in the house, where Mother sat with the hymnbook.

He suspected that something important was hidden behind all this. If only he could catch sight of it...

It was too warm. And besides it was a holiday. Sunday outside of time.

He turned over on his stomach. She lay completely still beside him. Taking a nap apparently.

How quietly and unobtrusively people moved among one another here. No unnecessary noise, no importunity on anyone's part.

A couple of teenagers had been eating the sandwiches they had brought, their Sunday dinner. Now they quietly folded the paper wrapping and put it into one of the litter baskets. There wasn't a discarded piece of paper in the entire area. No one found it necessary to make a mess in order to be a real man here. Something was happening here. Norway had changed. *This* part of Norway in any case.

Sometimes he would catch himself thinking that he was rather fond of this city which had become his home. Much of what was otherwise happening in the world at this time reminded him troublingly of his boyhood years – it was as though he saw some gigantic servants' quarters before him, filled with a bunch of poor devils who were afraid of the dark and sat there bragging themselves big and strong, and the one who was coarsest of all was the winner.

And in the house sat Mother with the hymnbook. But that was too dreary and boring, in spite of all.

And people sneaked across the dark yard, afraid of the high starry sky, afraid of the dark abyss, shuttling from one thing to another, small and powerless. No improvement possible, people ran true to form, it probably had to be that way since it was that way, there was a lot of nastiness and evil in the world, but that couldn't be helped, what could a tiny human being do? Best not to make enemies of the strong and dangerous ones, best not doubt, best of all not *see*, because if you saw you had to doubt; the best thing you could do was to shut yourself up inside your quiet domestic happiness and let the world take care of itself. Caution, caution, caution...

But here, in the open, in the sunshine by the sea, here something was happening nevertheless. Here something was springing up that, one fine day, could bowl over a little of everything.

The day when sufficiently many people knew that it was a joy to be alive, that love was beautiful – good heavens, what would that lead to! Had anyone thought about the consequences! How come these beaches weren't banned!

All at once he felt a stab of envy.

When he thought how much better off these teenagers were than he and his peers. How much more cheerful, more joyous, their life was.

It made his blood boil.

Yes. They had cheated him of ten years of his youth.

Caution, caution, caution – bah! He had those years coming. He wasn't forty, he was thirty!

Oh, really! No, sirree! Age was embedded in the bones and the vegetative system, it was no use trying to lie your way out of it. The old metaphor was right. Life was a web, each day was a thread in the web. Exuberant days added colour to the web, grey days made for a grey web, that was all the difference. Tell an old convict who is released sixty years old after being confined since he was twenty – for theft, and later for robbery, fencing stolen property, assault and battery, premeditated murder, everything a man learns to do when the government truly takes him in hand – tell him that now he must be sure to make up for lost time and enjoy the happy days of youth, and he will turn a pair of pale, arteriosclerotic eyes on you and say, 'What?'

Alas!

Years that have come to an end do not come again. Said the poet...

She nudged him. 'You look as though you're doing something unusual. Are you thinking?'

'Yes, my little saucebox. I'm thinking. I'm thinking as follows: the sun cancels out class distinctions. The sun builds a new society – or tries to. I'm looking at these people here. They're handsome, and become ever more handsome, more joyous, more free and more decent toward one another, simply because the sun is shining on them. But then a long winter is coming. If only our summer were two months longer, then we would be healthier, freer, more natural and courageous, would refuse to be cowed and put up with tyrants...'

'You mean – if we had as long a summer as Italy?'

'Yes – no – nonsense. It's impossible to talk to you.'

'I simply meant – it depends, doesn't it, on what you use your health for?'

He recalled something from last year. They brought a professional boxer to him – a magnificent body which had virtually been pounded into a piece of dough. His nose was completely smashed. A nasty business.

He looked at her. 'How can you know about such things? It's true, what you just said.'

She laughed. 'Oh, don't forget I work in a beauty parlour.'

He turned on his back again, felt how the sun was smoothing him out, solving several of life's riddles in its own way.

Vague thoughts came and went like shadows in his consciousness.

Vera. Who was she? A curious stroke of luck...

Ramstad, who had actually provided him with this holiday... A curious fellow.

His thoughts had no substance, like clouds that didn't manage to block out the sun.

Then something strange happened. He must have been dozing, for he awoke with a sense that something was wrong.

He opened his eyes.

A man stood there looking at him. It was a man he didn't know. He was standing on the small path a couple of metres off. A man younger than himself, with an impassive face. When the man noticed he was being observed, he went on.

Had he been standing there long? It could've been just a moment. It could be a chance thing.

He turned towards Vera. She was facing the other way. 'A man was standing here. Did he know you, do you think?'

She gave a start. She had been napping. 'Was a man standing here?'

She looked where he pointed. The man wasn't very far away. 'Where? Oh, there. No – or, come to think, perhaps I do know him.'

He thought she looked rather preoccupied.

It could be his imagination.

They took another swim. They sat out on the float. Afterwards they sat on their bathrobes smoking a cigarette. People were beginning to leave. Some clouds that meant business appeared.

Consulting their stomachs, they quickly agreed: yes, they were hungry.

They went to get dressed.

This time he finished first.

While he stood waiting outside, a man came out of the changing room; he glanced at him twice as he walked by.

Who was he? He had seen him before, a long time ago. Turning around to look at the man, he recognized him by his gait. It was the fellow who'd been staring at them. Not bad-looking, by the way – tall and thin, plainly dressed.

Then Vera came, bright and summery, tanned, with brown powder on her nose.

They sat under a parasol by the top balustrade. There was food and wine and music and sunshine. On the terrace farther down people were dining in their swimsuits. Still farther down there were some pine trees, whose reddish-brown trunks silhouetted against the blue water were reminiscent of bad paintings; but as reality it was quite attractive.

The dinner was pleasant. He was sluggish, the sun had done its job well. He felt a massive well-being flow through him – it was like sitting in a boat while drifting down a clear, calm stream.

They chatted back and forth about many things; he forgot to quiz her about herself. Only a couple of times did he notice, like a shadow, the familiar thought: he should have been doing something else. He should have been somewhere else...

It went away again. Today he was on holiday, exempt from everything, even from his customary scruples. He had found himself a little byroad, a little permitted byroad.

For a while she was lost in thought. He saw how her face changed, she was far away and not happy. He waited until she was present again.

'You were far away now.'

She looked at him. She had a pair of remarkably open eyes. 'Yes. I was thinking about something.'

'And you weren't particularly happy?'

She didn't answer right away. 'A bit up and down, perhaps. But this has been a lovely day.'

She placed her hand on his for a brief second.

They left shortly afterwards. The sun hung low among the pine-tree crowns.

The road was almost deserted. It was the quiet hour between afternoon and evening.

He noticed that she was watching him. He took a quick look at her and caught her eye. Suddenly his passive calm was gone. His hands trembled slightly on the wheel as he turned the car onto a small side road he knew of and stopped. His heart was in his mouth as he turned toward her, all quivering nerves. She still had that helpless look in her eyes. The next moment she let herself fall heavily onto him, burying her head on his breast.

He sat there stroking her hair. 'Come, come. Poor little thing.'

He was here, in the car, and he was not. He was sitting in a boat with her, drifting down a clear, calm stream; he heard and didn't hear a roar some place down below, growing louder and louder – they were drifting backward with the current, with clear, still water all around, drifting toward the brink of the fall, which they could only hear, not see, hearing without really hearing – the roar grew louder and louder, she had raised her face toward him, her eyes begging for something, for help, for forgetfulness, while the current grew stronger, sucking them more and more rapidly downward, till they were caught in the whirlpool...

The roar on the road behind them had reached its maximum and quickly died down. It was a racing car on its way to the city. He had understood that all along.

Then they were once more sitting in Ramstad's place. 'At home,' he said.

She said nothing, only smiled one of her teeny-weeny smiles.

It was getting dark. He lighted the floor lamp before the fireplace and the reading lamp over by the couch and wandered from one room to another for a while. She lay down on the couch, curling up like a puppy. He iced a soda and went into the study to fetch a decanter from the cabinet. He stopped to take a look around in there. He had seen something or other there yesterday and thought he would look more closely later. What was it? He must have put it aside and forgotten about it. He couldn't remember what it was.

When he entered the living room again, she was asleep, with her hands under her cheek.

The sun must have tired her out.

He found a chair and sat quietly watching her. Her face looked much younger in her sleep, and she appeared much smaller on the big couch. Like a little child on a raft.

The window was open. The wind soughed gently through the trees, a car honked down by Palace Park. A couple, a man and a woman, were talking in soft hushed tones right below. The woman let out a laugh, a low, cooing laugh.

The evening was strangely quiet, so that every sound stood out clearly, which usually happens only on quiet evenings in the depths of the forest or down by the sea.

She was breathing quite slowly for a while, her face filled with a profound peace. He couldn't bring himself to disturb her. A loudspeaker was turned on somewhere nearby, evensong most likely. As he sat there watching her, the shrill sound felt like blasphemy.

Suddenly she began moaning lightly, and her face became twisted. A tear trickled out. Again she moaned, more loudly, and mumbled, 'No! No!'

He went over and placed his hand on her shoulder. She started up and looked around, bewildered. Then she saw him.

'Oh, it's you.'

He couldn't tell whether she was relieved or disappointed.

'I think you were dreaming.'

'Yes, I had a dream.'

'A bad one?'

'Yes – no. Well, I guess it was something bad. I can't recall. It's gone already.'

'You were crying.'

'Was I?'

A flutter, as of bats' wings, in one's memory. 'It's mainly in the evening that I cry.'

Suddenly there was that helpless expression in her eyes once more.

They drifted off together, far away from the whole world, from all people. There was fear in her eyes, and tears. 'Hold me! Oh, hold me!' Then they were caught in the whirlpool.

Afterwards, as she lay with her head against his shoulder, breathing slowly and deeply, he thought, so this is her – and me.

He sensed the fragrance of her hair, fresh and aromatic, as of bog grass and heather.

Later, when he was in his own apartment and had gone to bed, he lay awake looking into the dark.

His last night here at home.

He saw nothing, only the night, a dark space without an end. He could be anywhere, far out to sea for all that.

*

A side road, he thought.

A little side road.

Probably a trifle for her too. A little girl from a beauty parlour.

It was late in the night. Through the open window came the noise of voices. A flock of young boys and girls were chatting down at the corner. He heard the boys' rough, uneven laughter, still slightly marked by their voices breaking, and the girls' little giggles and squeals. A pole was banged nervously against the curb, and then dragged along a fence, making a rattling noise. He could envisage the entire group. Especially the boys – their insecure postures, poor skin, brazen airs, lust and fear, ardent dreams, lonely falls from grace, remorse and shame. Nowhere to go with a girl. No courage to go anywhere either.

No room of their own. Or perhaps a rented room with an odious landlady on the watch behind the door.

He didn't need to see that group. He could certainly remember that state.

Youth...

And now?

Torn loose... far out to sea...

City Blocks in Shadow

It was wonderful to wake up one morning and have no definite obligation. He drew a few sighs of relief before rising. Free as a bird.

It felt strange.

He should probably make some plans.

He had taken a vacation before, of course. Every year – at the seaside in the summer, or in the mountains in the autumn. In more recent years he had usually taken a week in the mountains in late winter as well, but before Easter, oh, he'd become so genteel! But those vacations had been part of his regular life. They had been public, planned in broad daylight and carried out according to a programme, like office hours transferred to a different place – hunting, hiking on the plateau, dinner, stories, card games, or skiing tours, dinner, card games, dancing.

This was something new.

What did he mean to do?

Go on a journey back to the past. Find the old crossroads again.

It sounded strange in the light of day.

He wrote a letter to Agnete. He let her know that he probably wouldn't be coming down for some time. It turned out that the old unfinished dissertation on focal infection had suddenly caught his interest again. He would see whether he could finish it this autumn. But his own material wasn't sufficient, so he was forced to make some trips to various hospitals. Consequently, he would rarely be at home and had notified the maid. He was taking a vacation from his practice for the time being and had arranged for a locum. Take care of yourself.

It was a disgustingly untruthful letter, of course. Didn't he have a guilty conscience vis-à-vis Agnete?

No. He did not.

On account of a number of different things he didn't think about – which he never thought about, which he didn't even *want* to think about, and which, besides, were forgotten and forgiven long ago, dead and buried for ever – he did *not* have a guilty conscience vis-à-vis Agnete.

Anyway, he wasn't lying. He *did* mean to resume work on that dissertation, after all. He would go down and pick it up this minute.

He did go down and pick it up. Stowed the manuscript, reports, and card files into his attaché case. Looked around the office – it was like a leave-taking. Then he latched the door behind him.

Later, after packing a couple of suitcases and moving as planned, he sat for a while at Ramstad's writing table, staring into vacancy.

What now?

This was the hour when he used to make his rounds in the clinic.

There were many things you could say about such daily habits. They had a deadening effect, sure. But they were a support as well.

Creepers needed something to lean on.

So what did he want?

Hm. It seemed a bit unclear.

An unclear attempt to find clarity.

Clarity about what?

About his values.

What values?

The values he lived by. What he had gained. What he had lost. What he had dreamed about and later forgotten...

No! He wasn't used to sitting idle like this, just thinking.

Fortunately there existed some concrete tasks. And the first one was self-evident.

Where was Håkenrud?

He wasn't listed in the telephone book. Nor in the city directory. But he remembered where he lived. During the year he associated with him he'd been up there many a time. Håkenrud lived in an old, ramshackle wooden house somewhere behind Thereses gate, above the old terminus of the Homansby tram. He didn't remember the name of the street, didn't know if it belonged to Oslo or Aker, didn't even know whether it was a regular street, it looked more like a path. But he remembered clearly where the house stood, inside an old overgrown garden. Håkenrud lived there with his old mother and an ancient maid. His father was dead, he'd been a tinsmith, one of the philosophical kind. He was a leftist of the genuine old class and had participated both in the battles of 1884 and in the controversies in the old Workers' Association, and thought it was fine for his son to become a socialist, march in the parade on May 1, and associate with many odd characters; it won his approval. Then he lay down and died. And the son continued to live in the old wooden house behind the lilac arbour, the redcurrant bushes and hoary apple trees, which strangely enough bore excellent Gravensteins.

They had sat up there smoking and talking themselves hoarse many a time. The clique consisted chiefly of peasant students. There were also some working class bohemians from Kristiania. New Norwegian and socialism, that was the programme. The present society had to be overthrown and New Norwegian introduced. Moreover, Kristiania was to be razed to the ground – at least, the inhabitants were to be chased into the woods and regular Norwegians given a chance.

On and off Håkenrud studied law. He was a slacker as a student; but there was no great hurry, the tinsmith had left a few kroner.

He didn't recognize the neighbourhood. There were no longer any wooden houses here, no indeed. Terraced houses and new blocks of flats, some of them in the so-called modernist style. They had experimented with curved façades, with low, wide windows that would be extremely drafty in the winter, and a new patented plaster which made large rosettes as it dried and fell off in picturesque flakes. He knew immediately that no Håkenrud lived in any of these buildings. Håkenrud was a devotee of the society of the future, where everything was regulated just so, like a machine, but to live in he absolutely preferred an old, unpractical and cosy wooden villa with a privy in the garden.

He walked down Ullevålsveien again. There was yet another place he meant to look up today. On the way he dropped in at a bookseller's and glanced at a government yearbook. It had occurred to him that Håkenrud might have become a civil servant and could be found there. You could expect pretty much anything from Håkenrud.

But no.

How could he have disappeared without a trace!

He was alive, that he knew. He had seen him, after all. Just by chance, in the crowded street. They had nodded to one another. Time had taken them out of each other's orbits.

Yes, and come to think of it – he hadn't seen him for several years.

For all he knew, Håkenrud could be dead by now.

No, he wasn't likely to be dead. Håkenrud was healthy and tenacious of life, it would be just like him to live in some field in Aker or Bærum, as far as possible from all sewage and water systems, and support himself by gardening.

He could go to the national registration office to find out. That must be the sort of thing such things were for.

But – to go creeping about and play detective...

He didn't feel like going to the national registration office.

He had got as far down as Akersbakken. There he turned left, reached the top and continued on to where the view opens to the northeast, to Sagene and Grefsen.

Here it was. He entered a gate and climbed the front steps. He went all the way up.

There were new names everywhere. He still couldn't recall her surname, but it certainly wasn't any of these names.

He had known that beforehand.

He remained standing outside the gate for a while.

Over there, on the other side, under the trees, was where they used to stand to say goodbye.

Where could he find Håkenrud?

He reviewed the whole group in his thoughts. One was a medical student, he was now a district doctor in the West Country. There was a law student, aside from Håkenrud himself, his name was Cramer; he'd become an attorney and politician and was now in Trondheim. One was a philologist – what was his name? He was already going downhill and about to give up his studies, and later he seemed to have gone completely to the dogs, swallowed up by the darkness.

And then there was Nilssen, the pale idealist. He was safe and sound.

Good grief, Nilssen. Nilssen and his Adam's apple! Nilssen, who was so skinny and so overwrought and had such a fine voice that he could, without embarrassment, even without the others feeling too embarrassed, say *idealism* as easily as someone else said good morning or nice weather. He would use that word on all occasions, and then his Adam's apple went up and down, as if he were keeping the fine word in a bag and tossed it out from there. It must have been that Adam's apple which made them put up with him – what did Håkenrud say: 'You are a terrible swindler, Nilssen, but you have a first-class Adam's apple.'

Now he didn't have an Adam's apple anymore. As the years passed and Nilssen landed a municipal job, he had become extremely fat.

It was, come to think, Nilssen – and then Cramer, a future member of the Storting from Trondheim – who had put an end to his, Knut Holmen's, political interests. To those of several others too, no doubt. It was when the two of them were getting a foot in the door and, later, receiving real perks – quite small at first, like the bones thrown to little dogs – it was then he began to ask himself if that was the point of it all. If he was the only one who hadn't understood that much. If, that is, he wasn't quite simply a fool.

But now he was no longer a fool. He had used his studies, all those gruelling years, to get a foot in the door himself. Cramer, Nilssen and himself were probably the three in the whole clique who had done best for themselves, as the phrase goes.

He could go up to Nilssen right now, look him full in the face, firmly, honestly and openly, press his hand and say: *idealism!*

No, he didn't think he would look up Nilssen.

There had been a couple more, but he couldn't remember them.

Incidentally, it was quite strange how little he remembered from that period. He had a feeling that there was some essential thing or other he'd forgotten – something that would lead him straight to what he was looking for. If only he could remember what it was he ought to remember...

He was again standing in front of Ramstad's house in the little side street. He looked at his watch: half-past twelve. Result so far: nil.

There was nothing for him to do up there. It occurred to him that he might just as well take a walk through the neighbourhoods where he had lived during his early years as a student. Perhaps something or other there could put him on the right track.

He had lived in furnished rooms in Oslo for ten years all told, in twenty or thirty different places. Right behind Ramstad's house were a number of streets where such rooms were available. He walked in that direction.

It wasn't merely a matter of the first few streets. A succession of city blocks stretched behind other city blocks. You could walk and walk...

He did recognize the neighbourhood, street by street, but discovered that he hadn't remembered how grey and drab these streets were. Distance had, despite everything, overlaid them with a touch of romance – a kind of romance of greyness. You had to see them at close quarters again to realize how irredeemably commonplace they were.

The streets intersected at right and oblique angles, and some of them actually lay in the sun. Nevertheless, it was as though all lay in shadow. Though they carried traffic – banging and screeching trams, honking cars, old rattling wagons that produced an earsplitting noise on the badly-laid cobbles – it was as though the walls of the houses, the windows and entranceways, even the streets and the pavements were covered with dust and cobwebs. Long-standing hopelessness, money worries and petty debts, malice and resentment and remorse, gateway gossip, stolen pleasures and contrite sobriety, penny-pinching and Christianity, poor sanitation and outdoor privies, women in the door crack and milk bottles by the doors, drunkenness and uproar on Saturday, and blackclad widows and orphans with hymnbooks in their hands on Sunday morning – all this and much more of the same had in the slow course of the years mingled with the paint and the cement and left a shadow over these dreary neighbourhoods. A shadow that radiated from them, from deep inside, and covered them like a grey mist, reaching higher than the rooftops.

This was where the ten thousand tiny stores were to be found, very often in basement rooms built in times past to evade a building regulation that was defunct long ago. Shoemaker's shops, dairies, dry goods stores with picture postcards and soap and Christmas tree decorations, delicatessens with herring cakes and egg baskets and hoary meat patties in the window. With bells above the entrance door, which tinkled for every customer, and mistrustful faces glimpsed in the chink of the door to the back room.

Most inexplicable were all the shoemaker's shops with all those lame shoemakers. They always had wiry dark hair, like a brush, above a pale face with a dark bristly beard. They always talked politics over their leather aprons in their filthy workshops. What if it had occurred to them just once to tidy up the floor a bit and make the place a tad more inviting, leaving the future society to take care of itself for a few minutes? But no.

What did they live on, all those shoemakers?

From the fact it cost you dearly to be poor.

From mending shoes that long ago were so worn that it would've been more economical to buy new ones, if the owner could have come up with so many kroner at one time.

They didn't exactly live in clover, for there were many others who had to make a living from the same source – the milk suppliers who delivered milk a little later in these parts of town, the bakers who got rid of yesterday's bread, the art publishers who could sell discontinued picture postcards, all the milliner's shops which sold the latest fashion from the year before last. And all the small craftsmen and other tradesmen who made a modest and miserable living from one another's hardship.

Strange that some things could stay unchanged throughout so many years in a world where everything was changing. He was passing a corner with a delicatessen where he'd dropped by a hundred times. This store was unique in that it had a sleigh bell over the door instead of an ordinary bell. It was quite strange to be greeted by this solemn sound, which was so honoured in his home village, every time you went in to buy an old loaf of bread or a bit of margarine. It was twenty years ago, but he could tell by a glance – the sleigh bell was hanging there. Those meat patties in the window were also unmistakable; it was almost like meeting an old friend again after years of absence.

Across the street was a picture postcard shop, where they used to display Christmas tree decorations. Were they still hanging there?

They were. In the month of August. Christmas tree candles and clips, shiny coloured tissue paper, and silver and gold tinsel. And ancient picture postcards of angels with gold dust on their wings. The shoemaker's shop was next door. He could make out the brush-like hair of the master himself in the gloom in there; he was sitting in the middle of his chaos of tools and lasts and patches of leather and tattered, gaping boots, pulling a cobbler's thread through the sole of an old shoe with grumpy tugs.

'They don't know anything better, and so they don't miss anything' – wasn't that roughly what his present friends used to say after a first-class dinner?

Year after year he hadn't known, or dared to know, that there existed a different Oslo, one that was better than this. Grey years in shadow and poverty; if a stolen pleasure came his way once in a while, he had to pay for it with worry and a sense of guilt. Having to steal on tiptoe, in the hush of night, through long entrance halls which always creaked and moaned just outside the door to the landlady's bedroom. Dread beforehand. Dread for weeks afterwards. That was his carefree youth.

He had rambled down many streets and had passed several places where he had lived. It wasn't always easy to remember the particular places, they were so alike. He had entered a small side street; he hadn't made a note of the name, but knew he was acquainted with it. He passed a dark hole of a gate, dismal even in broad daylight. One leaf of the double door was open, he glimpsed a rotten wooden floor that rose toward a gravelled courtyard farther back. A couple of sheet iron rubbish bins could be seen in there. It all had a familiar air about it; he went inside. There was a doorway on each side of the courtyard; the one on the right just led to an entry, the flat of the corner grocer, the one on the left to the inside stairway.

He felt rather numb.

Here it was.

He had lived here a few months in late autumn; he used to leave the house before full daylight and return after dark – that must've been why he didn't recognize the place right away.

He walked out into the street again and stood there looking at the house.

It was that window on the second floor. He remembered the room.

A round table with a small square tablecloth. There was an old ink spot on the tablecloth which looked like a Negro's face. A little mirror hung above the washstand; there was something wrong with it, you always turned bluish pale, like a ghost, when you looked in that mirror. The door from the hallway was yellow. However, what he remembered was the doorway – that black doorway with the landlady in the middle of it. Motionless and mute like a pillar of salt, until she opened her mouth and let out a screaming torrent of words, venom and bile and big ugly toads. He wasn't likely ever to forget that shrill, shrieking voice.

To experience the highest bliss, the finest happiness anyone has known – and be taken by the scruff of your neck and dipped into a stinking sewer...

The corner down there was where they stood, afterwards.

How she wept!

Without a word, couldn't find words – she just wept and clung to him, as though the world was slipping away from under her in a ruinous storm and she had only him to hold on to.

And he stood there, strangely absent, clutching her and trying to speak calmly to her.

There, Helga.

There, Helga.

But inside he was stiff and numb.

He stood there motionless, on the same spot. He was afraid to move, he remembered – as if the world had really slipped away and they were standing on the only patch of land the slide hadn't taken.

The weather was awful too, incidentally, with driving sleet all around.

He never saw her again.

The next day he received a telegram from his father, packed and left immediately. The notice the landlady screamed out that night and took back with bitter tears the next morning, remained in force. And *she* was sick in bed when he rushed by to let her know he had to go home for a few days. He was not admitted. He still remembered the sour face of her mother in the chink of the door.

Never again.

He was home for two months – then his mother died. Next came that year by the coast, and only then did he get back to Oslo.

They exchanged a few letters early on.

Why didn't he try to get back to her? There was no one else, after all.

He didn't know.

He only knew this: In the following years this experience was lodged inside him as a fright. It sat there, working secretly. Oh, so secretly. A quiet, sneaking fear that kept him from giving himself completely to anyone.

Better be careful, to avoid ending up in the sewer.

He knew he still had this pale fear inside him.

What was the landlady's name?

Something with En. Enerhaugen – Enebak? No. Enersen. Mrs Enersen. Married to a postman. She had two boys with him.

How old might she be? Fifty – no, far from it. The boys were nine and six years old. Thirty something, maybe. He had never given it a thought at the time. He was twenty. She seemed ancient to him.

Her husband suffered from heart disease and had been sent to the country. She loved that husband of hers. She cheated and took the best chair away from his room after he'd rented it and sent it up to her husband. He received in its place an old rocking chair. From then on her boys hadn't had a chair to rock in – funny, he hadn't thought of that until now.

Suddenly he saw her in a new way – thin, tormented, weighed down by worries, thirty years old and without a breadwinner and a husband. Without a husband. And in the adjacent room the young lodger had a lady visitor. Now they put out the light – *she* could see that as she sat in a dark room to save on expenses. Now they were whispering and kissing each other, that she could hear, having stolen up to the door and standing with her ear against it in a state of excitement that could be nothing else than moral indignation.

She waited, quivering with rage, until she could tell they were about to leave. But then...

Well, well.

He climbed the brown winding staircase. He felt like seeing whether she still lived there.

Oh yes. The two apartments on the second floor had been combined now. A nameplate read:

Mrs Minda Enersen. Rooms to let.

A number of visiting cards were fastened with drawing pins to one of the door frames.

So her husband must have departed this life.

Poor woman.

And now she could go about her duties and listen at doors, take measures to maintain order in her own house, and transform fine things into something shameful.

He felt sorry for her. He hated her with a hatred that took his breath away.

It had happened twenty years ago. It felt as if it were yesterday.

He glanced at his watch. Good grief. Ten to four. How time passed.

Vera finished work at four and was coming by straight from work.

Yes, it had come to that.

He felt as though he were fleeing from something when he ran down the stairs, slipped through the gate into daylight, and increased his speed to get back to Ramstad's apartment ahead of Vera.

The next morning he sat in Ramstad's empty apartment, trying to figure out – he didn't know what.

Well, yes. The past.

Why had his youthful years turned out as they did? Why had that incident affected him so strongly? Why had he allowed himself to slip into his present existence? Why was he stuck in it, if it didn't suit him?

Now and then yesterday, when he was together with Vera, he felt he was very close to a solution. For a moment he felt the same now. Wait, wait a moment. He understood, he almost understood...

It disappeared again. There was always something he didn't understand, and so he understood nothing.

At the same time he had an unpleasant feeling that he was a malingerer sitting here.

After all, it was something quite different he should've been doing at this time of day. Should've been at the clinic, making his rounds.

Why was he sitting here?

Ugh!

There were just too many things he didn't care to think about. He picked up his hat and went out.

In those empty morning hours he again found himself wandering in the same shadowy neighbourhoods, among large grey blocks of flats, where something you would consider unsolvable had been solved – where they had succeeded in joining desert and anthill into an inseparable unity.

What did he want here?

Did he believe that the vanished past was waiting for him here, among these grey concrete walls?

There must be something he hoped to find here – an explanation. Something he had lost? Something he had never found?

If only you could remember everything you'd forgotten!

Something he did remember: the evening he met Helga at Håkenrud's place – no, he didn't remember it at all, didn't remember why she was there, what other people were there, when it took place – remembered only that he was watching a young girl, looking into a pair of eyes, into eyes that returned his look. And it was as though everything else vanished, became unimportant, and something new, something incomprehensible, fabulously fine and rich opened the door wide to him. That was how it must feel to have been blind and suddenly recover one's eyesight again on a mild, clear day full of colours.

Afterwards? Well, afterwards she was the one.

They walked around together for a whole autumn. Walked one street after another, one road after another, in and beyond the city. They had no place where they could go in. They had no money, couldn't go to her home, because both her parents were very religious, practising a harsh Christianity; everything to do with sex was evil, even within marriage children should only be begotten with weeping and gnashing of teeth. Helga was the next youngest, she was number nine – oh yes, with weeping and gnashing of teeth they had got as far as ten. Nor could they go to his room; Mrs Enersen had immediately informed him that she would have no truck with female visitors. And he had bowed and put up with it. He himself came from a pious and decent home.

He recalled things in glimpses. It was like walking in the dark, with a light flaring up and showing a picture, a situation; then it became dark again, until another light flared up and showed another picture.

Mostly he saw streets. Long autumn streets in the rain. Short dark side streets where they could stand relatively unseen. He saw the tall dark trees diagonally across the street from where she lived. They provided shelter both from light and rain. Once they stood there for three hours while it poured.

Oh, how they tramped that autumn. In all kinds of weather – but now, thinking back, it seemed to him as though it was raining all the time. Rain, rain, rain, and on and off sticky, wet snow that came sailing along – a condensation in his memory, of course, although autumn in Oslo could be nasty. It was as if it were in league with higher powers and said: all joy is forbidden! Because of people's sins during the summer, it shall now rain for forty days and forty nights, until melancholy rises to fifteen cubits above the tallest mountain.

But they had a good time together all the same, in the rain and the slush. The contact with his circle of friends, with all those discussions about the society of the future, got lost during those weeks. It looked like she became the society of the future for him. Oh, what a society that was going to be, their society of the future!

They walked and walked, trembling with cold, had constantly wet feet and a good time. He could recall his own happiness as he returned home in the evening, when his heart grew all too big inside him, and all too light, lifting him up so that he made huge jumps in the street, like someone disturbed.

They never touched each other. That is, they didn't cross the line to the greatest, the ultimate. The prohibition was too deeply implanted in them both. They could probably have kept walking like that to the end of days, if not...

It was a late autumn evening, in November. The weather was unusually rough; it was pitch-dark, with rain and slush and a bitter north wind. They had met and were wandering in the streets. She had stolen away from home. She always had to steal away from home, all their shared hours were stolen hours.

She was ill that evening and shouldn't have been out at all. It was probably the flu coming on, she was feverish. He could remember her shiny eyes and her cheeks flushed with fever. She had an attack of the shivers that made her teeth chatter. And so they did what they had never dared before – they sneaked up to his place.

It wasn't warm in the room. But the stove had been prepared for lighting. She was so shivery that he had to give her his overcoat to drape over her own coat. He lighted the fire, left the door to the stove open, and put her in a chair right in front of it. It quickly got warm. The stove became glowing. *She* became glowing. Off with the overcoat. Off with her coat. Off with her hat. Her hair cascaded. What fabulous hair she had. Wiry like a mane and long, all the way to her hips. Yes, that's the way it was in those days. He saw her with her hair down for the first time that evening – and the last.

He did understand a few things now that he hadn't understood then. How both of them, without stopping to think, exploited that fever of hers.

She was virginal and scared, he was inexperienced and scared. Her modesty would most likely have been insurmountable in ordinary circumstances, but now she was unwell. She felt so warm that some of her clothes *had* to come off.

And he experienced that one miracle. Nineteen years of threats and terrors and fear dropped off her like a bundle of old rags in the course of five minutes – until she stood there as God had created her, free, happy, ecstatic.

She was the one he betrayed. Not immediately, not in one day, but little by little, slowly and stealthily, using caution, caution, caution.

And at the same time he betrayed himself – the vast expansion of his mind that autumn, so vast that he remembered that also as a miracle, those times when he was capable of remembering that period. Those times when he *dared* remember. It happened more and more seldom, that he knew now.

Did it have to end like that?

He walked and walked. He pondered and pondered. But he seemed to be walking in circles.

He was grappling with all those bygone years, rummaging in them, holding them up, turning and twisting them as he searched for something – something that had got lost to him with the years. It was a curious game, like looking for a shadow among shadows.

No, it wasn't a game. For he noticed one thing: all this lay on him like a weight. It was as if he were groaning under a heavy burden. As if the present, even life itself, were lost to him, and he himself became a shadow, groaning under a burden of shadows.

He walked like this for hours on end every morning. It happened that he started running. For there was no time to lose! It was a question – if not of life, then – of something else, which he – which he –

He knew little about what he was looking for, didn't find anything, couldn't go forward.

It was this shadow world that Vera released him from every day at four.

It was a relief.

This little love affair had become something he rested up in, away from the hunt for something larger, more violent and difficult.

Vera was so close. She was *real*. She was something he could touch and feel – yes, that's what she was.

Away from all dark shadows and big feelings – they simply went out to dinner together, staying in the world of prose.

Officially he wasn't even in town, so he couldn't show up in the usual places. They went to restaurants that he, at least, was not familiar with. They looked them up in the business pages of the telephone book. There were many of them. And they were pleasant. Oslo had certainly grown larger during these years, while he had grown older.

He liked these dinners.

Why?

Perhaps simply because for nearly the first time he could go out with someone he was in love with – yes, why not use that word, why did it always have to be the grand passion? – and wine and dine her well, knowing all along that he could afford it. Oh, how seldom he'd had the opportunity to do that in his life. With Agnete it had never been like that, she was an old-fashioned homebody – to that old bootjack, her father, the very word 'restaurant' had a ring of frivolity and bohemianism, which he wanted none of; and her mother, who no doubt might have liked both restaurants and bohemia, was thoroughly cowed and never dared open her mouth.

After dinner came a drive, as a rule. It was fun to give her a ride. She was exceptionally good at acting sophisticated, with that Egyptian queen air of hers, but enjoyed like a child being grown-up and going for a spin. Afterwards they went home to their place, as they called it. And then it usually got late.

What was he looking for in her?

He didn't know.

Well, yes, one thing. In the morning he walked around looking for something, trying to recall something. But what he was looking for was probably too big. It instilled fear.

And so he looked for forgetfulness. And he found it with Vera. She awakened his desire – and stilled it. Awakened it again and stilled it.

He couldn't help recalling an old phrase: the well of forgetfulness.

But strange things would happen – once in a while it felt as if the shadows he was chasing were right behind him, chasing *him*. Then he knew he could turn rather tense and frantic when he was with her. Until he reached what he was striving for and forgot everything.

She was his defence – something near which defended him against the far away.

But it could happen that she gave him a fright. There was something about her wildness – no, she didn't cry any more, but now and then when she was most wild and caused him to be at his wildest, in those moments when, according to prevailing notions, they should be at the height of intimacy, when her eyes no longer saw him, when it was as if her eyes glazed over, then something like fear would shoot through him: What is it she wants to forget? Where is she now?

And he gazed searchingly at her, without knowing whether he hoped or feared to find what he was searching for.

Then what was far away could be a defence against what

was near. The shadows were there, whispering comfortingly: you should have been somewhere else. You should have had someone else...

She captivated him. She captivated him against his will.

How?

Did he know?

She was attractive, that was always something. When she sat on the wide couch, half covered by the blanket, that slim bronzed, golden torso of hers rose like a mysterious flower. Those challenging breasts, that bold mouth, that flaring hair which she flung back with a careless jerk of her head – was that it?

He didn't know. But at times he felt that, on the contrary, this was something that left him relatively cold, or made him hostile. Something that ought to be broken. That this was nothing but a façade, a mask. That behind it there lay something, he didn't know what, which he tried to reach again and again – and which she frantically defended and refused to let him get to.

But why brood? Brooding on such things never led to anything. She had crossed his path while he was out looking for something else. Maybe he had crossed her way in the same manner. Each of them would, most likely, end up as one of the lesser experiences in the other's life.

He told her little about himself.

He *knew* little about himself in this period. And told her less. Better not say too much.

She confused him.

For instance, her never questioning him about anything. Neither his feelings nor – nor anything. Her never trying to extract any promises or declarations from him.

She knew he was married – that she knew already that time four years ago. But never a word.

Was that sort of thing to be expected of a woman?

And about herself, about the shape of her life until now – not a word. About who had been part of her life – not a syllable. It was uncanny. He had tried to approach it a couple of times, but she had changed the topic, supple as an eel. He didn't know where he was with her.

A woman should be open and devoted and cheerful, and sad and wild, and gentle and illogical, and unpredictable, but above all simple, so you could feel secure and know where you were with her.

She hated her work. But one thing she maintained passionately: She would never get married.

'I would probably become the sort of wife who gets tired of her husband after a couple of years and has to keep it hidden, because he supports me, and seeks solace elsewhere and keeps *that* hidden, and gets wrinkles of disappointment in my face and hate my husband for it, and hate my lover because he cannot marry me, and hate every human being and get a hateful look in my face and a mean streak in all my thoughts, and have to go to a beauty parlour to become innocent and pretty again, and lose my sense of shame so I sit there trotting out with everything to the young women taking care of me...

'No, thanks. Then I'd rather work in a beauty parlour.'

Pause.

'What's the name of the parlour where you're working?'

She told him.

Pause.

It was a first-class parlour. Agnete was a client, he knew.

Something was weighing upon her.

She would suddenly behave wildly and erratically – clinging to him with unrestrained fervour and then, the next moment, letting go and turning her back on him. Once he caught a glimpse of her face as she turned away.

'But you're crying!'

Pushing her hair back from her forehead and laughing, she said, 'Now and then I feel so happy that I cry.'

He asked no more questions. He understood she didn't want to delve into it.

One time she said suddenly, 'You should've known me long ago.' And softly she added, 'And I you long ago.'

Another time she said, 'Oh, hold me tight – really tight. Will you?'

Another time, in a sort of frenzy, 'Oh, you should've been free! Really free.'

'Like you?'

Laughing, she replied in an entirely different tone, quite lightly, 'Yes. Like me.'

Once she said, snuggling up to him, 'Oh, poor me! Poor me!'

'What do you mean?'

'Oh, nothing.'

She was by no means wild all the time. Sometimes she was tired and went to sleep in his arms. He would lie there watching her calm face. It was pale under her golden tan, and infinitely calm. Too calm. It could have been cut in stone. When she woke up, it was as though life returned from deep inside her. Her eyes were the last to come alive – slowly, reluctantly. She gave the impression of looking at him with blind eyes, which became seeing only little by little. And then, a little later still, she recognized him and smiled.

Sometimes she gave him the shivers.

He walked her home to where she lived, late at night. The nights were clear, the August sky dark and deep, with bright stars. Sometimes they would stop and look. They never had to wait long to see a shooting star – it was that time of year. Then he could feel her hand grasp his wrist. Looking up at him, she would say, 'I wished for something. Do you believe in such things?'

'Yes and no. I believe in the power of it – of believing.'

He didn't know whether she understood what he meant.

Once she suddenly leaned her head against him and said, 'I wished that you could help me.'

Afterwards he walked back – through lonely streets to a stranger's house.

The days passed and he hadn't got anywhere. The old

crossroads? He had found some roads he knew – and those he didn't want to walk a second time. Those he wanted to walk he couldn't find.

Where could he have broken the ring, the ring of shadows which surrounded his youth?

Perhaps it was fidelity that he lacked. If he had held on to everything more firmly – friends, ideas, his interests of those days...

One morning when he was asking such unanswerable questions as he was wandering about in these neighbourhoods where time had stood still while it flew, he suddenly noticed a couple of windows he thought he ought to recognize. One wide and one narrow window, and between them a few steps that led down to a narrow door. Half basement, half ground floor. A few potted flowers stood on the sill behind the narrow window.

Here it was. The name was still there, at an angle across the wide window, with large neat letters, which could've been taken straight out of a copybook for elementary school. The letters had been worn thin and blurred by the sleet and rain of many winters. 'Temperance Café Sunbeam' – he remembered the gloomy premises, where not a single beam of sun ever entered, hence the name.

This was where they foregathered in the evenings, when they hadn't found any pretext for going up to Håkenrud. This was where they sat in a closely knit group, each with his cup of coffee and lighted pipe, until the room was enveloped in a fog of smoke, as dense as a tightly stuffed sack – this was where they were fighting the World War and deciding the fate of the world, or dreaming their more private dreams of exploits they would carry out – at some future time. In politics, science, sex. Just wait!!

Politics was taking its course.

The books lay waiting at home.

Women were not allowed.

Sure, here it was.

He walked in.

It felt like a shock. It almost took his breath away. Here he'd walked around in the old neighbourhoods and believed he'd entered fully into time past, but all at once he really was there, as if the past had been quietly waiting for him here, among these gloomy walls.

Everything was intact. The low smoke-stained ceiling, with a bit of extra soot in the corners; the dusty cobwebs in the corner over the door to the living quarters. That rancid smell of grease from the greyish-yellow doughnuts on the counter; the brown factory-made spindleback chairs which always creaked when you sat on them but were incredibly sturdy all the same; the brown, poorly wiped rings after coffee cups on the pale-blue marble tables round about; the lines of bitterness framing the mouth of the girl behind the counter – it had to be a new girl, of course, for she wasn't much over twenty, but she was a remarkably accurate reprint.

A picture of the Saviour on the cross hung above the counter. A close-up of the same with the crown of thorns hung in the small adjoining room. He remembered the old well-worn joke that these pictures had been donated by patrons in memory of their sufferings when they partook of the merchandise of the place.

Remember, the earth is a vale of tears! was written in invisible but painstaking script everywhere. You shouldn't come here for the sake of pleasure but to ingest what was needful before once more walking out into the inevitable.

'Coffee, please,' he said to the sour girl behind the counter and entered the adjoining room.

This was where they used to sit. Around that table over there, on those chairs, in that sofa with holes in the upholstery. The spittoon stood beside the table, and right behind it the coat stand, resembling a gallows for special occasions: Please, hang yourself!

A shadow detached itself from the shadows over by the stove – the place was steeped in a half-light.

'Hello, Holmen.'

That dry, creaky voice – it was like a nudge from that past he was thinking about. He knew that voice, all right.

'Oh, hello, Hagen. Funny seeing you here.'

'Hm. To me, it seems funnier seeing you here,' Hagen replied crisply, but added in a more conciliatory tone, 'Do you mind if I move my coffee cup over to you? It's really lighter where you're sitting – and it would be nice to have a little chat. It's been a long time.'

It was twenty years since the last time.

He made his move by stages, very fussily. He had always been rather fussy, Hagen had. Coffee, coffeepot, newspaper. He went to fetch his hat and overcoat and galoshes, too.

Overcoat and galoshes in this fine weather! But Hagen had always been cautious that way. The weather was, after all, one of those things you could never take for granted.

Holmen thought in amazement, how come he hadn't remembered Hagen? He had, after all, belonged to the clique all along, had even been one of the its most enthusiastic members. Something of an agitator.

'I happen to come here quite often,' Hagen said. 'I happen to, yeah. I've got used to the premises. I still live in the old place around the corner, and so... Well, I've taken over the adjoining room too now. The old landlady is dead. She died, yes. But the daughter – well, you remember her, right? With a slight limp. And a small hump? Yes, that's right. She has taken over the apartment. So I rent from her now. Yes, things change... And so, you see, I've continued coming here. That I have. It's conveniently located and... I'm like that, you know, I take root easily. I am where I am. I like to strike roots. Yeah. You were different, of course, in many ways – more flighty, if I may say so – you've done well I gather, haven't you? I thought I'd heard something to that effect. And you're married? Well, well... No, I'm not married. I've got used to being a bachelor, and so... Oh yes, I'm in the same office. Down by the railways. Nine to two, four to six. Well, I do have a somewhat more responsible position now, of course. Somewhat more responsible, yes. I've been promoted a bit, can't complain. I've done quite well, even if I say so myself.'

A quiet, self-satisfied smile appeared on his face, as if it had been hiding behind a curtain all along and only waited for the cue.

He sat in silence a while.

'Oh yes. Considerably more responsible. So I could doubtless have negotiated continuous office hours if I'd wanted to, but... I feel I'd somehow got used to these hours. I already had them twenty years ago, you know.

'Twenty years ago, yeah. Twenty years ago... ' Hagen lost himself in memories. 'Yeah,' he said a couple of times. 'Yeah.'

He glanced fleetingly at Holmen. You could easily see that Holmen's frivolous light suit awakened his displeasure. He himself was respectably dressed in a dark-grey outfit which was suitable for all seasons.

'Hm – well, you've become a well-known personage in this town, haven't you, Holmen? Well-known, that's for sure. Of course, a doctor must advertise, that's true. The rest of us go about our duties more on the quiet. But you aren't active politically, are you? No, no. I suppose you've become more of a bourgeois as the years have gone by, too, eh? It usually goes hand in hand with age and success. It's the law of life. People are like that. But as for me, I hold on to the old ideas, oh yeah. The thoughts and ideas I had at that time. I am and will continue to be a good social democrat. Once I've formed an opinion, I'm inclined to stick with it, yep.'

That heartily satisfied smile again appeared on his face and remained there a while. To be replaced by an expression of profound concern.

'Come to think, Holmen, while we're talking, you couldn't suggest a remedy against sluggish digestion, could you? It's really the only serious concern that I have. Occasionally days will pass – and it seems to me that it's getting worse with time. I've actually thought about you on and off – that if I came across you I would ask your advice – no, I haven't been to the doctor – these doctors, they – they can charge big fees, but – five kroner for a few minutes – bloodsuckers! Uh, pardon me – but I certainly thought that, if I met you some day, I would... '

He looked with an air of satisfaction mingled with suspicion at the prescription that Holmen, after some questions, wrote out for him.

'Håkenrud? Where he is?'

Hagen blew his nose carefully and stared long and searchingly at his handkerchief.

'I'm darned if I know. Well, I did have a sort of contact with him for a few years, until – let me see – well, until nineteen twenty-two or -three. It was a bit difficult at times, he became a little too much of a Bolshevik for me in the end. He betrayed many of our old ideas when this revolution came about in Russia. But I did see him on and off. I'm not in the habit of letting down old friends. But then that old mother of his died – well, first she and then the old servant. It all happened in the space of a month. And afterwards Håkenrud didn't seem to feel comfortable in the old house. The same year, in the autumn, he sold the whole caboodle and applied for, and got, a position out of town. Well, he had a law degree under his belt by then, you know... No, I don't know where it was.

'I believe they said there was a story about a girl, too. Who didn't want to have him. Hm, I suppose such things do happen. Something of the sort was said anyway. But I, for my part, am not in the habit of listening to gossip, so I don't know anything about that.'

Holmen sat and listened to him. Heard and didn't hear. Now he could ask – strange that it was so difficult to ask – Hagen wouldn't understand a thing anyway, no more now than before, his imagination didn't take him in that direction, or in any direction for that matter.

Hagen looked at his watch, put his coffee cup on the tray, picked up the two remaining sugar lumps and wrapped them carefully in his paper napkin, which he put in his pocket. Then he got up.

'Well, the office is calling. Look, it's a quarter to four.'

He went over to the coat stand and began putting on his galoshes.

'By the way, Hagen!' Holmen spoke hurriedly and stumblingly, in a husky voice. 'You who remember so much, do you remember Helga?'

Hagen made a half turn, one foot into his galoshes.

'Who? Helga? Which Helga?'

Holmen stammered slightly. 'I'll be damned, but... No, I can't remember. I think we just called her Helga. She came along to Håkenrud a few times.'

'Helga?' Hagen finished putting on his galoshes and draped his overcoat over his arm. 'Helga?'

Then he shook his head.

No, Hagen didn't remember Helga.

Ready to leave, he turned to Holmen, visibly animated, but with a dignified reserve.

'Well, Holmen, it was nice to see you again and chat about the old days. Strange that it's such a long time ago, all things considered. It seems as if it were yesterday.'

He walked out.

He had always had a kink in his body when he walked, as if he'd been chopped off at the middle at some time and poorly put together again. It was as though he pushed off with his bottom at each step. That kink had become more pronounced over the years. Perhaps it was because he'd developed a paunch. By nature he was a thin person, but he'd developed a distinct thickening around the middle, as if he'd tied a knot in himself to make certain to remember something he mustn't forget.

A little later Holmen got up, paid and left.

He took a last look at the premises.

Unchanged?

Yes – no. Perhaps you couldn't preserve the past hermetically, after all.

It was five to four. Quick, quick, back to Ramstad's place.

One day Vera came back from work and told him that she was on holiday. It had come about rather unexpectedly, a few days earlier than she thought. But she didn't have a great deal to take care of.

Where was she going?

To a guest house down south, with a woman friend. Her friend had arranged it.

So. She was going away. Leaving him behind here. In this apartment.

He knew instantly that he couldn't stand this apartment.

It was stupid – but no doubt it was because it wasn't *his*. He didn't feel undisturbed here. He often noticed it.

He would notice it when he was together with Vera. When they were joking and laughing, and the game, without their knowing how, became serious – when the smiles stiffened on their lips and their breathing grew shorter and a gleam that resembled fear appeared in their eyes – *was* it fear, perhaps? Was there an area where desire and fear merged? He didn't know – but knew that it was that way with him, that when desire or happiness rose above a certain level, fear cropped up. As though it were written somewhere with invisible script: to this point and no further! And here, in this apartment, fear arose as a fear of being disturbed.

'Why are you so preoccupied?' Vera had asked a couple of times. 'Are you thinking about something in particular?'

Well, yes. He had thought – against his will he had thought, what if Ramstad came home? What if he were suddenly standing in the doorway! As if that was conceivable. And – as if it would matter if it were. He would raise his brows a bit, smile the world's smallest smile, apologize for intruding and withdraw.

'No, I'm not thinking about anything in particular,' he said.

Now he suddenly thought, what if we could get away from this damn apartment!

'Can you wait here a moment?' he asked Vera. 'I'll just make a couple of phone calls.'

He went into the study where the telephone was and called up an estate agent he'd used a few times.

Did he know of some nice place down by the sea that was

available immediately?

The agent was astonished. A strange coincidence! Exactly an hour ago he'd been informed about a house – it had been rented for the whole summer to a painter and his family, it was so beautiful there, grand, first-class scenery, first-class, but the painter's mother had suddenly died, and that had changed things, so an hour ago...

It was down in the Tønsberg area. An excellent house, right by the sea, a farm nearby, general store half an hour away. Completely undisturbed. Two hundred kroner for the whole of August. It could be taken over today, if necessary. And first-class scenery. First-class.

He remained seated for a moment after putting down the receiver.

He felt almost alarmed.

This was going too smoothly.

There were several things lately that had gone a little too smoothly. Almost as if – yes, as if a trap had been set for him.

Suddenly he knew what it reminded him of. Of the pits he'd seen in the mountains. They had fallen into decay now, but still. When a reindeer got onto one of the trails leading towards the pit, everything went so easily, so completely of itself. No difficulties, no bumps on the road. All it had to do was to walk and walk, a nice comfortable distance downhill. And then – there it lay in the pit.

It was sheer nonsense. He was not superstitious, and he knew that *destiny* had not set a trap for him. If a trap was set for him, it was he himself, his own psyche, that set it – that much he knew.

But this was going much too easily. He almost felt alarmed.

He felt as if a trap was set for him.

Vera fixed a pair of scrutinizing eyes on him. Then, slowly, she became glad. Then she became delighted. He hadn't seen her like that before.

Her friend? Oh, pooh, that could be taken care of. Such friends took offence sooner or later anyway. Besides, this friend had a boyfriend down there on the quiet.

She suddenly turned silent. 'And we'll get away from this detestable apartment!' she said.

This was Thursday. Four days had passed of the fourteen. When he thought back, it seemed a little eternity.

Friday morning they drove down.

By the Sea

They had to leave the car at the storekeeper's. From there only a dirt road led south to where they were going. That is, it didn't quite take them there, only up to Lars, who had the keys; he lived on the last farm out by the sea, and from his place there was a path across the rocks all the way to the house, so it was no problem finding it. Oh yes, the storekeeper had a tarpaulin he could cover the car with. Anyway, they could drive it into the old stable. Yes, he could send a boy with a cart south with their luggage and provisions. Beer? Soda? Of course. The word no seemed unknown to the storekeeper.

The dirt road wound onward, first over fields and between houses, then through a wilderness area with knolls and undergrowth. The soil was dry and sandy in the wheel tracks, but the brushwood grew dense and vigorous; there were aspens and birches and alder trees and pines, as well as masses of blackberry bushes with red fruit. They couldn't see the ocean, but after walking a while they could hear it to the left; the ground swell beat lazily against the rocks, sounding like a sober, deep and booming conversation between two mighty ones. A number of thrushes chattered in the brushwood, a few gulls were rowing high in the sky. The faint breeze that brushed them every time they walked through open terrain had a fresh taste of salt water. They passed a few horses and a herd of grazing cows. A small dun-coloured horse came up at once and sniffed at Vera – all animals liked her, she even, deplorably, attracted fleas.

A small brown calf came over as she stood chatting with the

horse, it hadn't learned bovine decorum yet, was curious and toddled after them for a while to see what kind of animals they were. Its mother let out an admonitory snort from its innermost belly; the calf turned and toddled back, but turned around to look at Vera one more time. 'Moo!' it said.

Sure enough, it should obviously have had another mother, it should have been somewhere else!

They walked for some twenty minutes, then the landscape opened up, the wind blew more strongly, and before them lay a few farms, fields and meadows, red outhouses and low white main buildings. And right next to them was the ocean. It was so huge all at once that they had to stop for a while.

Lars was sitting in the yard mending something big that you might think was a salmon net, so like as not it was something else. He was wearing a black peaked cap with a shiny visor and had a beard fringing his chin, like Terje Viken. The stubble was old, at least from last Sunday, and he himself was getting on for seventy, but that didn't bother him at all.

They became friends then and there.

He pointed with his pipe: the house sat behind that rock.

They could get fish, eggs, vegetables and chickens from Lars. And he used to fetch bread, butter and other necessities from the storekeeper's.

Knut Holmen was called Dr Holm for the present. That was all right.

They walked across the bare rock.

It was a wonderful house. A closed veranda faced south; it abutted on a room with a fireplace that also served as a dining room. In the back lay the kitchen, with a flower garden outside and a tall, dense thicket farther back, and the bedroom, with a large window facing south. A staircase led from the room with the open fireplace to two more bedrooms, so they could have guests if they wished. But they might not wish to.

The house sat there snugly, just as if it had been placed there by a fisherman, which was actually the case – the large room with the fireplace was the original house. To the north was the thicket, to the east, on the other side of the sound, lay a high deserted islet, which offered shelter from the wind, and to the west a long rocky ridge with smooth grey flanks extended south; it resembled a beached whale that couldn't get seaborne again. In front of the house was a flat grassy yard, and from there stretched a heathery moor; it slanted evenly down a hundred metres or so, all the way to the boulders at the water's edge. There was a little cove down there, with a mooring place, boat and boatshed, and a bathing hut.

Bumblebees were buzzing everywhere. The heather had just begun to bloom.

This place was too good to be true. It looked like a dream. When they had been through all the rooms upstairs and downstairs, had sat in the chairs before the fireplace, on the wall bench at the table, and in the deck chairs on the veranda, had smelled the trellised roses on the west wall and were on their way down to the water, Vera had to turn back and touch the yellow ochre wall.

Yes, it was real.

Oh, how liberating to come here, away from the city and the mad rush through the streets all day long. It was as if he'd been released from a tether, as if a burden had been lifted off his back.

Wasn't it strange? These fourteen days were supposed to be a respite, a time when he freed himself of his tether, removed the burden from his back, straightened up and looked about him. But without knowing how it came about, he had found himself running in circles on another tether, with a new burden on his back.

It was those shadowy neighbourhoods. Or rather, it was the city itself. Yes – and that apartment, which was not his own, where he could never feel at ease. And the office and clinic, which were nearby. And Agnete, who might come to the city at any time.

Here it was different.

Neither of them had left an address. Neither of them could receive any mail. They didn't subscribe to any newspapers. They knew nobody in the place, as far as they could tell. They were alone, with a stolid fisherman-farmer as their sole neighbour. And out there, directly in front, they had the open sea. You felt free and calm in your mind simply by looking at it.

He drew a deep sigh. The fresh air, filled with bitter iodine and sweet honey, flowed like a healing power through his veins. Shadows and anxieties retreated. For a few timeless days and nights they would be allowed to be free human beings, to enjoy the moment without a thought of past or future.

*

Far out there were some islets. On one of the islets was a lighthouse, which sent a pencil of rays, a white fan of light, around the horizon from dusk to dawn: three times, then a pause, three times and then a pause.

The islets afforded protection from the large breakers, but the swell hit the shore. A slow, slow rhythm. Now and then it rose, becoming a thundering rhythmical suction. It was the shadow of time here, in the realm of the timeless.

There was a whistling buoy somewhere out in the ocean, and when the sound of the ground swell rose above a certain volume, the buoy began to give warning: 'Whoo-oo!' And then again: 'Whoo-oo!'

It sounded like a chained sea monster complaining to the moon.

It was their watchdog.

One of the flat smooth rocks lying beside the great whale had a dip along the middle, a trench the width of a man that sloped down into the water. There must have been a boulder there at some time, sliding back and forth in the surf. The stone had disappeared, taken by the waves perhaps, after a job well done; but the trench was left behind, fine and polished, without a crack or wrinkle.

That stone had taken its time. Oh, how it had taken its time!

In the morning, before breakfast, they lay down on their backs in the trench and let themselves be pulled out into the water by the undertow. It was just as exciting every time. It was also cold, of course, so early in the morning. That anybody could wish to inflict such pain on themselves! But it gave them a first-rate appetite. Then they went up and prepared breakfast.

Shortly afterwards the hot hours came round. Those flat slabs of rock got as warm as an oven.

Sometimes it happened that the sun lit a fire in them, making them look at one another with wild, alien eyes and forget everything – in the middle of the flat stone slab, in the middle of the day. But mostly they just lazed about, dozing a bit, turning slightly now and then as they slowly became brown like newly baked bread.

They looked out at the sea with indolent eyes. A sailboat or two glided quietly along out there, a motorboat or two chopped the silence into small fragments.

Or they were seized by the spirit of inquiry and lay on their stomachs on the outermost rocks for hours, watching the incredibly rich life that was stirring in one of the innermost warm puddles of water – it swarmed and crawled, in and out, among the large-leaved tropical seaweed. Tiny little transparent, cross-striped small fry came scurrying with military precision in shoals of hundreds, looking like a rigidly disciplined school on vacation. Sometime last spring their parents had obviously done something without benefit of clergy in the vicinity of this puddle. Some other creatures, which looked like transparent horseshoe nails with a curve at the lower end and ran along on their own without either horse or shoes, turned out, on closer scrutiny, to be half-grown uncooked shrimps that kept to the shallows while training on the sly. An old sand-covered chopping board cut in the shape of a flounder and thrown away out here by an earlier summer visitor, suddenly began stirring and was not a chopping board but a flounder.

Everything would've been idyllic if the crab hadn't come into the world with its disgusting legs reminiscent of a spider, and its treacherous flank attacks.

Neither of them had ever dreamt of feeling like a persecuted, half-grown shrimp, fearing and hating the crab like the very devil. But now they did.

That one hadn't become a zoologist was tragic both for oneself and zoology. But much could still be made good...

Then they would hear Lars clear his throat. He came walking along on the other side of the whale. He always coughed loudly and penetratingly a couple of times, as though he were lost in thought, before he mounted the back of the whale, which gave him a view of the house and the open space in front of it. Then they put on their bathrobes and went to meet him. He was delivering vegetables or eggs or whatever it might be. Afterwards he sat chatting for a while. He seemed to have almost as much time as the ground swell. Or as that boulder. Whatever had happened to it.

And the evening and the morning were the first, the second and the third day. Long happy days and nights, slow swells of time that merged with eternity.

The nights were mild, the water was warm, the sky without a cloud. Had there ever been a summer like this?

In the evening they lay and listened to the sound of the deep rolling waves. It seemed more solemn then than during the day. A glimpse of the fan of light from the lighthouse reached them through the wide window. Occasionally they could see a small cluster of lights moving far out; they tried to guess what kind of boat it might be, whether it was bound for far away, and whether it would've been fun to go along.

The slow song of the waves rocked them to sleep – or awakened them, so that they sought each other out in the dim light. Her eyes shone in the shadows, they were phosphorescent, like the eyes of a savage. What was it he glimpsed in her face – happiness or fear? Now and then she would call out his name, as if she were in danger. Afterwards she slept like a child – one second and she was gone, breathing deeply and calmly, almost inaudibly. He would lie watching her a long time.

Had this young girl really given herself to him? Without ulterior motives, without a secret purpose? Could such things still be possible in a world where everything was calculation and ulterior motives?

Did he dare believe in it? If only, only he dared believe in it.

What was so special about these nights?

They were so solemn.

Was it this place, perhaps? The open sea and the clear sky? The vast stillness which made every sound stand out like a star in the night sky?

Was it the safety? And at the same time the beacon from the lighthouse out there, which gave warning time and again of underwater reefs and danger?

Was it something in himself?

Solemnity and fear – why did those two things always appear together?

Why did fear always follow hard on the heels of happiness, as shadow follows the sun?

He didn't know.

He couldn't help recalling a sentence which often occurred to him, he didn't know if he'd come up with it himself or had read it somewhere a long time ago: *Forgotten fear of forgotten transgressions lies like shadows on our lives.*

The moon was waxing at this time. It stamped a bevelled white quadrangle on the floor and spread a shadowless half-light in the room. He would lie watching her in the half-light. And then he sometimes felt the way he had felt now and then in the city. Her absolute calm awakened a wondering restlessness in him: who was she, this strange woman lying there? And who was *he*? In these moments, when the night and the moonlight and the breakers and his own pleasant languor joined forces and shoved his common sense aside, there were times when he thought: This wasn't him, couldn't be him. *He* was always in many places and in none. One of his shadows was running around in some shadowy city neighbourhoods, another sat in an empty office, and still other shadows were in other places, and one was here...

Then he must have fallen asleep, for he awoke from the sun having come around the corner of the house and directing its first beams at his pillow. It was broad daylight, the smell of seaweed and blooming heather came in through the window crack, and there wasn't even any ground swell, only the lapping of a summer tide. Before them they had a long sunny day, and all shadows were far away.

He never grew tired of watching and observing her. She was so different from one time to another, that must be it. But simultaneously he had the feeling that, if he could really learn to see, he would discover that she was one and the same all along.

He himself was not one, that he well knew; but he suspected that she was and that this was her secret. He never tired of being on the watch for that secret.

Her skin was transparent, like marble or china. Even though she'd been bronzed by the sun, her skin seemed cool. But when she was aroused, in the grip of desire, he could see warmth coming to the surface of her skin, as if the china suddenly began to glow, and he had the feeling that he *was creating life*. It must be this feeling of creating something that had such a stimulating effect. So he thought, anyway. Possibly.

She was proud of herself, but in a simple, sincere way, like a child. When she stood before him stark naked, bold and enraptured, slowly turning around with her hands behind her neck so that her arms resembled the handles of a jar, she reminded him with her curved lines of a daringly and audaciously formed vase from ancient times.

And then, all at once, he saw it. Those old vases and jars were built around the female body, its lines were echoed in them. They were tenderly and lovingly formed vessels. Alas! It was *that* secret which had been lost, leading to the decline of the potter's craft. The old artisans knew what they were thinking of while they were making their vases and jars.

One day she said, 'I don't believe in this.'

'In what?'

'In – all this. It's too good. You know?

'Do you think anybody can be allowed to be perfectly happy – to love and be loved, for example – without having to pay for it? I have a feeling that we're *stealing*.

'Yes, there must be a penalty for being so happy. Something terrible is bound to happen.'

She suddenly shivered and clung to him. He stroked her hair. Her uneasiness made him feel at ease.

'Oh, my dear! From whom are we stealing? From nobody.'

She looked up at him. 'There's nothing wrong or ugly as long as we love one another. Is there?'

'No, there's nothing wrong. Nothing ugly.'

She whispered, 'The only thing that's hateful – that's ugly – is the thought that you will some day leave me.'

Was a change in the weather coming? A couple of nights both slept uneasily.

He was asleep and dreaming. He awoke from her stroking his forehead. 'What is it, my love?'

He looked at her, bewildered. Who was she? Oh – it was her! He drew a sigh of relief.

'What? Oh, I was dreaming – something or other. Someone was calling me, I think. It was – no, now it's gone.'

He slept lightly and woke from her tossing and turning. He brushed her forehead lightly with his hand. She started up. In the sheen from the moon he could see she was frightened. Then she recognized him and calmed down. 'Oh, thank God – it's you!'

'Were you dreaming?

'Yes, I think so. It was something – no, now it's gone.'

What had they left behind which they didn't want to think about?

The thought of Agnete emerged now and then. Sometimes it bothered him a little. He knew now that it had bothered him a little already in Oslo. He pushed it away then – it could wait. He pushed it away now – he couldn't do anything from here in any case. But had he known that this – that these different things – would develop and go so – well, so far – he should perhaps already then have – well what?

Yes, absolutely. Already then.

Not that Agnete had any claim on him – for she hadn't. Absolutely not.

Besides, they had agreed that each of them should feel perfectly free. With responsibility, of course. So that was not it.

But he liked to have order in things. And this thing lay behind him, out of order.

This thing? What?

There were the children, too. The thought of them popped up occasionally. But the children, that was something quite different. That was really something quite different. He pushed those thoughts aside.

What was the use of thinking about all this now!

And so he wouldn't think about it. But he had a feeling that – well, it was comical, simply comical, but the idea had taken firm hold on him – that all this lay somewhere thinking about *him*.

There was something else too. *His work*.

Was he dissatisfied with his work? Did he want to reorient it, was that it? In a more scientific, a more social direction?

He knew it was not yet too late. More than one path was open to him. But time was getting short. And all this, together with much else, he had to clear up in the course of these famous fourteen days he was stealing from eternity. But time was passing. And he hadn't made any headway so far. Soon he would have to... no, it wasn't too late yet, but time was getting short.

And then there was another thing: how was Strand coping with his patients?

All things considered, Strand was a clumsy ox. A bumbler. If only he wasn't destroying too much. He thought of this and that patient – there he really ought to have given Strand more precise instructions. Strand would be sure not to understand, bumbler that he was.

But, of course, he would take advantage of the opportunity to make himself important now – try to feather his nest, snatch a patient or two in earnest. He could picture him, fat and round, good-natured and ingratiating. Yes, of course! he says, rubbing his hands. Dr Holmen is an excellent physician, of course he is, a first-rate physician – well trained, with post-graduate study in both Berlin and Paris – scientific talent too – though he has never utilized it; we had expected a great deal from him precisely *there* – his interests may be somewhat scattered – I've often said to myself he should perhaps have been something quite different, an author or mathematician, who knows? He has a distinctly logical mind, you know, oh yes, distinctly so, but he's maybe less naturally fitted for simple and practical matters, which as physicians we often have to manage – clumsy with his hands, actually, quite a bumbler – I remember an operation where we worked together...

Yes, that operation he would be sure to remember. The dirty dog.

And then there was a third thing: *Her*.

It was truly unbelievable. Here he had set aside a fortnight to clear up a couple of simple things – well, quite a number of things, as a matter of fact – and instead he went off down to the seashore and was hanging around here with a quite different girl, while the one he really – yes, *really* – had done his utmost to find – for that he had, right? He had – was going God knows where waiting for him to...

Or perhaps she had pulled herself together and called him or tried to find him? But then he had cunningly arranged everything in such a way that she couldn't meet up with him. You would almost think he had taken care on purpose to –

No, stop now. There must be a limit to this nonsense. To begin with, it would never occur to her to telephone. Well, that first evening perhaps, just as he himself was caught up in sheer madness that first evening. But later, now, twenty years later? When she didn't even in those early years, when she knew he was in town... Well, did she know that? He for his part had never seen her and had made certain that he would never hear any news of her either –

No, stop now, stop. There must be a limit even to remorse. *Her* he would find, even if heaven and hell – just as soon as he...

Yes. Just as soon as he... Then he would find her without delay.

There was still a fourth thing. What was the situation at home? Had Agnete come back? If not – if she wasn't there – what about all the mail that was certain to have arrived in the meantime? All those letters that perhaps needed to be answered? He could see in his mind's eye heaps of letters all over the floor of the hallway as high as the letter box in the door, so that the postman had to take a stick along and push the letters inside – no, rubbish, that devout morning help came every morning to check, after all. Oh? Did she? How could he know that? Who the hell can trust such pious Christian souls!

But in any case – there might be registered letters. Or letters from patients. No, they came to the office. Well, was that any better? Or there might be letters from the broker concerning his securities. What if they had fallen? No, they had gone up; anyway, he had orders to sell if they fell. Yes, but he ought to write, no, he wouldn't write, people might be lying in wait anywhere to get hold of his address ...

The thought of all these letters came up repeatedly. He had

forced himself to be orderly in his correspondence, much against his sluggish disposition, in fact. But precisely because of that...

These letters were really the only thing that bothered him. Well, and then the broker. And then the thought of *her*, of course. And the fortnight that would soon be over. And Strand. And Agnete. And the children – no, not the children, those thoughts he pushed aside. He wouldn't think about the children, absolutely not.

The stupid thing was that now and then all this added up to the familiar thought which followed him like the pixie wherever he went:

You should be doing something else.

You should be somewhere else.

One day at breakfast a trivial incident occurred.

They were using some white plates with a blue pattern. A dark-blue double stripe ran along the slanting upper part, looking like a fenced-in path that ran in a large circle around the plates.

That day a small beetle had strayed onto this path. Some honey was lying in the middle of the plate, and it was no doubt the smell of the honey that had attracted it; but then it had landed in between the two blue fences. It ran and ran to reach the honey, ran tirelessly in a circle around and around the plate – it never gave up and never came closer.

When they had watched it for a few minutes, he took a match and gave it a push to get it over the line. Then it became scared, opened its shell slightly and – look, it had wings, it could fly! It flew off. But the smell of honey drew it – it came flying back again; led by an unfortunate instinct, it again alighted between the two blue lines and began running.

'Let's go out!' he said.

He had become disheartened.

Things began to happen that were similar to those in the city.

She would be tempestuous and erratic and fly at him for no

reason. 'Oh! You coward! Cautious and conventional! Bound by a thousand scruples! Why can't you be brave and strong! Unscrupulous! Brutal and coarse – why not! But brave and strong! Oh! You should be able to grab me, fold me up, stick me in your pocket and walk off with me!'

She shook him in a fit of infatuated rage.

He was familiar with that sort of outburst and took it calmly.

To tell the truth, he liked such things.

One day he found her sitting by herself down by the shore. She didn't look happy, but when she noticed his inquiring glance, she tossed her hair back from her eyes and laughed.

'Ugh! Isn't it stupid? Here you are, with a reputation among your friends for having a good head on your shoulders, a clear head, a quick head, I don't know – oh, tell me, Vera, explain to us, Vera, you who have such a good head – that's what they say, all of them; but when there is something really critical, I mean something important, something to do with myself, all of me, then this good head of mine fails me completely, or it works so slowly that it might just as well have gone home and to bed. Isn't it stupid?'

'Really? What are you thinking of?'

'Thinking of? Oh, nothing special.'

The same evening, after they had gone to bed, he again noticed that something was wrong. She was so thoughtful. He turned her around and said, 'What's the matter?'

But she wouldn't tell him.

'Oh, I'm so ashamed.' She hid her head on his breast.

'What is it, then?'

She didn't dare tell him. He could feel she was blushing.

'Well, I guess I'll have to tell you all the same – but, you see, I don't mean anything by it – no – yes – I just mean – it's not that I want to force you, and it doesn't have to mean anything, and it *won't* mean anything, and it doesn't bind you, it's *not* a question of that – and you must forgive me in advance but – do you think you could tell me, I love you?'

They were difficult words to say, he knew that. But here they were alone, far away from people, no one could see them and laugh at him.

He said it.

She turned away. 'And you will always love me, will you?'

'Yes, I'll always love you.'

She lay perfectly still, her eyes turned away; but he could hear her whispering: '*Always – love – you.*'

It was later that same night that she said to him, 'Hide me! Pick me up and put me in your pocket. I don't want to be alone any more. Oh, I've been so alone. When I think about it, and about it getting to be like that again, I'd rather die.

'But I don't want to get married, do I?

'And I don't want to fritter my life away.

'Do you know – sometimes I think I'm cut out to be one of those little hens that gather the chicks around them and are otherwise taken care of.

'Do you ever wish you could die?'

He laughed. 'Oh no. I wish I could live for ever.'

He thought, she's not as strong as she seemed. I must be good to her.

And suddenly he felt he became warm and glad – from springs so deep he didn't know he possessed them.

That night he dreamed a strange dream.

He was in a foreign city. The weather was nasty, with showers of rain and sleet and strong gusts of wind. It was late evening, well into the autumn. He was going somewhere but couldn't remember exactly where, it must've been far, he certainly thought it was far, very far... He was walking down a street which felt unfamiliar, so he thought he'd better find a taxi. Suddenly he was standing in a city square, it was dark, he saw umbrellas glistening with water. He took his seat in the taxi and it started off. Stop – he hadn't said where he was going, so he knocked on the pane wanting to shout, Stop, I'm going to – but then he didn't remember where he was going; that made him even more uneasy, he knocked on the pane and yelled,

Stop, I'm going to... Perhaps the driver could tell him where he was going? But the driver didn't turn his head, he might not even have heard his knocking on the pane, might not have heard his knocking, might not have heard his... just drove faster and faster. He felt more and more afraid and knocked on the window, knocked on the window... The driver didn't even turn his head, just drove on, turning a corner so fast that he was thrown into a corner of the car and had to hold on, not knowing where they were or where they were going. He could only see the driver's head, a woman's head, motionless, he didn't know whether he knew her, and if he knew her it was terrible, and if he didn't know her it was terrible, and in front of them was nothing but darkness.

'What's the matter with you?' she said. 'You had a bad dream, I think. You know, you were whimpering like a little dog.'

He was still haunted by fear.

Outside, light was breaking, a faint grey daylight.

In the evening the next day he suddenly noticed that she was gone. He wandered about for a while, thinking she would soon turn up. Half an hour went by, she didn't show up. He began feeling uneasy.

An hour passed.

Was she inside the house?

He went in. 'Vera!'

No one answered.

He went through the whole house, upstairs and downstairs, but didn't find her. He called her name but received no reply.

Suddenly he was seized with a certainty that brooked no argument: she had left. She had packed and left. He didn't take the time to check whether she had packed, ran out of the house and took the quickest inland path. 'Vera!'

He ran so hard he groaned. 'Vera!'

'Hello. What is it?'

She was sitting up on the moor.

'I – I – '

She didn't seem to be surprised. 'I walked up here. It was just that – I needed to be alone for a bit.'

She looked at him. 'You see – well, I've thought several times I should talk to you about it, but –

'I wasn't very happy that first evening in the city. Or at all to begin with. There was something which I found extremely difficult. And now and then I get reminded of it – '

'Can you tell me about it?'

'I don't know. It was – I felt betrayed. No, I don't think I can talk about it. Later sometime, maybe.'

She hid her face on his chest.

'Stroke my hair a little, will you?'

That evening he told her about Helga.

They were still sitting up on the heathery moor, looking out on the ocean. Both were silent; they didn't have to say anything, nothing separated them right now. It was quiet everywhere, the wind had abated, the sea was calm, it was as though the mild August evening was itself at rest. Suddenly he said, not knowing why he had to say it, 'Listen, do you recall the evening we met? Actually, I'd hoped to find another woman. Someone I hadn't seen for twenty years.'

He told her about the meeting on Drammensveien.

She sat quite still, listening.

'Was that old experience so fine and intense, then, since it came so alive again twenty years afterwards?'

'Yes. No. Oh yes. It's so strange.'

Before knowing how it had happened, he sat there telling her the old story, heedless of the fact that such things shouldn't be related to another woman.

She was quiet for a moment. 'And you never saw her since?'

'No, never.'

'And – why not, do you think?'

'I don't know. But – something occurs to me now, something I haven't thought of before. I remember having a dream that night – no, it wasn't a dream, it was a nightmare; I started up several times, awakened by my own fear, and went back to sleep, then started up again – I dreamed the whole thing again, but only the hideous, dreadful part of it. And then, every time, it was my mother who stood in the doorway.

'My mother was very strict. She belonged to an old pietist family. She left us once when I was a child. She did come back later, but...

'They had decided they couldn't afford to have any more children. So, she thought, they shouldn't be together that way any more, she and Father. She forced it through. And my father, who was only human, apparently happened to take a fancy to one of the maids once. There were some violent scenes, that I know. And so my mother left head over heels and without warning. She didn't want to be in a house where a hussy had lain in her bed.

'Well, I didn't get this explanation until long afterwards. And as usually happens in the countryside – I got it first in the servants' quarters. They had their own way of telling such things in the servants' quarters.

'I don't recall very much from that time. I don't know how much I saw or heard or understood. I suppose I didn't understand a great deal anyway – I was the youngest child, four or five years old. But I remember that afternoon in late autumn after she had left. Remember it so vividly. Father had set out after her to persuade her to come home again. My older siblings were away, I don't know where. The house was empty. I knew that, and I didn't want to know. I ran through the rooms calling my mother. Through one room after another, calling her. It seems quite strange now when I think about it, I know I ran from room to room radiant with joy, full of intense expectation – oh, she was sure, quite sure, to be in the next room, waiting for me. It was growing dark, and such old country houses are extremely large at dusk. Full of delighted expectation, I ran and ran calling her, my calls reechoed from the empty walls. Only when I had run through the house twice did I understand that she was gone, and understand that I had known it all along. I stood alone in an empty room, where it got darker and darker, and I knew it was my fault that she had left. That is what I remember most clearly. That I stood there alone, and it was my fault that she had left.

'No, I don't understand what it all means; I'm not even close to understanding it. But I remember a saying – have you heard it? I often think of it: 'Forgotten fear of forgotten transgressions lies like shadows on our lives.''

He didn't know what was the matter with him; he didn't understand much of himself this evening – suddenly he hunched up and hid his head in her lap, impetuously, as if he wanted to hide from the whole world for all eternity.

'Forgive me!' he mumbled. 'I'm behaving like a child.'

She just sat still, stroking his hair very gently.

That evening up on the moor she told him for the first time something about herself.

She knew he had seen her father in the hospital. Her father dropped by there once, quite drunk, and cried awfully.

It was when her mother died that be began to take one drink too many. She was eleven when her mother died. Afterwards she took care of the house, while going to middle school on the side.

'What was the true story of that ear inflammation? Had you been beaten?'

He had all along had a suspicion of what had caused it.

'He was good as gold when sober,' she said. 'Well, at other times too. But he could get a bit violent – sort of – '

'Did he beat you often?'

'No, no,' she said quickly. 'And never except when he was drunk. Anyway, I wasn't a very good girl, I suspect.

'That time – when I got the inflammation – I had actually moved away from home and was only visiting. That's when it happened. Ugh – it was all so commonplace, you could've read it in a book.'

'Yes?'

'No, it was only that Father wanted me to marry someone he knew. And then he wanted to forbid me to associate with a horrid communist I knew.'

'Aren't you a communist or something of the kind yourself?'

She shook her head. 'I don't know what I am. Why does one have to be something with a name on it, anyway? But Andreas – '

She thought it over for a moment. 'I think he taught me to *see*. That is to say, I had seen a few things myself too, of course, it's not possible to live in a working-class block of one-room apartments without seeing something. I wonder if that's not the one advantage a poor man's children have over others. Such children aren't quite so blind. They can't avoid getting to know a little bit about what life is like. God knows, though, whether it really is an advantage.

'Yes, I had seen a few things. But at the same time I must have thought that this was how things were, and that they would remain that way. But Andreas knew a lot about how everything could and should be.'

She sat another moment, smiling to herself.

'Poor Andreas!'

'But you weren't to associate with him?'

'No.

'Father was a Christian,' she suddenly said. 'Well, he was a union man, too, and a socialist and all. But he was also a Christian. I mean – in earnest. That's why he felt such awful remorse every time he'd been drunk. But his remorse was just *too* awful – so he had to drink a bit now and then to forget about it.

'The man Father wanted me to marry was also religious. They were members of the same association, he and Father. And then he had an excellent store. And I worked in a bookstore for a hundred kroner a month. And Father worked at the planing mill for about twice that amount. So that store – '

'How could he make such different things go together?'

She laughed. 'Haven't you heard about people who have stalls in their brains? Like in a cow barn, you know, with one cow in each stall? That's how Father was. In one stall he had Christianity. But in other stalls he had other things – like socialism. And revolt – all authority is a bad thing. And – children must obey their parents in all things. And in other stalls – well, a man can hardly have grown up where he grew up without having absorbed a peculiar kind of cynicism – that women exist for one thing only – besides toiling for their husbands.

'All in all he was a good citizen, Father was. You should've seen how delighted he was when the Crown Prince got engaged and drove through town with his intended. He had to see them several times. He took shortcuts to get ahead of them again. He had studied the itinerary.'

Pause.

'And how come you managed to get through that childhood unharmed?'

She looked at him in surprise. 'Unharmed? Oh, but – *remember that he loved me, too.* I knew he did. And besides, was it really that horrible? After all, most people have to go through worse.

'I suppose there is basically only one rule for such things. If you come through, it hasn't been that bad. If you don't, then it's been too hard.'

It had got late. The lighthouse had already been sending that silent fan of beams around and around for a long time. The sea was calm, but there seemed to be some ground swell, because now and then they heard the whistling buoy: 'Whoo-oo! Whoo-oo!' It was the only sound to be heard. The dew was falling, the fragrance of the heather had become stronger.

Neither of them said anything. He was feeling so calm, calmer than he could ever remember having been. He felt whole, and part of a wholeness. Nothing separated him from himself, nothing separated him from her.

Three days left. Two days left. One day left.

He had carried out a secret decision – he had sent in an ad to *Aftenposten* – he wanted a couple of rooms with telephone and bath. They must have a place to meet.

He had given some thought to whether he should tell her already now, but had refrained. It was just too exquisite to imagine her delighted surprise the moment she could see it all finished.

On the last day they went around saying goodbye to the place, talked a bit with Lars's dun-coloured horse, walked up to the observation point and looked out over the ocean. Ocean, ocean, ocean on three sides. Everything else became so small. Even the rock they were standing on, the very centre of the earth, became so small. Only the ocean was big – changing, immutable, indifferent.

She was gone for a while in the afternoon. He saw her going up to the heather-covered moor. When she came down again, her eyes were red-rimmed.

He noticed that she went around touching things, when she thought he wasn't looking – the flat smooth rock where they had lain sunning themselves, the red wall of the bathing hut down at the mooring, the stairs in front of the veranda where they had sat so often, talking about little things and looking out upon the ocean. She even bent down and quickly brushed the grass-covered ground with her hand – it was a place with tufts of grass and small corn mayweeds where they had often been sitting. Noticing it gave him a queer feeling for a moment.

No, he wouldn't tell her anything. It would be a surprise. Look, Vera, this is our place...

Agnete? The office? He hadn't quite thought it through yet.

It was slightly cooler this evening. They were sitting before the big old fireplace. They were burning dry old heather in it. It crackled and flared up. She was gazing at the fire, at the glowing embers, following with her eyes the little eager flames that rushed up a twig, sparkled like a small fireworks and went out right afterwards, while the twig became a glowing thread that turned into grey ashes and collapsed.

'Well, the week is gone,' she said.

'Ten days,' he corrected her.

She didn't seem to hear him.

He didn't drive home to Oscars gate. After they had dined in the little restaurant and he had brought her to her door, he turned and drove down to the Continental. He needed some time to think things through.

As he stood at the broad window in the room at the Continental, he suddenly felt anxious. Where was she? He turned and faced the room. But, of course, she wasn't there.

He had noticed this anxiety now and then the last few days. Perhaps every time he didn't see her. But then she came, he had her there and calmed down again. Now she was not there.

He felt an aching desire to have her with him.

He stared out through the window again. It was dark outside, and the lights were lit. Lights and more lights, groups of lights, cones of light, clusters of lights, hanging street lamps swaying gently in the wind – and in between there was darkness. But the darkness was full of shiny eyes – cars that sped up and down, turned and swept the street before them with their searchlights, turned their fronts in your direction and stared at you with large eyes of light – they resembled giant beetles rushing off in the fabulous world of a dark future. In each car sat one or more people. Unknown people.

How many cars there were. Vacation was over, motorcar traffic had increased.

Suddenly the city struck him as being extremely large – large and strange and dark. A light here and there in a forest of darkness.

How many did he know here, in a city of three to four hundred thousand people? Two thousand? Far from it. One thousand? Did he *know* one thousand? Hah – a hundred, maybe – but he didn't know them. Ten – but he didn't know them either. One – himself.

But he didn't know himself.

What kind of centre were his thoughts circling around, again and again?

He didn't know her.

How curious – as long as you had a person near you, especially if there were only the two of you, the very proximity stopped you from thinking about this – that you really didn't know that strange person at all.

He knew nothing about her. As good as nothing. Well, that is to say, in a way he knew perhaps everything – if only he could *see*; if only he could connect the dots and draw conclusions from what he had seen and heard.

He had seen to the very bottom of her.

Yes, but there it was dark. He had looked down into a darkness. A glimpse, warmth, and darkness.

Who was she?

He knew where she worked, what her opinion was about her work, and about a little of everything besides. He knew how she sat and stood and walked, how she leaned against a man and looked at him – how her face changed.

He no longer thought in words but in pictures – clear, luminous glimpses of pictures with darkness in between.

Down there, the motorcars were speeding off; they sort of felt their way with their cones of light, turned a pair of glowing eyes on him now and then, and sped on. Behind them, behind the traffic and the lights and the people, lay Palace Park, pitch-dark. And above it the autumn sky, vast and dark.

She had given the impression of saying goodbye.

Where Are You?

He opened his eyes in a state of anxiety. He wasn't where he ought to be. Where was he? Oh, of course...

He got out of bed and raised the window blind. The room was filled with a cold, hostile autumnal light. Well, there seemed to be a sort of sunlight, the sky was as clear as milk that had gone blue and sour; but there was no thicket, no heather, no ground swell, no ocean. Was this the view he found to be mysterious and uncanny yesterday evening? It wasn't the least bit mysterious. But uncanny it was – uncannily trivial; it consisted of ten thousand ugly little things that added up to one single threatening fact – it sneered at him through the window: now you are in Oslo again, and everything is in a mess around you, nothing has been solved, nothing is as it should be.

The fortnight was gone. What had become of the time? *Gone*. He refused to understand it. Just think of everything he'd hoped to accomplish in these two weeks! Everything he'd meant to figure out, everything he'd meant to get back to and move forward to.

What was the result?

Vera.

But so what? What did he *want*? To be with Vera – of course, of course; but he *couldn't* do that in the long run without talking to Agnete, and he couldn't talk to Agnete until he knew more about what he wanted with Vera. And then there was *her* – the other one – Helga, yes, precisely, Helga, what about her? After all, he couldn't know anything absolutely certain about Vera until he'd met Helga – and he couldn't find Helga until he'd met Håkenrud, and he couldn't find Håkenrud until he had... And he *had* to see Helga, that was the big – nonsense, this was nothing but a phonograph record, a twenty-year-old phonograph record. But what about his work, and the children, and the clinic, and... and...

Directly in front of him was the rear of the National Theatre. What a dismal and depressing building.

If only he could get hold of a giant club and smash it to bits!

Theatre crisis! Humph! Just look at that giant department store for old dust. Last generation's empty words and gestures are accepted for preservation. NB. NB. We carry everything in the antiquated category. Withered intellectual life and warmed-over passion are demonstrated every evening from eight to half-past ten by has-been talents and former female beauties. Come and see! How remarkable that the public wasn't storming the ticket window!

If only they were capable of making one sincere effort, however misunderstood, however mistaken, but sincere! But no, here as everywhere ten thousand secondary considerations ruled the roost, everything was to wither at birth!

He seemed to have got out of bed on the wrong side this morning. Away with these speculations! Get down to concrete tasks!

Hot coffee, eggs and rolls helped his mood somewhat.

He made a great decision and called home. Not in order to talk to anybody, but to find out whether anyone picked up the phone.

No one did. So nobody had returned home yet. That meant nobody would come home this week. It afforded a breathing space.

What a relief!

Then it only remained to call Strand and the clinic. For one thing he suddenly knew with absolute certainty: resume his practice now, reenter his old life? Not a chance! Rather die!

Strand wasn't even surprised.

That was the good thing about such phlegmatic people; they even lacked the energy to be surprised.

Next concrete task: *Aftenposten*, pick up replies to the ad, look at rooms, ooh.

'Quiet gentleman. Separate entrance' had been a success. There was a heap of replies. He eliminated the most impossible ones, kept a bunch of seven or eight and went out to the car.

And now he had to find his new place.

He drove around. And old experiences became new. He had always perceived all landladies as his natural enemies, which they also undeniably were, as a rule; what is more, he had viewed them as he did large dangerous animals. Oh dear! A bent old woman up at Fagerborg Church showed him into the parlour and the living room. The living room could be converted to a bedroom– she showed him a narrow couch that could accommodate a body. There was furniture upholstered with red plush, which had been considered elegant in its time; there were pictures, photographs and knick-knacks. It was her most precious possession, memories of better times, which that old arthritic woman had to peddle to strangers. He could tell by the polite, anxious look in her eyes how she hated him.

Up by Sankthanshaugen he came across something that was a bit better. Two passable rooms facing north, with the entrance to one located near the front steps. The innermost room had a telephone.

The landlady looked like most others. He asked a few of the usual questions. Was it quiet there? He must have absolute quiet, no disturbance. Because of a project he was engaged on. Certainly, it was quiet as the grave, the landlady said, ingratiatingly. There were no noisy people in the building. He took another good look at the place. The thought of driving around to look at more such rooms made him feel so melancholy that he decided he might just as well take these right away.

They settled a few practical questions – some pictures had to be taken down from the wall and the work table moved over to the window.

Suddenly it was as if the sour mood from the morning was blown away. Now he had a couple of rooms, even though they were nothing to boast of. But good heavens, what difference did that make? Vera! Vera! Now we'll have a bit of time to ourselves. A bit of time, Vera! Just wait!

That strange joy he had felt now and then recently – quite often, in fact, most recently – was there once again, rising and rising within him. If only he could sing! But, sorry to say, he couldn't carry a tune.

He walked around whistling while packing up at the Continental.

It was almost four o'clock when he was through with the little move.

Vera had *one* advantage among many others – you always knew what she was up to, at any rate in the morning. That was more than you could say about most women.

Should he show up in front of the door?

No. Men who stood waiting outside a place of business had always struck him as slightly comical.

Besides there were several things he had to take care of first, purchases to make, this and that to put in order in the apartment.

He drove down to the Grand Café, wrote a brief letter and had it sent up by messenger. He gave his address and proposed that she drop by at seven o'clock.

Would she be wide-eyed!

Yes, Vera. I couldn't return home. I've taken lodgings here. I have no idea yet what the future has in store, but I couldn't return home again – because I... Yes, Vera, I've discovered that I...

Oh, would she be wide-eyed!

Around six o'clock he was back again, after making the round of the wine shop, the flower shop, the grocery and the tobacconist.

A vase? A dish for fruit?

The landlady was running in and out.

He arranged and rearranged things, and then again rearranged them.

His heart was beating rather nervously.

It wasn't really that long ago. Twenty-four hours, not even that.

What time was it? A quarter to seven.

He had to arrange things better. That lamp looked terrible, he must remember to buy a decent shade.

Strange how his heart was beating.

Seven!

He took his stand by the window.

There! No.

There? No.

He continually saw her coming far off in the street.

He'd better sit down a moment. She wouldn't come sooner because he was standing.

*

Better look out the window. Perhaps it wasn't so easy to find this place, after all?

Maybe he'd better walk down to the entrance? No, no, he had to stand here, on the lookout.

Had he written down the wrong address, *after all*? No. He pictured to himself every word he wrote. No, he was afraid he'd written down the correct address.

The street was alive for a while after seven, then it went dead; it livened up again shortly before eight, before lying dead once more. Then it livened up a few minutes to nine. Afterwards it went completely silent.

She didn't come.

He always slept poorly the first night in a new place, The street was noisy, with a constant traffic of milk trucks from seven o'clock in the morning. Nor was the building quiet; the shrill sound of alarm clocks and rattle from the kitchens reached him through several walls and floors.

Shortly after nine he called the beauty parlour.

'Miss Boye? She's on vacation!' the lady answered.

'But – '

'She's on vacation. She'll be back in a week.'

She hung up.

She was on vacation, would be back in a week. But –

So she had extended her vacation.

But why hadn't she let him know? Good God – she must've thought he'd gone back home, to the bosom of his family. What answers had he given to those cautious questions of hers: 'Just wait!' As if that was an answer! He had wanted to surprise her, make her happy, and bask in his own grandeur and graciousness – ugh!

What had he said to her: you'll hear from me!

So gracious, oh, so gracious!

She had stood there receiving His Highness's announcement with a wee little silent smile. She didn't look particularly happy, and he noticed it and thought, Wait, just wait!

Yesterday he was the one who had to wait.

So she had extended her vacation and had been too proud to call him.

Or – what if she had pushed aside all considerations and called? Then there would have been no answer. After all, he had very cunningly seen to that, master arranger that he was!

And so she'd left. Had called up that damn guest house, wherever it was – which he hadn't even tried to find out – and packed her bag, but not without stopping a couple of times to stare at nothing – oh, he could see it all in his mind's eye.

And *he!*

If it was true what some people said, that society was sustained by all those blockheads, then he was one of the pillars of society.

Well. This was, of course, lucky for the woman friend, who

would have company all of a sudden. What was her name? He had forgotten, naturally, or made sure he wouldn't find out. Neither the name of the guest house nor of the friend. Strange that he remembered Vera's name – how in the world had he managed that? And he even remembered his own name! He'd better write his name on a tag while he remembered it, and keep it in his pocket just in case: Dr Knut Holmen, talented man, send him – yes, send him *there!*

In reality, perhaps he should be grateful. In this way he had all of a sudden been presented with oodles of time. Mountains and valleys of time, oceans of time.

What in the world was he to dream up? Maybe he could start examining those old crossroads again, those extremely interesting old crossroads – oh, go to hell!

Test one's values...

Ramstad. He could call Ramstad. Thank him for the loan of his apartment and – well, in short, call Ramstad. He must have come back by now.

He called Ramstad.

The telephone rang and rang in his ear; no one picked it up.

He called Ramstad's office; it had suddenly become extremely urgent for him to get hold of Ramstad.

'Dr Ramstad? He's on vacation. Will be back in a week.'

The speaker hung up.

He sat near the telephone, his head empty.

The house was quiet now.

The emptiness and the silence hummed in his ear, faintly and subtly, like a mosquito.

What was it that this stillness reminded him of? Oh, the dial tone, that empty sound from remote ages and places – just turn the dial quickly, my friend, and you'll get in touch with someone or other who is quite near.

Empty and silent. Not an idea, not a thought.

'Silent as the grave!' his landlady had said. Quite true, except for the fact that the place was a confounded echo chamber at night.

Was he to sit in this room and be buried alive in all eternity, while life rushed away from him out there?

He cast a glance around the room and knew he already hated it, as though all those dreary furnished rooms of his youth were rolled into one – as if all the poverty, hopelessness, and endless yearning of his youth had been sitting here waiting for him. He grabbed his hat and dashed out.

Outside, the sun was shining – sharp, dazzling sun. The razor-sharp light hurt one's eyes.

A lovely day. Not a cloud in the sky.

Not a cloud.

And oceans of time. There were no limits now to what he could accomplish.

Where should he go? What should he set to work on?

Totally at a loss, in the end he went down to his broker.

The broker was delighted to see him. Well, where had he been all this time! The broker had called and called – no, only pleasant news, exclusively pleasant news. Things were going brilliantly – well, that was to say, *the world* was going straight to hell, of course, as anyone could see, but all securities were rising and rising – copper was rising, nickel was rising – just yesterday his securities made a huge upward jump; after all, the situation had worsened considerably yesterday!

The broker was calculating.

'You've made over six thousand since August 1. More than one thousand of it just yesterday. Quite nice, eh?'

Quite nice.

He had started this game a couple of years ago – turned over to the broker one thousand kroner he'd made on a patient who died in his care. He played on margin, following the broker's advice. The earnings had been steady, and he could scarcely lose as long as the world was the way it was; still, he settled up every month and deposited half of his net gain in an account to pay for possible losses. It was sheer blindfold play on his part, except for the fact that, on principle, he favoured disaster securities, that is to say, copper and suchlike, which would inevitably rise in value when the world was threatened with war. When everything went thoroughly wrong, his securities obediently made a jump. If everything was headed straight for the bottomless pit, he would become a rich man.

Well. So what? *He* couldn't change the world. He couldn't stop the insane game of the big shots. So it must surely be permitted to profit a bit from it, on a small scale.

But at times he would be superstitious. He didn't always like to win.

The broker rubbed his hands. Oh yes, things were on quite a roll. And when Holland gave up the gold standard in the near future, there would be another rise. And in the Far East, dark clouds were also gathering – quite dark clouds.

His head empty, he descended the stairs.

Funny – it was here, in his broker's office, that he'd first met Ramstad. And, in reality, it was Ramstad who had given him the principle he gambled by. Funny.

Oceans of time.

He went on a ramble through the northern and western suburbs – Sagene, Ullevål Hageby, Smestad. He walked and walked without noticing very much where he was going, one road or street was just as good as any other.

At length he looked at his watch. He'd been walking for a couple of hours. Where was he?

In front of the house in Parkveien where Vera lived. He knew immediately: he had walked in a large spiral, which had finally ended here. Well. Then he might just as well –

He climbed the stairs, found the card among the others in the row beside the door, and rang the bell. A maid in a white apron and something white on her head opened the front door.

No, Miss Boye wasn't there. She was on vacation.

Could he have her address? It was to do with some work, he added, confused.

He was examined quickly from top to toe.

'One moment!' The maid disappeared, the door closed. After a short while she returned.

'She is at Geilo. She didn't leave a more precise address.'

The door slammed shut.

Geilo. He seemed to remember distinctly that that guest house was situated by the sea.

He went to the small restaurant up at Bislet, where he and Vera had dined a few times. The place was deserted now. Though there may have been some people there, all the same.

Evening came at last. It even got so late that he could go to bed.

Where had he been all evening? Oh yes, at that cinema. And had seen –

He couldn't recall what he'd seen. Oh yes, first there had been a Mickey Mouse film, which was funny. He distinctly remembered that it was funny.

*

Something was happening behind his back. If only he could see what it was, then it wouldn't be a bit dangerous. But something was happening behind his back which was so dangerous that he didn't dare turn around for anything in the world to see what it was. He only glimpsed its shadow, and if he could turn around he would recognize it and be released from the stone so he could turn around, but he had turned to stone and couldn't move.

He woke up and knew at once what he would do. He looked at the time – half past seven. He had plenty of time. The Bergen train left at nine.

He immediately got out of bed, walked through the hallway to the bathroom, took a quick shower, turned on the cold water – wonderful!

It was wonderful to know what you wanted. Wonderful, wonderful. He began to whistle while shaving.

Then all he had to do was pack the necessary clothes for four to five days. There would be excursions in the mountains, maybe in rainy weather.

What comfort to notice that his brain was alive again. After five minutes everything necessary had found its way into his suitcase, and he knew he hadn't forgotten anything. He locked up the manuscript in the other suitcase – there!

It was still half an hour before the train left.

Was the landlady up?

She was up. He gave her the necessary information, paying no attention to her curious glance. Then he went back to his room, called up the garage and asked them to pick up his car, and called a taxi for himself.

There were few people in the street. What a fresh and beautiful morning. Why didn't people get up a bit earlier and take a walk before going to the office! But how many knew their own good?

He'd been lucky with his travelling companion – a skinny Englishman who was probably capable of going round the world without exchanging a word with the other travellers. What a blessing for others the English spleen was! This one was going fishing. A silent sport. And playing bridge in the evening, maybe. A silent game. Could someone explain how the English language had acquired over one hundred thousand words!

Now the train could feel free to leave.

Now it was leaving!

He took along a couple of newspapers and went to the dining car to get his breakfast. Nothing could beat such an early breakfast in the dining car when the weather was fine, the landscape fine, the journey fine, and the end of the journey fine – hooray!

Bacon and eggs, rolls, milk, marmalade, coffee.

And a pipe.

And the world was going to hell, evidently. But it was probably just a trick so that his securities could go up.

Oh, Vera!

The train thundered through Nordmarka, its white steam bubbling cheerfully from the locomotive, as if the train was waving to the landscape with a huge handkerchief. Now the whistle went, giving out a plaintive, anxious sound, and he suddenly felt uneasy – he was susceptible to impressions today – then it went into the mountain, it got dark, he felt depressed; but it was only a brief depression, and they came out on the other side to new views.

He was seated in his compartment again. The Englishman was reading a book about angling and was as silent as one of the big fishes he was reading about.

A few hours more and he would arrive, and meet her.

*

Vera, I've been blind, I've been deaf. Can you forgive me? I was chasing dead old shadows and didn't see it was life itself I was holding in my hands, I turned my head away, refusing to see, refusing to know. I know that now, Vera. Is it too late? Tell me it's not too late. Vera, I don't understand what was the matter with me – oh yes, I know, I realize that you meant danger, that's how I felt, you awakened something in me that was stronger than anything I had experienced before, and I became afraid, I think I became afraid of losing my freedom – the freedom that consists in being dead – I've been dead, Vera, I've been dead for years, while believing that there lay the true art of living. I don't wish to go back there any more, to that endless desert I called life. I don't, I don't, I don't... I found you while chasing someone else, no, I wasn't chasing anyone else, I was running away from something and found you, and won you, and didn't dare think I'd won you – out of fear of awaking one day and having lost you. Vera –

His face must have expressed something. The Englishman looked up from a big fish and sent him a disapproving glance, before turning the page to an even bigger fish.

Ah, he was full of joyous anticipation. To see the happy surprise in her eyes. Talk with her. Chat with her. See that little smile break through. It had been a rare sight those last few days.

And all the things they would do. Hiking in the mountains.

He would teach her about mountain plants, hear her laugh...

Were the colours starting to come out in the mountains now? No, it was probably too early. You had to have a few nights of frost first.

Her woman friend? Oh, to hell with her friend. Come to think, they could take her along on an excursion and be nice to her.

The train chugged: Vera and Vera and Vera and Vera...

Slowly, the hours went by. The train had passed Hønefoss and Nesbyen and began to work its way up Hallingdal Valley. What a long country. What an endlessly long valley. Steep barren hillsides, poor soil and fox farms. It was quite understandable that the greatest pleasure of the Hallingdal people in the old days had been to leave the valley behind and go up into the mountains to shoot reindeer and people from neighbouring Valdres.

The railway line made one turn after another, but the same great natural beauty was there after every turn. It became too much of a good thing, the repetition lost its mystery, it was, sorry to say, like watching a hundred attractive chorus girls dancing in step. *That*, too, was no longer beauty but monotony, and mentally stultifying – it was like rushing through one room after another in a large, empty house.

What was happening to him? Soon they would be there, soon he was to get off the train.

Get off and track down –

Drop by the post office, perhaps, and inquire about her? Go and ferret her out –

Tag along after her like a beggar –

They were getting close now. The train let out a sharp, piercing whistle before the last turn. Now it slowed down, now it steamed slowly into the station. People everywhere.

He had taken cover near one of the windows in the corridor.

She didn't seem to be on the station, in any case.

He stepped out, suitcase in hand, and looked about him right and left with quick glances.

There was no one to be seen.

What now? Find lodgings in a hotel?

He deposited his suitcase at the station and at the same time hastily checked the train times. Then he went out again.

There was no one to be seen.

What now, indeed.

He ought to go in again and make inquiries.

He stepped out into the road.

The dreary railway town stretched up and down along the road, like a refuse heap of monstrous buildings. The warm autumn colours hadn't yet come out. The hillsides and the mountains sat one behind the other, cold and bluish green, in the thin, clear mountain air, without distance, without extenuating circumstances.

The whole landscape struck him like a vast, empty, deserted room. He shivered with cold in the sunshine.

This was senseless. He had travelled all this way up here, excited like a child!

Not during the last hour.

He could bide his time, of course. He could look around a little while and then take a room in Holm's Hotel.

He walked up the road between shopkeepers, posting stations and boarding houses.

Up there, on a path, a couple was walking.

No.

Someone was coming towards him.

He had smoked too much lately, his heart was not in good shape.

No.

He probably ought to leave off tobacco for a while – he recognized these attacks of cold sweat.

Over there someone was coming – and there, in front of that cottage...

No.

How odd. He felt dizzy too.

He sat down on the stone fence.

Sitting like that, he probably looked just like a biggish stone in the fence.

It was dinnertime now and she couldn't be out, that was clear.

There it was again, that hollow sensation in the region of his heart; it was as though someone was sitting somewhere or other sucking and sucking the heart out of his chest with an invisible suction pump.

Over there came a group of three – and one of them –

No.

He looked at his watch, stood up quickly and started walking.

Time was getting short. Now it was really getting short.

He quickened his pace.

There was the station.

He could check into Holm's Hotel and bide his time. It was lovely up here, after all. He could go hiking up Hafsdalen Valley and think things over. That would be the solution.

There he heard the sound of the Oslo-bound train.

He ran into the station, up to the ticket window, got a ticket and took a deep breath, as though he'd just barely been rescued from a great danger.

The train thundered in, the locomotive spewing steam and trickling water. Four or five tourists got off.

No.

His knees numb, he climbed the two steps of the car. At the last moment a couple came running – a man and a woman.

No.

The station master signalled, the train whistled and screeched and started moving. He had to hold on to the door of the back platform, seized all at once with an absurd desire to jump off; but now the train was under way. There the first turn was coming up.

Now he could no longer see the station.

He could get off at the next station and take a taxi up again, that was no problem.

He remained standing out on the platform until they had passed the first two stations. Then he went inside and sat down.

Don't think now. Don't think.

He stepped out of the train in Oslo in the evening, beaten and aching in every limb, dead tired, as if in this one day he'd made a round trip through all the desert stretches in his life.

The next morning he went down to the garage, got into the car and drove off, out along Drammensveien, out of the city and south.

It wasn't even a decision. He just drove.

He had no suitcase with him today. No expectations either. He simply had to make this trip.

It was crazy, he knew.

She had said, by the sea.

He wanted to make this trip.

He let her rip through Lier, right through Drammen and farther out along the old road from Drammen to Holmestrand, a road that went up hill and down dale. There were few cars on the road, the worst ferry traffic seemed to be over for the year. But it was a fine summery day, with a mackerel sky in the south, otherwise not a cloud. It was warm and quiet.

Large flocks of thrushes and sparrows were gathered in the fields. Here and there combine harvesters were in action. Well, it was harvesting time.

Before Holmestrand the road made a turn over a small range of hills. The view of the fjord was so fine there.

He stopped the car, stepped out and sat down by the roadside.

Here they had taken a rest on their way back to the city. She sat on that stone over there, right beside him. That was three days ago.

The fjord appeared pale before him. A few fishermen were trying their luck, they were sharply silhouetted in their small boats, like ebony against silver.

On a hill near the road stood some giant birches. It might be an old burial mound. There were so many of them here, in Vestfold County. The birch leaves were just beginning to turn; they weren't yellow yet, but you could see that it wouldn't be long before they were.

During the last few nights he had been asking himself where her strange power came from.

He didn't know.

You can't know that kind of thing.

Things like that belonged to the mysteries. It was no use mulling over them.

But he'd been struck by the fact that, when he visualized her, pictured her to himself, dreamed her up, there was one thing he most often saw. Not only that, by the way – he could see her stand or walk, laugh, be serious...

But mostly he saw her face as it looked in the supreme moment of surrender.

No, not then. But just before. When he knew, now she was rising, now she was soaring.

Away from him? That was what he had often asked himself.

What was so special about that face?

Oh, he knew that all right. It was wild, free, untamed – and radiant. It radiated light. But it was more than that.

Oh, he knew very well.

It was *courageous*.

It radiated courage.

It was enraptured, wild, courageous – like a pilot as he begins to rise.

Yes. It was her courage he remembered. Some of it passed on to him, and he felt he rose to heights where he'd never been, except perhaps in dreams.

Then she left him. That's how he felt. At a certain point of the voyage she left him behind and continued rising.

And he – didn't dare follow her any further.

He was dizzy. Far too afraid of falling.

Too cowardly. Too full of doubt.

He looked back. He should have been somewhere else.

What happens to the doubter?

Back and forth. Back and forth. Forty years in the desert. Will never find his way out.

But...

She had, nevertheless, given him a glimpse of the Promised Land.

He left his car at the shopkeeper's. Taking no notice of the man's inquiring glance, he followed the road farther out.

The blackberries were beginning to ripen, the willow herb had shed its blossoms, otherwise everything was as it had been when they came here together.

Lars was completely unchanged at least. He even sat in the same place, mending something that looked exactly like the same net.

He asked Lars for the key.

Lars got up and went in to fetch it. He stood outside, leaning against the stone fence. No, no, the sunshine hadn't faded, everything was the same, nor had he expected anything else, he knew, knew, knew, after all...

Lars came back. 'So. You're going to stay here again?'

'No,' he answered shortly. And, as a kind of explanation, he mumbled, 'I've lost something.'

He quickly walked off over the rocks and up to the house.

It stood there the same as when they had left.

He unlocked the door and went in.

The whole thing was nothing but an empty ceremony.

The window shutters were closed, and it was semi-dark in there despite the open door. He walked through all the rooms upstairs and downstairs, quickly and nervously, as if he were afraid of the dark.

It was empty everywhere.

He returned to the empty room with the fireplace.

'Vera!'

'Vera!'

His call reechoed from walls and ceiling in the empty house.

Wandering around for a while, he came upon more than one familiar spot.

He came upon that flat stone up on the moor, where he discovered her that evening. He sat down there.

How quickly autumn had come – the heather had almost finished blooming.

He broke off a bunch and took in the wild, spicy fragrance of honey.

A belated bumblebee was still whirling about here. It seemed confused and in a rush, as if it were about to miss the train.

One really ought to soothe such a bumblebee, if only one could get on speaking terms with it: the train would surely wait.

He went down to the house again. He had plenty of time. He padded back and forth in the yard for a moment or two and went down to the mooring and the smooth rock.

Everything was as it had been.

This was where she walked about touching things that last evening.

There stood the tufts of grass and the small corn mayweeds which she bent down to and brushed with her hand.

He bent down and touched a small corn mayweed. It nodded lightly with its little white star-like head.

How quiet everything was today. No warning from the whistling buoy, not a stutter from motor boats. The murmur of the waves was so faint that it merged with the stillness.

He stood a little while looking outward.

He wasn't likely to come here again.

Then he went up to the house, locked the door, and went back to Lars over the rocks.

'Well, did you find what you'd lost?'

'No.'

He was about to go, but noticed that Lars was in the mood for a chat.

'You take it easy, don't you, Lars?'

Yes, Lars had come to that – one might as well take it easy.

We caught up with death soon enough – and age, well, *it* caught up with *us* soon enough. There was no rush.

Oh no. Nothing was really so much worth that it paid to

chase after it.

And the rest of creation, they knew. They were much wiser than us, in that way.

That big sow here, for example. If it could reason, it probably couldn't help thinking that human beings were foolish and vain creatures, chasing around and wearing themselves out instead of taking it easy and putting meat on their bones.

It sounded reasonable, what Lars said. Well, more than reasonable – rather like low-key wisdom. True, he could remember how the neighbour over there had dropped a kind of hint that Lars hadn't always taken life with such ease as now. Once long ago he would row three hours one way and three hours back every day for a whole summer to spend half an hour with his sweetheart. That was the bent-over old woman who stood over there feeding the sow.

But otherwise he was obviously right. There was no rush. No, there was no rush.

He happened to think of something. 'One week,' she had said, the lady on the telephone.

But was that so certain?

She could have come back today – and could have looked for him, called him up, in vain.

He said a quick goodbye to Lars, ran rather than walked back to his car and set off at top speed.

Nobody had called. Nobody had made inquiries.

There was no mail.

Back and Forth

The following days were a bit of a blur.

A good deal of the time he sat idle in his room – sat hour after hour waiting for a letter that never came, by a telephone that never rang. He sat looking out of the window until he thought he would remember for the rest of his life every stone in the pavement outside, every curtain in the house on the other side.

Old ladies used to sit like that.

He even had some flower pots on the windowsill.

When he could no longer bear to sit on a chair and bloom behind all the pots, he got up and took a walk inside. The room was relatively large; alongside the rag rug, which lay at a slight angle, he could walk seven paces forward and seven paces back.

He could make an hour pass in this way. Then it became too impossible and he went out.

And so he found himself running up and down the street again, exactly like a fortnight ago. No, not exactly, because now he avoided the old shadowy neighbourhoods like the plague; he'd had enough of them for twenty years or so. Now he headed for the outskirts, and from there farther on, out of the city.

Without clearly knowing how it had happened, he found himself walking far up in Nordmarka.

The first day he was wearing his usual summer clothes and light shoes, which was impractical, forcing him to stick to the beaten track. Later he put on proper gear so he could walk trails and cowpaths through the thickest forest. It was restful to walk yourself tired and exhausted up there. Your thoughts calmed down, the tension gave way. It was a period of quiet in the woods, he scarcely came across other living creatures, except flies, mosquitoes, ants, and a bird or two. If he met someone, it was usually a harmless berry picker with a tin pail in his hand and a wooden box on his back.

It was restful. But as soon as he turned around, restlessness wormed its way back again.

She could have returned. She could have been staying in a hut way up in the mountains and been unable to endure it. She had left without having received his letter, had written and sent her address, and had received his letter and come – or had sent a letter at least... She had received the letter and had telephoned, and was sitting waiting beside a telephone somewhere in the mountains... She had come back and was knocking on his door this very second...

A hundred other possibilities. He quickened his pace, and noticed it got worse and worse the more he quickened his pace.

Dripping wet and dog-tired, he came back to the two lonely rooms, where silence sat and waited for him.

The evenings were more difficult. The hollow ache was worse then, the emptiness was worse.

It was impossible to stay out, because something might happen at home. It was impossible to stay home, for something might happen outside. The newly lighted street lamps found him running along the streets hoping for the impossible, now just like a long, long time ago. Back and forth, back and forth, a regular run between two regular end points. He didn't know why he ran through precisely these streets; he ran there as if under coercion – maybe it was because he had walked there in a rather happy mood several times not very long ago.

This was the way he had run, up one street after another, hour after hour, evening after evening, for months, for years, in his beautiful youth eighteen, twenty, twenty-two years ago. Just imagine all the shoe soles he'd left behind as dust in the streets!

No, not quite this way. In those days he ran freely along unfamiliar streets, hoping at every street corner to run into the arms of the young girl he didn't yet know. Now he ran under compulsion along known streets, and what he hoped for he didn't know himself.

Late in the evening he went home, dead tired in body and soul, and to bed.

And now the house, ordinarily quiet as the grave, suddenly awakened to a strange life. A hundred tiny little sounds, barely audible to the average ear, were magnified by the nocturnal stillness and rose to a shrill tumult of hostile sound. Steps resounded down in the street, cars whizzed by and blew their horns at the corner, a conversation between two people standing at a front door with nothing more to say to each other was drawn out ad infinitum. One man had forgotten his front-door key and was whistling and whistling. A dog was howling far away. A shoe fell to the floor somewhere in the house. A sigh came from the wallpaper behind the bed, long and infinitely mournful, as if it would take its death of grief over the poor glueing. A fly fell and fell down on his hand, set on getting killed before it died. A bed creaked. A window catch sawed and sawed. From the floor above him came a slow, cautious coughing, with long pauses in between. Now there was a couple down in the street again, they weren't talking, they were whispering, 'Tsss! Tsss! Hee-hee-hee! Tss!'

Come seven o'clock, the milk trucks got going.

*

On Monday morning there was a letter for him. It was written on Sunday evening and was commendably brief.

'Don't look for me. Don't call me, I can't see you now. I can't talk to you. I hope to be able to explain everything quite soon, but I can't now.

Oh, please forgive me if I'm hurting you. I didn't mean to.
Vera'

Well.

That was that. He hadn't felt so calm for a week.

He asked the landlady to listen out for telephone calls. Then he took the shortest way to Nordmarka. He wandered about in a leisurely fashion up there for a few hours. Afterwards he couldn't remember having been bothered by a single thought.

He dined at Frognerseteren. He would indulge in a first-class dinner today; he recalled little of what he'd eaten or drunk in the last week.

In the afternoon he went back to the city.

Now he might as well go back home. His job must be said to have been done, for the time being. And Agnete had most likely arrived.

He called.

Agnete picked up the phone. He held his breath. She said hello a few times, then she put down the receiver.

Yes, he ought to return home now. There was no reason for doing otherwise. And so...

Never.

At the same moment the doorbell rang. They were talking out there. He recognized the voice of the postman.

The landlady knocked on his door and handed in a letter.

It was commendably brief.

'I *can't* talk with you now. *Can't.*
                    Can't.
                              Vera'

If he understood the letter correctly, she couldn't talk with him now.

What time was it? Six. Three minutes past six, to be quite precise. The evening lay open before him, he could do whatever he liked.

About half past ten he came walking through the northern section of Palace Park in the direction of Wergelandsveien. He'd been on a long ramble through the outskirts of the city; for the last hour or so he'd wandered back and forth at the north end of the park. Now he wanted to go home.

As he came out of the shadows among the trees, he caught sight of Ramstad and Vera on the other side of the street. They were walking up toward Parkveien.

He couldn't tell whether Vera saw him. Ramstad did see him, but didn't tip his hat.

Ramstad

For half an hour afterwards, he walked back and forth along the rag rug in his room. Then he heard someone whistle outside. He looked out.

Ramstad was standing down in the street.

'May I come up for a moment?' Ramstad said.

Holmen went down and opened the front door, and Ramstad twisted his long body past him. He had a nice tan from being in the mountains and seemed to be in tiptop form.

He put his hat on the couch and sat down in the best chair.

'So, this is where you're living. I heard about it and thought I might drop by. We have a small account to settle. But first – do you have a whisky?'

Holmen got out a bottle of whisky and glasses, and went into the bathroom for a couple of sodas. Ramstad downed a stiff shot to begin with, and then, with great care, uncapped a bottle of soda and made himself a half and half. He took a whopping mouthful of that too.

'Well' – he rummaged in his side pocket – 'there's that account. Let us see' – he got out a piece of paper – 'there's milk, ten half-litres at 0.18 kroner each, makes 1.80 kroner. Then cream for 3.20 kroner. Add to that twenty bread rolls at 0.07 kroner, totalling 1.40 kroner. Altogether 6.40 kroner. If you please, here's the receipt. Many thanks. That's it. Oh yes, you had evidently forgotten to cancel the order down in the dairy. And the owner is a conscientious lady, so when I came back a week ago – you see, I made a flying visit to the city a week ago – the whole staircase was full of milk bottles and rolls.

'Yeah – that was that.'

Ramstad took another big swallow. The whisky and soda hadn't lasted very long, the first one had been all but polished off.

Holmen was watching him. His Arabic-Negroid looks were more marked now that he was so tanned. His large heavy blue eyes appeared out of place in the dark face, as if they had been stolen.

Suddenly he saw one more thing. Oh, how he'd pondered over who Vera reminded him of! Now he saw who. It was clear enough. Some things in this world were less haphazard than they seemed. A great many things, actually.

She had looked bad, by the way.

He went out for a soda and put a couple more in the running water.

An Egyptian queen who looked like a Zulu – as a matter of fact, he thought he'd read somewhere that the Zulus were an Egyptian tribe which had wandered south.

He felt even more depressed than before.

Ramstad had finished his highball and took a stiff shot number two, before mixing another high-powered whisky and soda for himself. He had apparently taken it into his head to give that whisky bottle short shrift.

'Yeah!' he said with a sigh of satisfaction. 'Yeah!'

He gave Holmen a searching look

'Well, I can tell you that I did take the time to test my values. I have a certain bent for doing that, now and then, as you know.'

Another whopping mouthful.

It seemed he had a bent for letting others test their values as well.

'Maybe you'd like to hear a little about the result?'

He sent Holmen a lingering look from under those heavy eyelids.

'We could perhaps make a mini-confession to one another, eh? Because you have also tested *yours*, yes? I assume so.

'But anyway – as far as I'm concerned, I can at once make

the preliminary remark that my values have passed the test. That's how it appears to me, in any case. And now it would be interesting to hear what you think. But – I'm not bothering you, am I? You're certain I'm not bothering you? Because I have no desire to. Not under any circumstances.

'Test one's values, yeah.

'Seek out the truth, yeah.

'It's a dangerous habit, that. In fact, one probably ought to tell every single human being, "Do not leave the beaten track!" And above all, "Don't look too deeply into yourself. If you do, God only knows where you end up and what you will then see."'

'You know what? Truth is an explosive.

'Can you remember the fear that suddenly took hold of the physicists when they had thought up those new atomic theories and began to fiddle with splitting the atom? This was what they thought: Let's assume that we succeed in splitting an atom – won't the splitting spread from this first atom to the next, and from there to the next, and so on, until the entire cosmos in no time at all is shattered into nothing at all?

'You're familiar with that fear, aren't you? It's the primal fear, after all – the anxious conservative human being's fear of everything new. *Who can foresee the consequences* – have you heard that saying? What terrible things you can imagine happening if...!!!!

'Where do you think that fear comes from? Well, go on, have a guess!

'Shall I whisper it to you? *From the nursery!* Do you know that? Everything stems from the nursery – well, and from the bedroom, why not. Everything. Even Einstein's theory of relativity. Do you know what Einstein's theory of relativity is, in reality? An ingenious childish dream magnified to the point of fantasy and transferred to the cosmos.

'There is no absolute authority! Imagine the moment when that thought arises in the brain of a child. Daddy bosses me, but Mummy bosses Daddy, and I boss Mummy! All authority is relative. And the cosmos is limited, a nursery, but it expands from year to year.

'Well, you aren't an astronomer, are you? I gave a somewhat simplified picture of the theory of relativity, adapted to your understanding. Sorry.

'But, you know, such a childish dream can very well be correct. Approximately correct. Many childhood dreams are amazingly correct. And besides, it is precisely the task of our manhood to continue working on our childhood dreams and make them grand and fine and approximately correct.

'What were we talking about? Oh yes, about childhood dreams and the fear experienced by the conservative pillar of society. What is he so afraid of, do you think? Well, for instance: to let slip a fart at the table. Oh, horror! What terrible things might possibly happen if...!! Who would be able to foresee the consequences!! Wouldn't the Lord himself rise in dreadful wrath at the end of the table and...!!!

'But do you know what is behind this fright? A *desire*, an awfully dangerous *desire* precisely to let slip a fart at the table! Well, it does sound quite unbelievable that a good conservative pillar of society can harbour such desires, but he does! Let each of us search his own heart, if I may say so!

'Oh, if he only dared! But he doesn't. No, he doesn't dare to such a degree that he doesn't even dare to know that he doesn't dare – that he would like to, in other words. He doesn't dare to such a degree that his children and grandchildren do not dare either, as a rule – dreamed iniquities of that sort, you see, are visited upon the children unto the third and fourth generation of them who hate him, namely the father. This is what we call a good and moral upbringing. Hm! That stands to reason, doesn't it? What? What you don't dare to do yourself, no one else shall be allowed to do either. Otherwise, who could foresee the consequences?

'And those nasty radicals! To them, nothing is sacred, of them anything can be expected – they might, for example, be quite likely to allow themselves the most amazing things at society's ready-laid table.

'Danger, danger, danger, danger, danger, danger!! There

certainly is!

'But then there is a quite different type of pillar of society – well, I can see you have guessed it. The manufacturers of explosives, yes, and – yes, the active guardians of the sacred social order, for example, those who engage in secret exercises in street fighting, learn to throw bombs and grenades, and to shoot at moving targets representing workers – in short –

'A more dangerous type, eh? A more interesting type, eh?

'Shall I tell you what the childhood dreams of *those* people were like? Ah-ha! Let me whisper something in your ear: *I won't tell you*. Because, sure enough, you guessed it – you really are a star at guessing – yes, I belong to that type myself! But let me say this much: those dreams are something quite different from what we talked about before – they are truly explosive things, my friend – *high explosives*. Hah! That's another kettle of fish!

'Have you heard the story of Charcot's hysterical girl? Who in a high, holy trance split her dress from top to bottom with just one rough tug of one hand, while she simultaneously held it together for all she was worth with the other! Well... *Those* people certainly have reason to protect society, because they know a little about what dangers threaten it. Know? Oh yes, insofar as they have magnified their childhood dreams on a colossal scale and transferred them to the whole planet.

'Society must be preserved! For those sinister radicals can be expected to do what – well, what these men have dreamed of doing, *and which they do*, in their fashion.

'Oh, how I like those fellows! Those great restless souls who preserve law and order, the trust kingpins who collect wealth and spread poverty, the dismal vultures of war, the great, sanctimonious wreckers and destroyers.

'That really *is* something! Something other than people like you – nice, pious you – do you know what you are? *You are a miserable little pillar of society* – of the first-mentioned type, yes, precisely. Socialist? Are you *really* a socialist to boot? I might have guessed! But so what? All socialists are nothing but miserable little pillars of society!

'But we were talking about explosives, weren't we? And you reproached me for manufacturing explosives, or contributing to doing so, at any rate? Didn't you? You haven't said a word all evening? Oh yes, you have, and you definitely reproached me for making explosives, don't you think I can tell by the look on your face? So let me repeat to you that little saying, *Truth* is an explosive!

'No! Not those small truths of yours! Those I would compare to the small harmless sounds that nice little children – *don't* let out. I mean the real truths! *They* match the splitting of the atom, you see! Oh yes. Allow me to tell you in confidence: no one has yet succeeded in producing a splitting of the atom. It may well be that it really *would* spread to the cosmos – it may well be that such a splitting will be the last thing we all experience.

'And *truth*? The truth is no joke. Let us say, just by way of an experiment, that communism is the first short step in the direction of truth. What must communism dissolve above all? The *family*, which is the atom of the present social system. What holds the family together? A number of atomic forces, call it illusions: common interests, or a belief in common interests – common delusions, *common fears*.

'So, now you can say what I see you're thinking, that, if communism contains the truth, it's bound to replace all these delusions with true ideas. Nonsense! Pure nonsense. Because, first the atom must be split. And it's this splitting of the atom we're witnessing today. The preamble to it. And do you know what the funny thing is – the fine point? The fantastically fine point, which an ordinary person can only sit still and enjoy?

'That, believe it or not, it is *the protectors of the atom* who are splitting the atom! They are the fine and pious and devout people, the leading preservers of society – well, not such as you. You're simply a nice man! Excuse me, I don't mean to offend you. No, the *truly* devout, the sincere hypocrites, the constructive destroyers, the virtuous beasts of prey, the decorated criminals, all the warmongers with the Peace Prize, all the gangsters in uniform, all the sex murderers who go around preserving chastity – *those* are the ones who are splitting the atom! And they are at work everywhere, all over the world. It will be exciting to watch, eh? Whether the splitting will spread! And how it spreads! What if the things we're seeing today are the first warnings of the detonation that will shatter the planet?

'Oh no. It's best to be careful with the truth. Who can foresee the consequences?

'Do I contradict myself? Am I going in circles? Well, everyone goes in circles. The whole world goes in circles.

'*You* are going in circles, around a little disgrace from your childhood – oh, don't deny it, it's just that you don't remember, but I can tell by the expression on your face!'

Holmen was watching Ramstad, listening to him now and then, but otherwise thinking of something else.

There was something called the retroactive power of perception. Many things became simple and clear now. But he felt that his brain was working slowly, as if the wheels were turning in sand. That wasn't so strange, because every new little perception was a new humiliation.

The strangest thing was that letter. For now it came back to him. Oh well. When he entered the study that first evening, the letter was lying in the middle of the writing table, and the heavy soda opener lay askew on top of it, like a paperweight. And when he entered a while later, to fetch the soda opener, both it and the letter were gone. Good Lord, the moment he saw it he'd even thought, another letter from Ramstad – and then – gone. Gone from the table, gone from his memory. Vanished without a trace.

Without a trace? It had been lying there, well forgotten, and was added to other things he likewise hadn't remembered or wished to take notice of.

Thus arose, slowly, belief and trust, also called misgivings. Well, well.

No tears on that account. No tears altogether. The art of living consisted of taking pleasure in what there was to take pleasure in. For example, in the fact that a feeling of misgiving turned out to be correct.

Feeling? A simple matter of arithmetic.

Ramstad over there on the other side of the table was beginning to get drunk now. He was *set* on getting drunk, that much was clear. His eyelids hung like half-closed window shades over his heavy eyes, the little grumbler's smile in the corner of his mouth had grown broader. His face had acquired a deeper colour – he was flushed. He was clearly feeling great.

Holmen was playing with a purely scientific thought: whether one could alter this face. It wasn't all that bad just as it was either, but... Many women would probably say it was superb. But the cheekbones were somewhat too prominent. The bone nodules at the eyebrows likewise. And the nasal bone could've been a little higher – or lower, you could imagine it considerably lower too. You would probably have to press the whole face, remodel it, so to speak – that is, first design a mask which then could be slowly screwed down.

It was no easy task to refashion the face of a grown man. It had probably never been tried, in that way. It could scarcely be done altogether painlessly, the smile would no doubt stiffen little by little. But no blood must flow. There must be a way of carrying out this operation in an entirely aesthetic manner, without bloodshed.

What was he talking about over there? Oh yes – about women's rights from the creation of the world to now, and how it constituted a minor part of a greater topic, namely, Ramstad's relation to women.

His voice was slighly drawling – well, he'd downed half a bottle of whisky in a scant half hour – but otherwise it seemed his brain was functioning about the same as usual.

'Listen, Holmen – you're familiar with all these new theories about matriarchy and patriarchy, aren't you? You know that, in the Biblical account of creation, it says that sin came into the world, roughly speaking, six thousand years ago. Quite funny, then, isn't it, what the most recent research shows, that, roughly speaking, six thousand years ago matriarchy was succeeded by patriarchy: the mother was cast down from the throne where she'd sat as head of the family, and the father took his seat there in her place. From then on woman, that is to say love, became a commodity. And, with that, sin came into the world. From then on evil has accumulated and accumulated – greed and miserliness and hatred, cruelty that takes pleasure in oppression, and slavishness that puts up with being oppressed – well, you know that old story?

'And women have become most oppressed of all, haven't they? Women, along with all the joy of life which they represent to a special degree. Yeah. And we, who are slowly beginning to understand some of this, we, of course, ought to consider it our self-evident duty to liberate woman and thus ourselves from the curse of these thousands of years. That's clear, isn't it? It ought to be our duty to peel off layer after layer of violence and coercion and oppression, and the effects of these things on her body and soul – if necessary, we may, for some generations, have to accept the idea that the creature we are liberating will play all sorts of tricks on us and cut loose in every possible way and, among other things, turn life into a veritable hell for us, yes. But what did the fox say when he was being skinned? It's just a passing phase! That's what he said. And in a couple of hundred years, if God is merciful and all of us men act meek and noble and work away – and that we do, of course, don't we, that we do – then, no doubt, or hopefully, at least, or possibly at any rate, woman's awkward age will be past and the worst effects of the six thousand years of oppression overcome, so that woman can emerge as a new being, the way she was before the Fall, lovable and free, man's friend and playmate – and there shall be neither sin nor sorrow nor lament any more, for the former things are passed away!

'But I say unto you: Nonsense! I say. Yes, verily, verily: Nonsense! I say unto you. And I say unto you more: I grant you all that – that the trade in love came into the world through patriarchy, and calculation through trade, and duplicity and meanness through calculation, and the sin against a natural life through all this, and fear through sin, so that fear came to prevail among all people, since they all sinned. Yes, indeed! It's true. But that's only half the truth. And the other half is as follows: from time immemorial – and do you know what that means? It means from a time beyond human memory – from humanity's childhood, from the time when man and woman came into being – from as far back as that, woman has envied man his sex. Yes, precisely *that* one. Because it is an ornament, and even today every little girl thinks so from before she can say cake. Therefore she envies the little boy, feels inferior to him and would like to *be* that boy, but failing that she likes to be together with him, and these are the conflicting feelings from which woman's love is made, and will always be made, that is to say, primarily from envy and hatred and submission. *Yes*. Now I agree with myself. But even if I should disagree with myself from a purely theoretical perspective – which can happen – in practice I do not. I mean: in this instance. By which again I mean that *now*, at any rate, woman's love is primarily made up of these three above-mentioned ingredients: envy, hatred, and submission – shall I repeat them yet once more? And to whoever wants to suck the full sweetness out of the sweet sex, and avoid the stinging pain that is also called disappointment, distress and grief, to him I recommend to be aware of this fact. Which I am. Which you're not. Hence our difference.

'For you, you see, cling to the disappointments. You enjoy them. You revel in disappointments. Don't you think I can tell just from the expression on your face?

'But *I* – I say: Why sacrifice yourself to a dubious future when the only sure thing is that you thereby destroy an excellent present for yourself? We don't know what the future has in store. The life of the future must be allowed to be the future's business. My present life suffices me. You see, I've discovered that the future doesn't worry about *me*, so why should I worry about the future? And why should I think about the women of the future, as long as I can find so much pleasure in those of the present?

'So, in short: "They like it!" the man said, beating his wife.
'Ugly? Yes. Boorish? Yes. Mean? Yes. Brutal? Yes. But let me whisper a secret in your ear, a tiny little secret: they like it!

'Let her die by your hand. Isn't that what she wants?

'It's to the *master* she wants to give herself. To the *tyrant*. Not to the friend, whom she despises in secret, although she plays along with him, because he plays along with her.

'But remember: when I say this, I do not in any way put myself forward as a spokesman for crude, primitive cruelty. Oh no. Everything can be refined, cruelty as well. Let us refine it. Learn to rule. Learn to command. Let your *words*, should the occasion arise, have the effect of whiplashes.

'And one more thing: never be cruel to her without rewarding her. You must reward her generously. If you can't, you have no right to be cruel.

'Uhuh. You may say that all this is mean talk, that my philosophy is suspiciously reminiscent of that of the explosives manufacturers, who also feel a great sympathy for eternal peace – sometime in the future. Sir, I *am* an explosives manufacturer, as you know. And I won't conceal from you that I find a certain satisfaction in the fact that there is coherence in my view of life and that my philosophy is so suitable to my occupation. It eludes all control, including my own, whether my philosophy has sprung from my occupation or my occupation from my philosophy. You see, I've succeeded in turning the two things into one. Beat that one, if you can! Hah! What sort of philosophy can you pull out of your patients' throats?

'For that matter, I say to hell with all philosophy. And all views of life. And all preservers and destroyers of society. And all societies. And besides, almost everything and everybody.

'And besides, besides, besides I know – alas! – that my words are like water running off a duck's back. Beg your pardon! But anyone can see with half an eye that you're not made to rule. Skål!'

Holmen went through the hallway and into the bathroom to fetch some soda. He let the door remain open behind him.

He leaned his forehead against the windowpane and stood like that for a while.

It cooled him off.

It was dark outside. Midnight.

Was he still talking in there? No, he was taking a breather now. He probably needed the sight of a human being as a kind of driving force to keep the works running.

Why didn't he throw the man out?

No.

He had to see him. See more of him. See more, hear more.

So that's who he was. That fellow in there.

There was no alleviation of that pain, not the slightest bit.

He remembered the many conversations at home about the Ramstad family. His mother held up Ole Ramstad as a model.

Old Ramstad, as people called him, although he was by no means old, was a hard man, and very strict. The children were brought up with prayer and the rod. They had to stand behind their chairs until the parents had sat down, and to say grace by turns.

And in there sat the result.

The result? Seemingly, there was nothing wrong with the result. It appeared to be a great success.

What sort of result could *he* show?

He went back in with the soda.

Ramstad looked up.

'Oh, there you are! I missed you. Yes, for let me tell you – I appreciate you. Appreciate you more than you imagine. You haven't received the contrary impression, have you? What?

'You know – I've thought a bit about *your* case, too, since I got started anyway. Yes, because you interest me. Oh yes, very much.

'A very interesting case. Do you want me to tell you why? Well, because it's so ordinary. So banal! Good grief! You're someone who has aged a bit and is alarmed by it, because you've never been really young. That's all. It's bad, that's clear: not to have been young and to be about to grow old – yes, indeed, it's unpleasant. But most people have to pass through that state sooner or later.

'And do you know why this age thing *really* hits you like a crisis? Because you have nothing outside yourself. No *cause* that's greater than yourself. You aren't even a scientist! Well, don't get me too badly wrong. I don't exactly have in mind some great cause, with high rank and title, no, only something or other you could've associated yourself with while there was still time. But not now, it's too late now, you'd only do it out of panic and not out of an honest desire now. Such a cause is a remarkable thing. It doesn't grow old with you, it goes on living, you can invest your modest talent of independent strength of mind in it, it takes over what you possess of life when you yourself grow old and disappear. *That* is modern man's form of eternal life – or religion – call it what you like.

'But you have nothing of the kind, nothing beyond yourself. And do you know why? Because you've never been truly young. You were born old! That is, not *born*, but *brought up* to be old from when you turned seven. You've been filled with anxiety from the nursery on, just as one fills a jar with jam.

'Have you ever asked yourself: *why?*

'There must be a reason, after all?

'Let me teach you how you *really* should ask the question: *Who benefits from the fear?*

'Have you ever asked yourself that?

'Tell me: do you believe hundreds of millions of workers would allow themselves to be driven like cattle into the factories, and from the factories into unemployment, and from unemployment onto the battlefield, if fear hadn't been instilled into them from the moment they opened their eyes in this wonderful world?

'You're only one among millions. That's what makes you significant.

'But when a person realizes all this, as I do, I suppose that person will go out into the world and preach the gospel? Verily, verily – free yourselves from fear, free yourselves from oppression – or, more correctly: realize that you *cannot* do it, because the fear sits in your bones and the hollows of your knees, but see to it that a new generation grows up, a free and glad and happy generation – oh, Lord!'

Ramstad suddenly collapsed and became much smaller in his chair. He looked old and careworn all at once. He sat like this for quite a while, it looked as though he'd completely forgotten where he was. Then, abruptly, he straightened up and gave Holmen a keen look.

'Not likely! I don't do that! I don't preach any gospel! For – '

At this point he suddenly hissed, 'It serves the world right! Hah!'

Pause.

He again looked at Holmen. 'Tell me, anyway, why don't you throw me out? Let us imagine the possibility that I'm sitting here in order to see how far I can go. That can be an exciting sport, you know! Won't it soon go bang? A bit more – then it *must* go bang.

'No.

'No, because you're absolutely impossible. One can't get anywhere with you! There must be a limit to everything! You should be ashamed of yourself! Well. I can understand that, as a polite host, you think you must go to the greatest possible lengths, but...

'Oh, you're so polite! So polite it's suffocating!

'If someone came to you and said that a circle is rectangular, you'd reply something like this: you don't say? To me it appears slightly roundish!

'Hm. Why are we sitting here fighting anyway? What? We aren't fighting, you say? You didn't say anything, you say? Of course you said something. Thought something, at any rate. And the devil knows we're fighting. Of course we are! Skål! But why? Are we fighting about *her*? Or are we just fighting?

'What?

'It has occurred to me – what if it's not about *her* at all? Well, there must've been a *her* at the beginning, that I admit – to start the ball rolling, if you will. But now it is rolling, after all. And then?

'Couldn't it just as well have been chess? Or poker? Or – '

He fixed those large, slightly protruding eyes under their heavy lids on Holmen, as if he wanted to devour him.

'It's a question of who is the *stronger*, quite simply. *That* is it. It's *the two of us* now. Everything else is – what? What?'

He sat a moment. Then he said all of a sudden, 'When I was a boy we played an awful lot of finger-tug...'

He got carried away by the thought, you could see him growing eager. 'Can you play finger-tug, Holmen?'

Holmen felt a wild, absurd joy shoot through him. Could he play finger-tug! As a boy he didn't do much else. He and the other boys played finger-tug in every single break at school. And *he* was the champion. He knew that, once he'd hooked his finger around the finger of someone else, it would rather snap than straighten itself out.

'Well, I certainly know what it is,' he said. 'Sure, we can try.'

They hooked their fingers together. They dug their heels in and started pulling. Ramstad's lean face slowly turned red. There – the chairs tipped over and they were tugging on the floor, their legs intertwined and every muscle taut. Who would've thought the fellow, nothing but skin and bones, was so damn strong? Holmen quickly understood that Ramstad had proposed this because he himself had a finger that would rather snap than straighten itself out – well, it remained to be seen which finger would snap first. There the small side table tipped over, causing the newspapers to sail fan-like along the floor and the rug to bundle up under them – Holmen was the heavier one, he dragged Ramstad after him around the floor – there they overturned another chair, oh, what the hell, whee, he had a feeling that this was going very well, yeh, his finger would rather snap than... Ramstad was getting gorgeously red-faced now, his blue blood, or what? Or was it his philosophy, his view of life, which began seeping into his skin? Hey, hey, hey, now it was going well, he was a bit red in the face himself perhaps, but – oh ho, now Ramstad's finger was slowly starting to slide and his face turning blue – could it be that all his bragging had got stuck in his throat? Oh hey, hurray, there it straightened itself out.

Ramstad fell back, wringing wet and worn-out, like a rag. Holmen felt a bit warm and wet himself, that he wouldn't deny, but otherwise it had been nothing much.

A moment went by, then they both got up, calm, slightly embarrassed. They brushed themselves, straightened out the rug a bit, raised the chairs, picked up some newspapers. They didn't look at each other. A highball glass had fallen on the floor and broken. Strange, when did that happen? They didn't look at one another for quite a while. Ramstad shrugged his shoulders and muttered, 'Ridiculous!'

*

That seemed to be the end of it. No one said anything. At last Ramstad made a move. 'I'd better leave perhaps.'

Then he shot a glance at Holmen. 'By the way, do you think I don't know why you haven't thrown me out? You're dying to *hear* something, of course. You put up with everything in the hope of getting to *hear* something. So, what do you want to hear?'

All at once he hissed: 'You took the girl from me while I was away and couldn't defend myself.

'But, of course, I had arranged it all myself – was that what you thought?

'Possibly. That's beside the point. But I took her away from you while you were here and could defend yourself! That's the difference between the two of us!

'Yes, you're right. I laid her open to you on purpose. I wanted to test my values. Wanted to experience bodily how I would react. I knew she liked you. And I knew at the same time – from you I could always take her back whatever happened.

'Well. Was there anything more you wanted to know?

'You thought perhaps that she looked pretty bad this evening? Maybe you believe it was because she had been crying? Come, come. You who are a doctor and a man of experience and all must know that a hot girl can get dark circles under her eyes from other things as well, eh? Quite dark circles under her eyes, eh?

'*Quite* – you understand?'

It happened quickly. Ramstad had barely managed to get up when Holmen struck – he struck with both hands, struck at that large heavy eye and felt he hit home, struck at the stiff smile and felt he hit home.

Then everything went blank.

'Come on! Come around again!'

It was Ramstad.

Ramstad stood bent over him. He was lying – yes, he was lying on the floor. His face was wet – blood? He felt with his hand – no, it was water.

The door to the hallway flung open, he glimpsed a terrified landlady in a nightgown. Ramstad swept her out. 'Away! Out with you! We're just playing a little game! Away, you hear!'

The landlady was gone.

Some wisps of fog were floating around. The room was turning. He had a whopper of a headache. As for Ramstad – he looked a bit dim and his speech was extremely blurred – oh, his mouth was bleeding, and one eye was swelling – so blood had been shed anyhow.

Actually, he could probably manage to stand up. But he might just as well stay down. He was totally indifferent.

'There's no need to be afraid!' Ramstad said. 'I only struck the point of your chin. You're as whole and pretty as ever. I didn't want to spoil your chances by maiming you.'

He put on his hat, then turned to look at Holmen. 'It serves you right, because you were such a damn stuck-up fellow back home, in the village. Don't you think I remember you? Student and man of the world, you walked about puffing yourself up, not even looking in the direction of a shy twelve-year-old boy who admired and hated you. I'm telling you this, by the way, to offer you a kind of comfort, and if I've been unreasonable, I stand by it. Bye!'

He was gone.

Holmen remained lying on the floor another few moments.
There was no reason to hurry any more.

A Little Trip

He didn't quite know whether he slept or was awake as the night wore on. He seemed to be mostly awake. He was thinking about these last few hours, and the last few days before that, and the couple of weeks before that again. Was he thinking? No, he seemed more than anything else to be *seeing*, and there was one sight he was seeing all the time – a veil was rent and he saw something behind it, but the next moment he didn't see anything there, because a veil was rent and he saw something behind it, but once again a veil was rent, and again and again; there wasn't enough time to see anything properly, because what he looked at was always rent. Most likely, though, he wasn't properly awake, he seemed more than anything else to be dreaming.

'Oh no!' he heard himself whispering at one point. He was biting the sheet.

'Oh no!'

No, no!

Oh, oh! No, no!

At the same time he had the distinct feeling that all this was merely something he was repeating. It had all of it happened before at some time, a long time ago, he just wasn't able to recall anything, and it was that which was so tiring.

It was also unpleasant that all things became so large. It was no doubt due to the dark of night. The quite ordinary room grew to a vast space, and all the articles inside, which he could just barely make out, became huge, immovable, threatening and indifferent. But this vast room was just a small part of something much greater still that was perfectly calm and inexorable. It was unpleasant that everything was so large, it made him so small –

179

and because he was so small, everything became so large.

Daylight came at last, but it changed nothing,

He lay thinking about Ramstad.

He yearned for Ramstad. It had been so nice to have him here. He'd been talking a great deal and hadn't by any means been disagreeable all the time; he had more than once spoken about other things as well, and been quite friendly. And things weren't so large then, and he wasn't so alone.

He rose early and got dressed. As he was doing so, he mumbled something, but couldn't catch what he was saying.

He went out. It must've been very early in the morning, how early he didn't know, he'd forgotten to take his watch along.

He walked down to the underground. It had started running, at any rate. He got off at some station and set out through the woods. He had walked there before and knew where he was all the time.

A path diverged from the road and he followed it. He'd walked here before, all right.

He walked for what seemed a long time. He passed some marshes and crossed some stony ridges with sparse vegetation. Afterwards he found himself in a dense thicket. He walked a bit back and forth there, he was searching for something. He worked himself through denser and denser thickets. At long last he found it.

Then it was as though he woke up. He hadn't really slept, but still. What was he doing under this shelter? And the pocket-knife he was holding in his hand? Oh yes, he must have wanted to carve some names into a tree trunk, wasn't that it? But he didn't want to sit here.

He stood up and started walking; feeling he was a little scared, he began to run, which made him more scared, he noticed, so he contented himself with walking quite rapidly. He felt much better when he found the path again. It led down to the road, and the road led to the station. He couldn't lose his way now.

Had he been repeating himself from his childhood days again?

He'd heard that story often enough. That evening when he'd run through the empty house – when his father came back home, he was nowhere to be found. They searched everywhere, and at last they found him inside a dense thicket down in the pasture; it was late in the evening and dark when they found him. He had dug himself in among a knot of low spruces, as if he wanted to hide from the whole world forever.

Pure nonsense.

Woods on both sides. Just press on now, looking neither right nor left.

When he came home, Vera was waiting for him. He was too tired to be surprised.

'Well,' was all he said.

They didn't talk for a while.

He noticed that Vera was crying. 'Well, how are you doing?' he said.

She didn't answer.

'I got so scared,' she said in a low voice.

'You were scared? Why?'

She didn't answer.

A moment later she said, 'I spoke to Arne – to Ramstad this morning. Or rather, he called me. And I understood he'd dropped by your place yesterday. And so I got scared.'

'That was nothing to be scared about,' he said. 'Ramstad was downright friendly.'

She didn't look at him. 'He has talked a bit about you,' she said falteringly. 'During – during these days. He related something – from long ago – and today I got so scared. Where have you been?'

'Oh, I just took a little walk,' he said.

Pause.

She sat with her face turned away the whole time.

'That's why I had to come. By the way – ' She sat a moment without speaking.

'By the way – I guess it's only right to tell you what I said to him yesterday.'

Pause.

'That I'll have to keep to myself for a while. I can't any more...'

She was silent for a moment again.

'Oh, Knut – I'm not the least bit happy!'

He didn't say anything. He just took a deep breath, as if he hadn't been able to breathe for a long time.

That unbearable hollow feeling in his chest, which he finally understood must be stopped at any price, was gone. He was filled with a peace that was more than peace.

She was unhappy for his sake.

Did You Call Me?

A few days went by. He sat and waited. For whom? For what? Oh, nothing.

Eventually he knew: no one would come. When he heard footsteps on the stairs and his heart began pounding away, he knew all the time: it was not for him. Little by little this certainty reached such depths that he could even work a little when no one was on the stairs and the house was otherwise perfectly quiet.

One day – it was a Thursday, right after lunch, and he had come back from the little restaurant over in the side street and had just sat down at his work table – there came suddenly a knock on his door, without his having heard any footsteps on the staircase. He got up from his chair, but his knees were so weak that he had to sit down again for a second.

Then he quietly went to open the door.

Agnete stood in the doorway.

Of course. Who else?

Well.

He fell back a step, then felt annoyed and stepped forward again.

But Agnete didn't stand there at all like a pillar of salt, and by no means did she begin screeching. She was calm and friendliness incarnate. She came into the living room, looked about her with a faint smile and merely said, 'So, this is where you're hanging out.'

After a while she said, 'Aren't you going to ask me to sit down?'

'Certainly. Please sit down!' he said.

She sat down.

Why hadn't he talked to her before! He could just as well have done so. Then at least he wouldn't have had to stand there like a schoolboy caught cheating.

He stammered out a few sentences – he'd meant to talk to her about this for a long time – well, not exactly for a long time, because it really hadn't been a long time, but...

He felt irritable, ready to flare up at the first opportunity.

But she didn't give him any. She was just as calm and friendly all along; slightly ironic, to be sure, but that was her way.

Goodness, there was no reason why he should have any scruples on that account. Here she was, after all, and had even found her way to him entirely on her own.

'I have of course understood for a while that something was going on. I knew full well that when a man, I mean a really clever man, someone like you – when he wants to hide something from his wife, he does it with such care that she would have to be blind not to see that something was wrong. Do you know what you all remind me of? Do you remember those American gangster films ten or fifteen years ago? When the detectives stole around the corners so cautiously that you simply couldn't avoid noticing them? Yes, that's the way you men are. Oh, you're so sweet!'

She was looking about the room. She seemed to be enjoying herself, taking out her mirror and compact to powder her nose. Afterwards she looked about her once more. Her eyes came to rest on his work table. 'Ah. You're working too, I see?'

'Yes,' he said sheepishly, slowly getting heated.

She didn't look at him as she continued talking.

She had really dropped by to ask if he would drive her down to Hankø today and help her pack up after the summer. They weren't likely to go there for more weekends this year. And, after all, his car was standing in the street, so... And he had nothing against seeing the place again, did he? It was a long time since he'd been there.

All of a sudden it occurred to him that, actually, it was a good suggestion.

Just as soon that as anything else. It was a brilliant suggestion.

And what lay behind it – the whole reckoning which was bound to come, and which he had felt queasy and anxious about? Good that it came. Now that it was in fact completely indifferent whether it came or not. It was great that it came.

'Yes, let's drive down to Hankø,' he said. It was a brilliant idea.

He found himself driving quite fast. A little too fast maybe, but it was good to have something to concentrate your thoughts on.

The landscape left only the sort of scant impression you get when you drive fast – he saw the road rushing and rushing by under the car, faster and faster the closer it got, it was like driving towards a horizontal waterfall. The telephone poles were racing backwards, he tried to count them now and then, but always had to give up, there were so many other things to look out for. You couldn't manage to do everything. Here and there some people stood in front of a house; they belonged there, how strange! What did they find to do all their life long? Well, *long*? Oh yes, now and then it was long enough... He had himself belonged to such a place at one ime. That was long ago. It was the only thing that was long ago – no, everything was long ago.

Once in a while he thought, what an advantage that Agnete was so full of conventional considerations, of firm ideas about how one ought and ought not, and absolutely ought not, to behave. Oh yes, now and then it was an advantage to be married to a textbook on good manners. It came with a guarantee. A good bourgeois upbringing came with certain guarantees. There would be a reckoning according to the best drawing-room drama recipe, elegant, quiet, perhaps witty. Malicious? Yes. Sentimental? Hardly. Embarrassing? Out of the question. Thank God, Agnete did have certain qualities. He could picture her during the imminent conversation.

185

But one thing bothered him a bit – he couldn't see the denouement. And he couldn't see himself.

Calm. Just calm.

The road widened and became a street, the houses were squeezed together, there was a smell of cellulose. They were passing Moss. Afterwards the road, the rail fences and the telephone poles were there once more. He increased his speed.

She was talking beside him. Talking in a quiet and friendly way about this and that, exactly as usual, as in earlier days. It took a little while before she got started, that was all; but then she found her brief ironic opening sentence: 'Perhaps you are interested in hearing a little about how we've been doing while you were – in all those hospitals?'

Then she talked about the house, the maids, about the children, who had been so good, although Per was perhaps at a rather difficult age right now, about the others down there at Hankø. It was the usual thing. So and so had been out sailing with such and such and said she'd stayed the night, but no one had seen her there.

The moral of most stories was: it was comical to be in love, it was comical not to cheat on one another, it was comical to be cheated on, but most comical of all was to be caught in the act of cheating.

Drawing-room comedy.

Strange. At the same time these people were full of solemn feelings – they were preservers of society, defenders of morality and Christians on Sundays – or at least during the high festivals, if they happened to remember. Otherwise they were spiritists, Sufis, Krishnamurties, and yoga cultists, and believed in slimming pills and fortune-tellers. All in all, you can talk the worst filth in male company, come out with the most smutty insinuations in female company, but do not offend against the nobler feelings, and believe mightily in all kinds of purity! How did these assorted contradictory feelings manage to pass through the brains of those people? Well, the feelings probably made the stopover in such a boring place as brief as possible.

Agnete related the stories with small stylistic niceties and enjoyed them herself.

Meanwhile the telephone poles receded backwards – along with the rail fences, guard stones, the houses along the way, children on the front steps with their fingers in their mouths. The cut meadows lay meagre and greenish yellow on both sides of the road; in the fields the grain stubble remained, greyish white in the greyish-black soil, as lifeless as the beard stubble on the chin of an old man. The trees along the road were powdery-grey in front but curiously green and fresh at the back, a result effected, most likely, by the dew during the clear nights in this spell of dry weather. He reflected a bit on what he recalled from his physics classes about dew on clear nights, but gave it up.

He looked sideways to where she sat. He couldn't help admiring her clever, composed, cool disposition. She knew what was imminent just as well as he, well, better; for she had a plan she intended to carry out, she always did – and it was no doubt a quite hard, merciless plan, no sentimentality there, oh, he knew her – and there she sat beside him, friendly, pleasant, charming, and seemingly unconcerned as she chattered on about this and that. But he knew that neither what she said nor the way she said it would restrain her one jot once the battle was joined; under the smiling surface she was hard as nails, so hard that precisely because of that she could afford to be pleasant now, not being answerable for it afterwards, as a man would be. He couldn't help admiring her, admiring the woman in her, with an admiration resembling terror.

He increased his speed again during the last bit of road, down through the monotonous Østfold landscape. Here, on these desolate flats, in these stubborn hills, people lived all the year round. Well, perhaps they were happy.

His speed was getting rather high, maybe. They drove past

a farm. A hen escaped across the road, but at the last moment, when it already found itself safe in the ditch, it had an alluring idea. No! It should've been somewhere else!

It was incredible what a large amount of feathers there were on such a hen, it looked sufficient for an entire duvet.

The farmer stood in the yard.

It came to five kroner. Well, now the kids would eat chicken for once, instead of that everlasting pork.

He felt like a benefactor.

Agnete was fairly shocked. She couldn't stand witnessing accidents.

Afterwards the accident gave her new associations and she related more stories from Hankø. 'You don't say?' he answered. 'Really? Is that so?'

They arrived at the storekeeper's down by the ferry landing, parked the car and walked down to the dock. The small ferry was ready to leave, they didn't have to wait. The young boy said hello, calmly and politely. Yes, there were still some people out here, some, not many. Fourteen degrees in the water.

They walked side by side toward the interior. He carried the basket and the raincoats. It was grey and chilly, with a north wind, but no sign of rain. Though you could never know.

They passed the old hotel building, looking deserted now, like a stage set from the 1890s left behind by a roadshow. They came to the grass-grown road, with its old overgrown wheel tracks, which led through the pine forest and the moor to the house.

Autumn had arrived. The heather was past blooming, the blueberry bushes had turned blue. Here and there some fiery-red strawberry leaves stood out. They probably had the same dye stuff in them as the berries. The nature of each separate thing emerged in a new way in the autumn. The ground was dry, a smoke-like dust was stirred up by your feet, your shoe soles glided on tinder-dry grass, it rustled like dry snow against the skis. Winter, ah, winter...

*

Neither of them was talking any longer, she seemed to have given up on him. The road was long, the basket heavy, he had to change hands every once in a while.

At long last they were at the house. She got out the keys, unlocked the door and entered ahead of him. He went to get wood and lighted the fire – it began to burn with a flickering flame.

Then, supposedly, they only had to begin.

But she wasn't ready. She was putting things in order. Was tidying up, although it was tidy and nice enough already – by Jove, there she began to set the table!

'Are you going to eat?'

'No. But I'm setting the table, then it's done.'

He went to the cabinet, took out the bottle of whisky and poured himself a sizable drink. He took it straight. He felt rather cold. Come to think, if anything he felt rather warm.

Wouldn't it come soon?

No. She thought up one thing after another to put in order. She gathered some old flowers and threw them away, then went out for a moment and came in with another bunch. Women and flowers – by the way, they were pretty.

Then she began to wind the clock, that old cuckoo clock from the eighteen hundreds or so – oh well. Lighting a cigar, he noticed that his hand trembled. If one didn't know better, one might almost think he was scared.

'What time is it, Knut?'

It was a few minutes past seven.

He recognized this feeling from numerous times before, but didn't know its origin; it appeared to him that it had accompanied him as far back as he could remember, oh, longer, that it had always been a part of him, like the bark of

189

the tree from the very moment it sprang up from the ground – something inevitable was about to happen and he was nervous, nervous to the point of feeling sick, as though something unfathomably cruel, sombre and threatening was imminent, while he felt helplessly small and defenceless and therefore nervous to the point of feeling sick, but precisely for that reason wanted to plunge into it, quickly, hard, at any price. He recalled a story of someone on the rack looking at the irons being made red-hot while the torturers engaged in a leisurely conversation; suddenly he became insanely impatient and screamed, as if the red-hot iron were already stuck in him: Come on then, Christ Almighty, why don't you begin!

Nonsense! Now he was getting rather too noble, baring that everlasting soul of his. Look how nervous I am! Am I not noble and deep and remarkable, and don't I feel nervous? First, he was not nervous, second he had nothing to be nervous about, and third he was absolutely not nervous.

After all, he simply had to say to her: Listen. I've fallen in love, violently and miserably and hopelessly; hopelessly, do you hear! It's the only thing I can say. Yes, and that you'll have to give me some time. I know nothing about myself.

It was just that it wouldn't do to say such things. To your own wife? Impossible.

She would never be finished.

Was she also nervous? Was that why? All of a sudden sentimental feelings surged up in him, he felt warm and tender.

Ho, he was scared, he wanted peace. He worked on himself a bit and drove back his feeling of weakness.

Now she seemed to have finished tidying up. She came and sat down by the fireplace.

'Do you have a cigarette?'

'Here. Would you like a drink?'

'No, thanks.'

She smoked the cigarette, looking at the fire for a moment.

Outside, the wind was getting up. Was the rain coming at last? No, not a drop against the windowpanes. It was a north wind in any case, and that didn't bring rain.

'How could you be so stupid!' she said.

'What do you mean?'

She didn't look at him. 'Just imagine going to the seaside under a false name – and leaving the car at the storekeeper's, where everybody could see it.'

So that's where it came from. Well. He should have thought of that. He should have kept in mind the sexual curiosity, envy, malicious pleasure, and gossip that unite all women within a certain milieu like an underground network.

'Oh well,' he said. 'Firstly, I did not go under a false name (oh yes, you certainly did) and secondly – '

He gave up.

'And secondly?'

'Oh, nothing.'

It was no use trying to explain.

If he only could say, quite simply: Let's make peace. I admit you might have been entitled to greater sincerity, but we haven't sold ourselves to one another, you don't own me –

'You awakened some interest out there,' she said. 'Greater interest than you yourselves knew about, I think. You acted rather – free and easy, didn't you? Dr Holmen has started a private nudist colony. Can be viewed every day between ten and two. Good lookout points among the bushes. Not too bad an ad, eh?'

She was speaking in a light, friendly tone, not looking at him.

Now time was getting short, if peace was to be concluded.

'Who do you have this from?' he said.

'I don't mind telling you. From Mrs Gunnerus. And she had it from – but that doesn't really matter. It's all over town. People have certainly got something to talk about.'

Pause.

'You have nothing to say?'

He thought she looked almost imploringly at him.

'No.'

'Ugh! If at least you hadn't had such poor taste!' she said, getting up.

'If it had at least been one of *ours* – I mean, a *lady*, a cultivated woman. But such a – such a – '

She sat down again, resigned.

Now time was getting short, all right.

Mrs Gunnerus, really – Mrs Gunnerus of all people – oh sure, it might suit her quite well to tell this to Agnete.

'Mrs Gunnerus, really,' he said slowly. 'Mrs Gunnerus might do better to look after her own business. And by that I mean above all her husband, our friend Jens Gunnerus.

'Yes. Apropos Gunnerus, your friend Gunnerus, well, I ran into him in town recently – on my birthday, at the Continental – and he was together with a very pretty young lady, and Mrs Gunnerus was walking the street down below like a roaring lion – you know the Bible verse, don't you? "There is a lion in the way; a lion is in the streets..." And Gunnerus left the dining room unsuspecting, while I remained behind and was, frankly speaking, in some suspense, for if the three of them met outside, it would've become quite exciting; but they didn't meet, for Gunnerus didn't come out at all, he was swallowed up by the great nothingness, I mean, his great love.'

When he looked at her, he saw she had turned pale. Uncannily pale.

He felt the blood being drawn to his heart and knew he was turning pale himself, uncannily pale – he had perhaps – had perhaps got too close to hitting home this time.

Had he known before?

Known what? He had known nothing.

Had he known before?

Nonsense. You couldn't be certain there was anything to know.

Had he known before?

Known and known...

'Well, well,' she said, attempting a smile. 'Well, well – so you spy on people, do you? Try to, anyway – for sure, there are all sorts of ways of getting one's kicks.'

Pause.

They sat looking at one another for a moment.

'You know, I think I'll have a drink all the same!' she said of a sudden. She quickly got up and went over to the cabinet, found a glass, took the whisky bottle and poured herself a drink; but – it was a beer glass, and she poured it more than half full.

'What, are you crazy!' he said. But she had already swallowed it. She coughed, got tears in her eyes and couldn't speak for a while. She shuddered. 'Whew, how unpleasant! But I felt cold.'

If anything, it was rather warm in here.

*

She sat down again; she apparently needed a brief rest after that mouthful. She was looking at him. Her eyes were different – calmer, it seemed. She looked thoughtfully at him.

'So this is you,' she said. She looked at him again.

'Well, well, so this is you.'

He knew there was no rush any more. For now it was too late. Whew, it was rather cold here all the same.

She came from an unexpected corner. 'Will you have a bit of supper now, or do you want to wait?' She was friendly. A tad too silkily soft and friendly.

'Nothing for me, thanks.'

'No? Food calms one down, you know – and you seem so nervous. Here's the ashtray.'

He realized he'd been smoking his cigar without letup. The ash lay on the floor.

'Thanks, I'll skip it anyway. I'm not hungry.'

She jiggled her leg for a moment. Then she asked, concerned, 'You aren't sick, are you?'

'Sick? Why?'

'Oh, I just thought – '

'What?'

'Well – as anyone knows, such girls can make you nervous

– and sick too.'

She said it quite lightly. It was almost not uttered, that's how light it was. A sentence as light as a feather.

Calm now. Calm...

She laughed. 'Well, I must say – I certainly hadn't expected this. That a marriage can get slightly monotonous in the long run can't be helped, of course, but that you should fall for a streetwalker, who has even been a patient at Ullevål Hospital, that is... Yes, she has even been a patient at Ullevål. Perhaps you don't know? Four years ago.'

He was calm, completely calm, took a puff at the cigar, slowly blew the smoke out, and sat watching the ash a moment before he said, 'Yes, I know. But you must have been misinformed. She was admitted to Ullevål for an ear inflammation. I treated her myself.'

She didn't seem to hear what he was saying. After considering briefly, she said, as if absorbed in her own thoughts, 'But after all, many men prefer streetwalkers, people say, despite the risk. So there's nothing to be done about that, I suppose.'

'By *streetwalker* you mean a girl who supports herself by her sex, don't you?' he said. 'Living on immoral earnings I believe it's called in the law. But allow me to inform you – she doesn't do that. She *works* for a living. And in that she differs from many you know. She never married to earn her living that way.'

He hadn't meant to say this. He hadn't meant to say anything, for that matter. He had meant to let *her* say what she wanted – let her vent her rage as well, if that was what she needed. And then give her the necessary explanation – to which in all fairness she was entitled, by the way.

He hadn't meant to, but already as she talked he knew: she was about to succeed in driving him into that strange world in which the spiteful showdowns between spouses take place.

He already had the strange feeling that he was himself and yet not himself, that he was *floating* – stop, stop, she wasn't going to succeed. Calm, just calm.

She looked thoughtfully at him. 'If only I could understand

why I accepted you. But it was Mama. She had a soft spot for you. I believe it was because Papa couldn't stand you. And I had a soft spot for Mama.

'She believed that something great would come of you. Something great! Mama said. Imagine, that's what she said.

'She believed that something great would come – of you. And the man I loved was nothing at that time. Ruined by those years after the war and all that...

'And so I let myself be persuaded. And you got me.'

She made a brief pause. Then she continued angelically, 'Aren't you glad about that?'

He sat quite still.

That hit a sore spot. A little too neatly. He felt that all the secret, carefully stored resentment that collects and collects in a harmonious marriage of many years was beginning to stir. Hot springs of indignation were bursting within him, flowing together from many directions; they rose and rose, exerting pressure on the embankments.

'Oh yes, I'm glad about that!' he said. 'Oh yes, I do remember that.'

'Did you think I had forgotten that time! How you calculated and calculated, adding up the pros and cons?

'You chose me in the end. I presume I offered the highest bid. Do you think I have forgotten?

'And when you had chosen me, I was liquidated. How could I avoid seeing *him* in your eyes all day long? The eyes of a man I didn't even know, clever as you were. Do you think I've forgotten that?

'And when we visited my childhood home to say hello to my relatives – people who lead a quiet life and have the kind of good breeding that you and your likes lack all prerequisites for understanding – then you were so friendly and patronizing and nice to those poor farmers that it could pierce a stone to the quick. Do you think I've forgotten that?

'You've been spared from associating with them since. They weren't good enough for you.'

195

He said to himself: 'You've said enough now, more than enough.'

But she didn't seem to have heard what he said this time either – and it was just as well. She laughed, a rippling, melodious laughter.

'Seriously speaking, the only thing I find disgusting in this business – really disgusting – is the fact that I've let myself be treated by her – yes, I! Maybe even at the time when the whole town knew she was letting herself – be *treated* – by you. But now that part of her activities, at least, will come to an end. A complaint has been made against her – ah, perhaps you don't know? From several clients who refuse to put up with – that sort of thing. When you go to a so-called first-class parlour, you like to have a certain guarantee. Among other things, you would rather not risk being directly *infected* during such a treatment – and that is why steps have been taken, by *several* ladies – so now, I suppose, you can have her to yourself both day and night – well, that part of the time which falls to you, I mean. How does it feel, by the way, once you're in love with such a girl, such a streetwalker, that is, such a whore, beg pardon – and I do mean *in love*, which you must be, you are, aren't you? – how does it feel to sit alone waiting and waiting, knowing that now she is with one of the others? It must be rather strange, eh? Well, I don't know, having no experience, I'm so little emancipated that way, but I just think it must be quite strange. Maybe that's the feeling you value so highly? If only you had let me understand that! Or is she so delicious when you have her? Is she so delicious in bed that whore of yours? Delicious, but demanding, perhaps, eh? So in reality you're glad that she has several others? You know you've never been very demanding that way – a modest man, satisfied with little, isn't that how it goes? Ha-ha!'

It was odd to hear her utter all these unaccustomed words. He sat watching her. It was odd – he thought he could *see* those filthy words pop out of that beautiful, well-cared-for mouth of hers – see them leap into the air, flutter around, and settle like motley butterflies on the edge of the table and the mirror – he followed them with his eyes and found distraction in it.

'Oh, Knut! The whole town is laughing at you!'

She laughed, ripplingly and melodiously.

Stop, stop. Calm, now. Just calm. She wasn't going to succeed. He ought to analyze this conversation – find out how it had taken this unfortunate turn. Well, her right of ownership had been violated, that was true, and so she said... But she wasn't like that to begin with, so there must be something or other he'd said that – wait now, he'd said, she'd said, he'd said, she'd said – only analyze, only analyze, then this sickening feeling of *floating* would be sure to disappear – what was this business with Mrs Gunnerus, because that's where it began – Gunnerus? Began? – To float, yes – float – only analyze.

All of a sudden she had stopped laughing. She had become serious. What? It looked as though she was on the verge of tears.

On the verge of tears? No way. No sentimentality. Calm now. Analyze – so, Gunnerus – Gunnerus.

'They're laughing at me, are they?' he said. 'Yes, I'm ready to believe that. And how about *yourself*, my friend, yourself? And not on account of me, remember that.'

Was she on the verge of tears? Far from it. She raised her head like a charger.

'Let's end this conversation!' she said. 'It's leading nowhere. But there is – all the same – one thing I would like to know. Tell me – had you started your new life when you were down here the weekend of July 27? But no, it doesn't matter, not at all. It doesn't concern me. It doesn't even interest me.

'Oh yes. One thing I'd like to tell you. I understand why you absolutely had to be alone in town on your birthday. I hope you had a good time.

'But I almost think the two of you had *too* good a time. I mean when you set about writing a letter – to *me* – about that wonderful cigar you were smoking – which lay untouched in the box I had sent you. You enjoyed yourselves heartily then, huh? Over that cigar. She laughed then, huh? You had a delicious laugh at me together then, huh?'

Suddenly he knew: here he could stop her. Correct *that* misunderstanding at any rate, so she got rid of the insult that made her more wild than anything else.

'I didn't know her then!' he said. 'That's to say...' He had meant to continue: That's to say, I had of course had her as a patient once – but he gave up. She could continue.

She laughed demonstratively. 'That's to say – ha-ha-ha! That's to say! That's to say, you happened to know her nonetheless. You had treated her, after all! Ha-ha. But forget about that too – and the fact that you go on a trip with her and disgrace yourself and me before the whole world – your cigars and letters and your various public scandals are a matter of indifference to me.

'But that you throw out our maid and take this tart of yours into *our* home and play slap and tickle with her in *our* beds, that must – that must – shall I be forced to put up with *that*! Oh, that tart! In *my* bed!'

Her voice had been strident for a while. But at the last sentences it rose and rose, until it broke and passed into screaming sobs.

Calm, he thought, quite automatically, as if it were a magic word. Calm, now.

Calm. Calm. Calm now.

It felt like a curtain being ripped away.

Twenty years ago – and today. Twenty years ago. One day like twenty years and twenty years like one day.

She stood in the doorway, screaming, 'That tart – in *my* bed!'

Then she went up and pulled the bedspread aside, beat the sheet with her clenched fist and screamed.

She was foaming at the mouth. Was Agnete foaming at the mouth? Not yet. Not yet.

Why didn't she go up, pull the bedspread aside and beat the sheet? It was part of the act. Oh, come to think, there was no bed in there, that had been forgotten, a necessary stage prop was missing, a bed had to be provided – hey, a bed! My kingdom for a bed!

It hurt. It hurt like hell. And there, over by the mirror, stood Helga, stiff as a statue, deathly pale, without saying a word – and he, stiff, without saying a word, wanted only one thing, one single thing – to kill that landlady. Silence her. Strangle her. Clasp his hands around her throat. Not quickly. Quite slowly. And then squeeze, making the scream sink to a croak, her face turn blue and her eyes, bloodshot, force their way out of their sockets.

No, no. You must pull yourself together now. Pull yourself together. You are *here*. This is only Agnete, your own wife, your own lawful Agnete, married to you for six years.

He closed his eyes and opened them again. It didn't help. He couldn't get rid of the nauseating feeling that this wasn't real, that it was taking place on a stage, or that two things were happening at once, on top of one another, one within the other, like a double exposure. And he himself was in both places at once, and hence not altogether in either place, hovering somewhere in between and watching himself, how he took it – it was sickening and made him feel nauseous: to have experienced everything before and not experience anything properly now! He stuck a couple of fingers under his collar to get some air, but pulled his hand back double-quick. To be sure, that's how it was done on the stage, it was a theatrical trick, supposed to signify that you were having a hard time of it, that you were on the verge of being suffocated.

What was she saying as she stood over there, far away? Of no interest in and of itself, because all he had to do was to stop and think, he had doubtless heard it before, twenty years ago.

Ah, now he could hear it: 'But – fortunately – there have been others in *your* bed too. You understand? And in *mine* – with me! Ha-ha!'

She looked at him with shining eyes and her head thrown back. Her teeth gleamed wet and white, her knees opened and closed again.

She was drunk.

He took a fresh cigar from the box and lighted it carefully with the old one. He tossed the cigar butt into the fireplace.

'Is that so?' he said calmly. He thought she said something the same moment and asked, 'Who, did you say?'

She gave a loud laugh. 'Who? Huh, you would like to know, wouldn't you? But never mind, for the time being. Doesn't it suffice for you to know that you're a cuckold?'

Why the hell did he ask! He had the distinct impression, however – well, he'd noticed, or thought he'd noticed – that his hearing had been a little poorer lately. Had to get it examined, he'd rather not grow old and deaf.

He heard a scraping, grating sound behind him, coming from up on the wall – the door of the old cuckoo clock opened, the cuckoo jumped out and crowed, 'Cuckoo! Cuckoo! Cuckoo!'

Eight times. It sounded so merry. Then it slipped in again. He thought, really, that seems too arranged. Crude effects. She had got up. She looked at him as if she expected something. Stood staring expectantly at him.

She appeared to be in high spirits. She was fired up. Her eyes sparkled.

Actually, she was quite handsome. Blond and well-groomed. Her face a bit too regular perhaps. Rather dull? But many would find her handsome. He himself thought she was handsome. But a stranger – he who ought to know her reasonably well felt she was a stranger. He'd never seen her like this before, in such a mood.

'My cuckold!' She laughed.

Her eyes were shining. She wiggled her hips. Her bearing was somewhat overwrought. It was as though – yes, as though she were standing on a stage and feeling all eyes upon her. Every movement had a wild grace which he'd never seen in her before.

He thought: her I've been married to for six years.

Her I've lived with for six years.

Her I've slept with for six years.

Her I've thought I knew for six years.

He felt a bit jittery.

That tart who stood there wiggling her hips and screaming obscenities ... his wife for six years.

He must be drunk.

He closed his eyes, shook his head, opened his eyes again – she was standing there.

He was scared.

He said – his mouth said, 'I don't care who you've slept with.'

Didn't he care?

Indeed, it felt as though he didn't care.

She came closer. Of a sudden she was calm and friendly. She bent forward. 'So, you don't care? You don't care that I've cheated on you all these years? You don't care? Not at all?'

He repeated, like an echo: 'Not at all.'

'Then you also don't care at all' – she did a wiggle, moved a couple of steps, turned around amd took a few breaths before going on – 'who is the father of your children? Don't care at all – that *you*, at any rate, are not the father of either of them?'

He didn't say anything.

It was as though she herself felt she was far away now. She cried, 'Do you hear me? Why don't you say something? Do you hear me?'

He said, 'You should lower your voice. Somebody lives half an hour from here.'

He knew he smiled inwardly when he said that. She was so afraid of any kind of scandal.

She didn't hear him. She screamed, 'Do you hear! You aren't the father of any of my children! Someone else is their father! Someone else! A real man! A real man is the father of my children!'

Oh, a man. A real man. A – a scoundrel – a – a pitiful man –

What? Was she crying? Was she breaking down?

No. His eyes had misled him. Besides, he wasn't even looking at her.

He was simply smoking his cigar. He was on a picnic and

sat smoking a cigar. Smoking it very slowly. Now he put it down. Very slowly. Stood up. Turned towards her. No, she wasn't crying. Turned slowly towards her. She stood still looking at him.

They were in a film. A slow-motion film. Everything took an endlessly long time. He got up, it took an eternity. But the only thing in all this time that puzzled him was that he was really able to stand up – usually you couldn't do that in dreams. She was looking at him. She was breathing. He could see she was breathing – hard but slow. She took a step back. That, too, very slow. Slow film. Poorly directed. Ho-ho. Ho-ho. Very touching. Eight o'clock. It was beginning to grow dark outside. And the wind was rising. The same north wind apparently. So there wouldn't be any rain. Or – by Jove, there a few raindrops smacked against the windowpane. Well, a bit of rain now would be good for the farmers.

He walked slowly towards her. She stared at him and made a slow retreat.

He felt how calm he was. He walked – no, he didn't walk, he floated. He floated slowly through the air toward her. He felt he was setting an old wrong to rights when he raised his hands and put them slowly around her throat.

She barely fought back. She seemingly accepted what was coming, as if it were her fate. She pushed at his hands with hers, but without a will, lamely. Yes, that was it – her face took on a tinge of blue, her mouth opened, her eyes became large and staring, she groaned but said nothing.

He released his grip and said, 'I know you've lied many times this evening. But now I think you should tell the truth.'

She gasped a couple of times, pulled at his hands with hers, looking at him all along, panting and looking at him – then there was a flash of laughter in her eyes: 'Ha-ha-ha!'

Three short bursts of laughter. Then she coughed. He squeezed hard once more, feeling her powerless hands against his, and wrestled her to the floor; she twisted and turned under him, her eyes fixed in a wolfish stare. He released his grip.

'Time is running out. Tell me the truth!'

She coughed and cleared her throat. Then the look in her eyes became expressive once again – it triumphed,

She laughed, 'Ha-ha-ha!'

Her laughter, gross, hoarse and alien, grated on his ears.

'Tell me the truth!'

'What is it you want to know then, sweetheart?'

She was hoarse, she coughed, her voice broken, but she triumphed. Her eyes gleamed maliciously, her nostrils opened wide, her mouth laughed straight through coughing fits and grimaces. He shook her – caught her by the shoulders and shook her the way a child shakes a naughty doll. He knew this was a sign of powerlessness, and he knew that she knew. But damnit, it must be possible to shake her back to her senses, shake her straight again... Once, he recalled afterwards, he hit her on the cheek with the flat of his hand. Not hard, he thought, more like an attempt to bring her back to reason and common sense.

She laughed, screamed, bit him when he placed his hand over her mouth, coughed, groaned and used coarse words, which he'd never suspected she knew. A stream of words, occasionally completely meaningless. Now and then just triumphant screams. Now and then completely contradictory utterances, without coherence from one moment to the next.

'Tell me the truth!'

He groaned, he shook her. And she groaned, laughed, screamed, cried, laughed again. She was possessed by the devil.

'With all your friends! All your friends!' She laughed, frivolously, spitefully, teasingly. The next moment her voice melted – yes, indeed, though she was as hoarse as a raven, her voice melted as she said seductively, 'My love! Why don't you believe me?'

It was so well imitated that he knew he could've taken it for genuine. In the midst of his exasperation he grew frightened. But she was already someone else – full of scorn and hatred and gall. She hissed like a cat, 'Let me go! Blockhead! Numbskull!'

And then again, ingratiatingly, while she groaned with exertion – for they were fighting all along – 'What was it you wanted to know, my love?

'Oh! I've been as true to you as steel! Boo!'

All sorts of things mixed up. '*You*, a father to those two? Ha-ha-ha! You must be crazy! Then I would really have been down on my luck! Yes, yes, yes, you are their father, can't you understand a joke? Well? Just a joke, ha-ha-ha! Ha-ha-ha!'

She laughed in a way that made the joke somewhat dubious.

'So! You imagine you'll get to know who is – the father, don't you? Oh no! You can break every bone in my body, but – *no!* It's not you, in any case !

'Yeah! Kill me! Beat me! Kill me! Beat me. Kill... Oh, sure, sure, it *is* you, it *is* you, please, it *is* you, of course, I'm telling you, it is you, so are you satisfied now? What are we talking about anyway? Say, what were you asking me about?'

And in between there was constantly that laughter – when he released his grip on her throat, when he gave up out of sheer weariness, when he thought he must've shaken her head off her neck, there was always that laughter, 'Ha-ha-ha! Ha-ha-ha! Ha-ha-ha! Ha-ha-ha!'

'Tell me the truth!'

He panted it out, though he had long ago given up hope of learning any truth from her. He had long ago noticed that she didn't even hear what he was saying, she only knew there was something he wanted to know and that she could drive him to desperation. That was enough – she triumphed. What was truth and lies to her? She no longer knew the difference between one and the other – if she had ever known it. What was important to her were much more primitive things – sensations, to awaken and feel sensations, awaken hatred and feel lust.

He knew long ago what her fight was about. Everything about her betrayed it, her face, her movements – the little catlike movements as she twisted and turned under him, brushing him with her breasts, while she scratched and bit or laughed and screamed, or made her voice loving and seductive, husky as a raven, smiling and hissing – oh, she was triumphant now. She was far beyond truth and lies and triumphed, but he would teach her.

'Tell me the truth!'

She writhed under him, as strong as a man, supple as a snake. She laughed and hissed. He might just as well have asked a viper or a moonstruck cat to tell the truth. But he wasn't going to give up. Wouldn't give up. Mustn't give up. Some vague thoughts sailed through his head. This was an important battle – it meant a lot. Meant – a lot. A battle about principles. He was fighting for something great – something – great – there the chair tipped over – the fight of thousands of years taken up again here, on a living-room floor among the skerries, an unceasing battle never fought to the finish ... a battle for something high ... something sacred.

Truth against lust.

Insight against intoxication.

He would teach her.

Ha! Man's battle for thousands of years. *Man* – truth, desire for truth. *Woman* – lust and intoxication and darkness.

He would teach her!

It flashed through his head: *for* light – *against* darkness – *for* truth – *against* lust and lies ... an ancient battle – he would wring the truth out of her.

He would show her.

Because this was a battle about *power*, about raw power.

He would show her ... even if he had to, had to... He would show her – who had the power – no, the truth – even if he had to crush every bone in...

But she didn't let herself be crushed. She writhed under him, strong as a man, supple as a snake.

'Ha-ha-ha!'

'Tell me the truth!'

'Kill me! Yeah! Kill me!'

He tightened his grip around her throat. He shook her,

clutching her in a state of insane agitation.

Ah! Some drawing-room comedy this had turned into! Some – drawing-room – comedy – this had...

Her body tensed up so she touched the ground only with her heels and the back of her head, the whites of her eyes showing under her eyelids. But her lips smiled. She moaned, she rattled, but in the half-turned-up glance he read hatred and lust, insane lust.

And suddenly he knew, like an explosion – it was no different with him.

'Bloody hell!'

Abominable. Abominable.

A wave of shame shot through him. He took his hands off her, as if he'd been burned, let her lie where she was, stood up and turned his back on her. He felt dizzy and nauseous. He stood for a moment, it wore off, and he dropped into a chair. She was still lying on the floor, heaving restlessly, and he could see she was waiting. He saw the gleam in her eyes come and go for a while still.

Then she sat up. She remained on the floor without a word and without a glance at him, all hunched up – she appeared curiously small and ruffled, like a hen that had been run over.

He looked at her, remembered how she used to look and thought for a moment, What have I done?

Then she began to cry, in loud, heaving fits. It was unbearable, like hearing a child cry. Desperate, he mumbled, 'No, no!' He had the idea he must go and help Eve, who was sitting over there crying, but now it had really become as in a dream, and he couldn't budge.

It was abominable.

Outside it was raining hard, in uneven spells, which now and then rose to a drumfire against the windowpanes; rising still more, it became a steady pressure of sound, before dropping off again, as if the weather were catching its breath. Her sobs seemed to rise and fall in time with the rain. But that must be something he imagined.

She had stopped crying – or was it the rain that had halted? No, there the rain began once more; but she had stopped crying.

She simply hunched up where she sat.

How quiet it had become. Nothing but the wind and the rain outside, a peaceful sound. She sat so quietly – sat looking straight ahead of her. Her eyes had acquired a new expression. He didn't recognize it. She whispered something. What was she saying?

'Abominable. Abominable.'

The next moment she jumped up, ran past him, incredibly fast, and was gone – he felt the draft and heard the door slamming. What was it? Something in her eyes – he leaped up and took off after her.

She was already through the hall. The front door stood open after her, it kept banging in the wind. One jump and he was outside.

Pitch-dark and pouring rain. He was blind and confused for a second, then he had a glimpse of her running down the path to the pier. She showed white against the dark evening, he could make out the outline of her shoulders quite clearly and realized she'd taken the white Spanish shawl which used to hang in the hall and thrown it around herself. It was this that made her visible.

She ran down the path, fast and nimbly, like an animal. Now and then she spread her shawl to keep her balance, it fluttered about her like a pair of large white wings. He ran after as fast as he could, slipped and fell and got covered in dirt – no matter, he was soaking wet anyway, the rain felt like a weight on his shoulders and back. He was catching up with her, catching up – but there she stood at the edge of the pier. She flung the shawl back with a single grand gesture – then she was gone; but he, only a few steps behind her, threw off his jacket, squatted down at the end of the pier, tore off his shoes in two jerks and stared down – there! The water, black as night, washed angrily against the pillars of the jetty, he glimpsed her head in the light from a crest of foam right outside the pier. He plunged in, swallowed some water right away, felt the seawater like ice against his body, came up again, looked about him, swallowed a bit of water again – she was nowhere to be seen.

There she was, two metres away, but instantly gone; two strokes, and he was there and dived – then he had her.

'Agnete!'

She offered no resistance, her eyes were closed, he couldn't tell whether she was still conscious. They had drifted a good distance out and were drifting farther out as he struggled with her. How stupid he had never learned lifesaving.

Thank goodness for the neighbour's bathing hut, which they had cursed many a time, but now it was their salvation; they drifted directly towards it.

He managed to tow her up to the bathing hut stairway. It was steep and slippery. She was conscious, her eyes were open, but she had no strength and hung like a rag over his shoulders. He got himself up, step by step, but had to sit straight down on the pier afterwards. She was lying on her back across his knees without stirring, and when he bent down over her he noticed that her eyes were closed again. Her hair clung to her face in wisps, sticky and wet like seaweed; he brushed it aside with his hand. He got to his feet with her in his arms, remembered there was a path along the shore here and found it with his foot. It was narrow and quite slick from the rain, he slipped a couple of times and twisted his ankle, but without falling. She hung dead and heavy in his arms. He managed to carry her up the path and into the house, pushed the door to the living room open with his elbow, stepped across the floor and laid her on the sofa, then fell on the floor himself. When he picked himself up shortly afterwards and saw that the door was wide open, he dragged himself out and shut it. He remained standing out there a few moments, leaning against the wall.

When he came in again she was conscious. She had raised herself on her elbow and was looking in the direction of the door. He walked over and sat down on a chair beside the sofa; she wanted to say something, but suddenly her teeth started chattering so she couldn't talk. He brought the whisky bottle and the beer glass from the table at the fireplace, poured a stiff drink and had her swallow it. She let him do it, quiet and obedient as a child. He put some wood in the fireplace – it flared up – undressed her, rubbed her down with a bathrobe until she was burning hot, and sat her down in a chair before the fire. The yellow pine-pitch flames flickered over her golden brown skin.

He lifted her up and carried her to bed.

She lay still looking at him, her eyes shiny and her cheeks roseate with fever. Her hair had begun to dry, it rose in profusion around her head. Actually, she looked healthier and better than usual; but she did have some disfiguring blue spots on her throat.

Shaken by shivering, he noticed that his clothes hung on him like a cold slime. He took a stiff drink of whisky himself, for some reason or other he almost felt he'd earned it. Then he undressed, rubbed himself warm, got into his pyjamas, and felt the good warmth of dry clothes against his skin as he went around locking up and putting out the fire. It was still raining. The wind came in heavy gusts, almost like underground booms, the house shuddered every time.

She wasn't yet asleep when he came in and got into bed – she lay still and followed him with large, quiet eyes. He couldn't decide what they contained.

'How are you feeling? Better?'

She nodded.

Getting into bed, he was busy a moment arranging the blanket. When he turned toward her, she was quietly asleep, like a child, her head resting on her arm.

He lay there looking at the ceiling for a while. His head was empty and his body strangely absent. He didn't turn out the light. He'd better keep it burning tonight. He lay like this awhile. A fly was walking on the ceiling, he followed it with his eyes. It took a turn down to the bedside lamp, close enough to get its legs slightly burned. Then, bzzz – it flew up to the ceiling again and went on strolling on the white paint.

He opened his eyes. He must have slept, he still felt immersed in sleep, with only his head above the surface. He knew there was something he should have thought through, something that couldn't wait. Something or other he couldn't bear thinking about, which he had to think about, which could never be solved but which had to be solved immediately. His thoughts began to slide, he barely managed to reach out his hand and extinguish the lamp.

...which had to be solved...

...his head above the surface...

He felt he was sinking.

He got up, went over to the window and stood there awhile, leaning against the high windowsill. It was a fine, clear sunny day. Down in the field just beyond the river, a man was breaking in a big black stallion.

The man down there was letting the stallion make voltes. The big black stallion was running in circles.

It was he himself who was working with the stallion down there.

But suddenly there was some trouble with the reins, they wound themselves around his legs and he fell down. The stallion turned toward him, came up to him, big and black, sniffed at him– and then it turned about, unbearably slowly, in slow-motion cinema, and *struck*. A loud, dry cracking sound came from the bones that were broken.

He stood by the window, watching and feeling small. And the stallion turned about again, infinitely slowly, in slow-motion cinema, and sniffed at him. Then it began to turn slowly about again. And he lay down there, entangled in the reins, waiting, and he stood by the window up here watching, and he lay there waiting and he stood here watching, and he lay waiting and he stood watching, and he tried to edge his way toward the stallion, a bit closer, a bit closer, so the blow wouldn't be so crushing, and he stood and watched all this and cried in utmost dread: 'Shoot him! Fetch a gun and shoot him!' But behind him, above him, at a man's height, he heard a calm, slow voice: 'It's no use. Before we can get the gun, he'll be dead.'

And the big black stallion turned slowly, slowly around, and he tried to edge his way closer, slowly, slowly ... hey! ... then that loud, dry sound of bones cracking.

It was in the middle of the night and completely dark. It was still blowing hard and unevenly, and – oh yes, it was raining. He lay for a while looking out into the darkness. He was awake. It was good to be awake.

Odd. After all, he had never seen that incident with the man and the stallion, only heard about it in the servants' quarters.

He woke up once more. Someone had called him. He straightened up and looked about him. All was still. She was sleeping – she had turned on her other side and was facing him, but otherwise she was lying in the same position as in the evening.

A glimmer of dawn could just be made out through the windowpanes.

Had he misheard?

He got quietly out of bed, groped his way through the dark room, found the door and groped his way further. He remained standing on the open veranda facing east. Not a soul was to be seen or heard. Everything was deathly still, not a puff of wind, not a ripple of a wave, only the soft, sucking sound of the ground swell, which made the stillness even more audible. The rain had stopped, most of the sky was clear. It was semi-dark, neither night nor day.

He remained standing there looking out.

He couldn't make out the details of the landscape below and before him. The bay lay like a dark abyss down below, and the whole moor before him, the whole earth, was a single dark mass which ended in a jet-black jagged crest against the sky.

You could dimly perceive the dawn as a faint sheen of mother-of-pearl against the black crest.

High up in that thin crystalline sphere of the heavens stood a large cloud, pure and blue, sublime as a deity on the top side, heavy and clotted and bloody on the underside.

It must've been such a cloud people thought augured war in the old days, at a time when they thought that everything existed for the sake of humankind.

Still a little higher up a star was shining, one so much larger than the other stars that it seemed to be alone in the entire firmament. He wondered whether it was Venus, the morning star, but didn't know.

He dropped his eyes again, past the star, past the austere, bloody cloud down to the jet-black forest. He felt the first soft breath of the morning breeze and heard the first note from an early bird. It made everything even bigger and calmer and more austere.

He stood for a while staring outward, tiny and unnoticed in the midst of the great, austere vastness, which stared back at him, without sympathy, without offering solace, without seeing.

He heard the door behind him creak; it was Agnete, strangely small and childish in her nightgown and with bare feet. Her eyes were narrow, she was not yet fully awake.

She blinked and looked at him. 'I woke up. Did you call me?'

He shook his head. 'No, I didn't call you. Go back to bed.

'It's cold out here,' he added, to soften his words.

She quietly went in again and closed the door after her.

It had grown lighter. He could dimly make out the pier now. Something was lying down there – of course, his jacket, the shawl, his shoes. He made his way down the soft, wet path on his bare feet. The gravel hurt, and the ground gave him the cold, wet and unaccustomed feeling he'd so often had as a boy during the first days of spring, when he ran around barefoot – a fresh and fine sensation none the less – a poor boy's only privilege. He had begged to be allowed to walk barefoot as a boy.

The pieces of clothing down on the pier had once been clothes, that was about all you could say. The shawl looked as if it had lain underground for years. The jacket was a sorry sight, a dirty washrag. He'd been particularly fond of that suit, and had stolen a glance into the plate glass windows when he passed by.

He picked up the wet rags and carried them up.

Once again he remained standing on the veranda, staring out into space in search of an answer, but found none. No one had called him.

He remembered he'd sent her back without an answer and went in.

She lay awake when he came in. Staring straight ahead of her – he could make out her face, but not the expression of her eyes.

Just to say something, he said, 'I was down at the pier and picked up our clothes.'

'Yes?'

'They've seen their best days.'

'They have? When we've ironed and pressed them a bit, you'll see.'

They talked in subdued tones for a while, about little things.

'Do you have a headache?'

'Yes, a little.'

'Let me feel your pulse.'

He did.

'OK. It's normal. Then the whole thing will pass,' he said, knowing that something had to be kept at bay, kept at bay, kept at bay, or it would all begin afresh.

Suddenly she said, 'Are you very much in love with her?'

'Well, yes. I am. But she's left me.' He noticed he could say it calmly and naturally. How was it possible to be so sincere! But – no doubt is was because nothing else was worth the effort any longer.

He said, 'Agnete – have you always hated me?'

She turned her face toward him. He thought he could sense that she was astonished.

'Hated you? Me?'

Then it seemed she recalled something. 'No. At least, I don't think so. No – not always – not even lately. But quite often perhaps, lately.'

She waited a moment. 'I haven't been very happy lately.'

She waited a moment again. 'I suppose I couldn't forgive you that I loved someone else,' she said.

How still it was out there. Not a puff of wind could be heard. The storm had blown over.

It was still in here also. They talked quietly together.

Something had to be kept at bay.

Talk a little about small things.

He told her the true story of the cigar and the letter.

She turned toward him. 'Oh, if only you'd told me before. For I almost believe *that* was what hurt me the most – that you were sitting there laughing at me. If only you'd told me. But no – I guess you didn't have the time.'

It had grown lighter. He could make out her eyes. They had a faraway look.

He observed those eyes, which he'd seen so often. He couldn't decipher them. Were they loving? No. Scared? No. They seemed to be beyond all that, in a way. Mute, completely resigned.

What had she hoped would come of that conversation yesterday, which destroyed so much? He didn't know. Would probably never know.

Suddenly her eyes became clear and fully present. She looked searchingly at him. 'Listen, what I said yesterday – '

He became scared to death. He didn't know exactly what she meant to say, but knew that whatever she said now, it was a lie. And he couldn't bear to hear her lie. Not now.

'Let's talk about it some other time,' he said quickly.

'But you don't believe it, do you?'

'No, no. But let's not talk about it now.'

*

She was asleep again. He lay still, staring at the ceiling.

Never again. That was likely to be the only certainty to emerge from these days.

Never again would he look at the children as before. Never again watch for familiar features without fear.

Never again.

Odd that he had never doubted before. After all, every husband ought to doubt, how could he help it? Even if he lived with his wife on a desert island. There's always a shipping lane leading to desert islands.

Had he never doubted before?

Didn't know. Didn't know.

Never again.

Never again.

The sun was rising out there.

He woke up from her watching him. So he had gone to sleep at last, after all.

It was broad daylight.

'Well, how are you doing?' he asked.

'I think better, thank you. I'm just very tired.'

'It will pass.'

He suddenly felt that he was very hungry – he hadn't had a bite to eat since lunch yesterday. She hadn't either. He got up, went to the kitchen and prepared breakfast – lighted the fire, made coffee, fried eggs, toasted bread, prepared a large tray and carried it in. It looked quite cosy.

She didn't eat much. 'Well, how are you doing?'

'Much better, thanks. I think I'll be spared getting a cold.'

'That's great.'

They got up. Yesterday's clothes were sopping wet, that couldn't be helped. Fortunately they had something else in the closet, she several dresses of an older vintage, he an old sports suit for bad weather use.

They hung the wet clothes out to dry. It was clouding over – on and off there was a glimmer of sun, then it turned grey again. The clouds were scudding across the sky. End of August, end of summer. They got out their suitcases and began packing.

Agnete was usually very good at such things, but today she was slow. Occasionally she would stand bent over a suitcase for a long time without moving.

He pretended not to notice.

At long last they were finished. They closed and locked the suitcases, closed and locked the house.

She stopped to look about her for a while. 'It's a nice summer place.'

'Yes.'

He was looking out across the moor and the pine forest, out toward the blue ocean.

Between the tree trunks over there, you could make out Gunnerus' red house.

She noticed his glance.

They walked along side by side, in silence.

She dropped by the little house at Larsen's, delivered the keys and left a message. That was it.

The car stood where they had left it. He unlocked it and started the engine. She sat slightly hunched over beside him.

'Well, how are you doing?'

'Not badly, thanks.'

'Are you cold?'

'A little, perhaps.'

'When the engine has been going a while, it'll get better.'

He started, turned onto the road and accelerated. Although there was no reason to accelerate, no one was waiting for him.

He accelerated some more.

The road, telephone poles, rail fences, guard stones, stubble fields, grain on the pole, red and white buildings, people on the steps...

Everything looked fresher after the rain.

The landscape looked exactly like a quiet, peaceful inland hamlet. But the trees along the road were low and had their crowns bent northeast. Persistent cold winds from the ocean throughout all the previous years had seen to that. The ocean itself lay hidden behind the horizon.

The wind had caused some leaves to fall in the course of the night.

But Per looked like him. That he had heard often. Had heard it so often that...

In fact, he thought so himself. There was something about the eyes, the eyebrows – wasn't that him?

They had said he looked like him.

Who had said it?

His friends.

...all your friends...

...all your friends...

That was a lie, at least.

On the other hand – could he acquit any one?

How absurd – he couldn't.

Anything could be expected from each one of his so-called friends. For example, to be carrying on an affair with Agnete, not without consequences, at the same time as they were on friendly terms with him, drank his whisky, smoked his cigars, and slapped him on the shoulder and said, 'By Jove, that boy looks so much like you that...'

Wasn't there something called *Lifestyle in Bangkok*?

That was life Bangkok-style.

A fine state of affairs. A fine brood.

And his having so often heard that the boy looked like him, that was ... that was...

Little by little, Agnete felt better – she straightened up in her seat and looked at the landscape fleeing backward in the direction of Hankø.

'It's really quite pretty here, don't you think?'

217

'Oh, so-so.'

She opened her handbag, took out her compact and powdered her nose.

'You know – when I look around now and think of yesterday evening, I can't believe it. It seems to me like a dream. It must've been the storm that made us so beside ourselves. Don't you think so?'

'Maybe.'

Suddenly he felt there were no walls between him and her. He understood her as well as he understood himself. As he understood a small segment of himself... He could see straight through her, as through a glass of water.

There were two things she wanted yesterday. To defeat him, conquer him – and get even. But the two things tripped each other up, and she was tripped up by both.

And now she was in full swing *forgetting*. It appeared to her like a dream. And why? Not only because she had made a mess of things, but because what she'd said and done was in such direct conflict with what she thought a *lady* ought to say and do. Alas – under a slightly too strong pressure, her shell had been broken and terrible things had surged up from the depths of herself, but she didn't *understand* what came surging up, and now, afterwards, she was just appalled, and busy building the shell firmly around herself again, forgetting, pushing aside, turning her head away. All her warmth and passion, all her *worth* was down there, and it was that which bobbed up for a moment, in a distorted and unpleasant form, to be sure. She couldn't understand that.

She was still rather surprised at the thought of yesterday – was curious as well as afraid and appalled.

It would wear off quickly if she didn't receive help. She would forget all the important things and only remember the unimportant ones, one or two things which offended all too embarrassingly against the rules of good form – oh God, what did I say!

He ought to help her now. He knew he ought to help her. But he was stuck as if in a dream and couldn't.

Anyway, did he *understand* her? Did he even understand himself? She ought to be helped now. But did he understand himself?

'Well, how are you doing?'

'Much better, thanks.'

The road became wider, the houses huddled together like a flock of hens, they smelled the stench of cellulose as they drove through Moss.

But, in fact, he thought so himself. The eyes, the eyebrows –

Ho-ho! He who wished to see something, saw it. And besides – likeness, what did that mean? What about all the kings who little by little came to look like the peoples among which they lived? It wasn't at all necessary to imagine secretly employed lovers in the royal household. Enviromnent, imitation...

Children always imitated their parents – their so-called parents – in regard to facial expressions, movements – and yes, their feelings, which were influenced by the facial expressions and, in turn, influenced those expressions and, along with that, the features.

That was how heredity came about.

The road, rail fences, guard stones, trees. The telephone poles raced past. Past is past, is past, is past...

But they had never said that Eva looked like him. Eva was so feminine, small though she was. Everyone said she took after her mother.

So there one might rather be inclined to believe that everything was in order?

Stop, stop. Sometimes I gain nothing, and at other times I gain twice as much.

No. Zero was and remained zero.

And as far as Eva was concerned...

Was it he who had never been in doubt?

Agnete was so fond of Eva.

As for Eva...

All at once he knew that, as far as Eva was concerned, he'd been in doubt for a long time.

'Well, how are you doing?'

'All right, thanks.'

Around half-past two he pulled up in front of the entrance door.

She had become weaker again.

He helped her out, helped her up the stairs, supported her as she opened the front door. She leaned heavily against him.

They saw nobody in the living room at first. Then the maid came.

'Where are...'

He checked himself. But Anna answered anyway. 'Both the children are in the Frogner Park with Marie. They will be home around half-past three.'

Pause.

'Well, how do you feel now? You are rather pale. Let me take your pulse.'

'Knut,' she said softly. 'We must – I must...'

But he didn't dare.

'We have various things to discuss,' he said, 'but those things won't run away from us. And I have quite a lot to take care of right now – I'll call later this afternoon to hear how you're doing. You should go to bed, my dear, you really look tired.'

'So you'll call this afternoon?' she said.

'Definitely.'

Her humility was the worst part of it. Agnete humble, even grovelling – it was just too awful.

Running down the stairs, he mumbled, 'It's just too awful ... too awful.'

Journey's End

A few days went by which seemed hazy to him afterwards. They were quiet days, in a way. Nothing happened, or nothing essential anyway. As far as he knew. That is, now and then it was rather difficult to know whether anything had happened, or whether he'd just thought it or dreamed it.

He mostly stayed in his rooms. He took long trips there, settling things with himself.

Seven steps forward and seven steps back. That made fourteen steps in – let's see – eight seconds. That made one hundred and five steps a minute – it was an advantage to be good at mental arithmetic, a great advantage. That came to six thousand three hundred steps an hour, accordingly sixty-three thousand steps in ten hours. And he could easily walk ten hours a day when he had nothing else to do, nothing else at all to do. It amounted to roughly fifty kilometres a day. How far was it around the equator? He thought he'd heard something like forty thousand kilometres. How long would he have to walk back and forth here before he'd walked in a circle around the earth?

No, no, no, out of this. Out of this. Out of it. Out, out, out of it. What was she, really – a silly little goose, overrated by herself and everyone else because she was good-looking. Courage? Backbone? Bravery? Nonsense. An attractive girl. That was a fact. The rest was something you acquired a reputation for when you were attractive.

And extremely spoiled, like all attractive girls.

Away with you. And come into my heart, all you brave, worn-out, tired, sad, poor, down-and-out girls, who have faced defeat and humiliations a hundred times – who have lain quietly in your horrible rented rooms, crying and crying, abandoned by all, forgotten by all, loved by no one – trampled on, crushed – and who have got to your feet again, wiped your tears, faced your humiliation and gone forward, silent, tired, threadbare, in inexpensive, well-kept clothes – but greeting life with a smile and with a wiser face every time –

Away with you!

He made a movement, as if chasing away a fly.

So much for that.

Someone came up the stairs. What if it were her?

Hello, Vera.

She doesn't answer right away, just stands there looking at him. Then she says, You won't drop me, will you?

No.

Never?

Never.

Whatever happens?

Whatever happens.

Quiet.

Will you remember this moment?

Yes. As long as I live.

The steps went past, they weren't for him. He stood alone in an empty room and looked out on an empty street.

Well. So here he was, hoping for a miracle despite everything. It really was about time he knew: there would be no more miracles in his life.

He had spoken with Agnete by telephone a couple of times – they hadn't said very much to one another, he'd explained he needed a bit of time. And he hadn't been able to ask her about what he was thinking of all the time – whether the maid wouldn't drop by with the children sometime.

The thought of the children tormented him much worse than before. And strangely enough, not because of what Agnete had told him down at Hankø. That was just stuck in him, like a stone, something he couldn't touch. No, he was simply thinking about the children. And dreaming about them. He pictured them, or he heard them. They stood in the dark calling him.

One evening he came to his senses. He was together with Mrs Gunnerus; he'd spent several hours with her. He had met her by chance in the street. Her husband was abroad, on a business trip that had become rather drawn out. He understood quite well what she wanted. And he remembered he had thought, Well, why not down there too?

Her name was Adelheid, and she insisted he call her Hedda.

They were sitting in a pub for the time being. She was just jabbering away.

Everything was a mush in that small three-cornered head of hers – love and sheets, pillow cases and wall paper, insults and stair cleaning, tea things and morning help. 'Just imagine, you too like cauliflower with shrimps! I love it. Just imagine, you really are a bit in love with me? Do you dare tell me once more? I ought to get furious with you!'

Suddenly she said, 'And Agnete who has joined the Oxford Movement!'

That was when he came to his senses.

Mrs Gunnerus was more than willing to talk.

Oh yes, Agnete had joined the Oxford Movement. It happened the day before yesterday, at a religious tea party. She was transformed and had come forward and confessed. Yes, no, nothing dreadful, of course – what could that have been anyway?

Here Mrs Gunnerus gave him a couple of quick glances.

But she had admitted doing an injustice to a young lady who had annoyed her. That lady had actually lost her job, the poor thing.

Mrs Gunnerus was getting herself into a tangle. It gradually became quite evident from her confusion and ardent denials that she had herself been a party to the letter sent to the beauty parlour.

He didn't exactly remember how he managed to get her

home. It happened quickly.

Pfui! he thought, as he walked back and forth in his own place again. It was himself he felt like spitting on.

He felt nauseated and weary.

He had one, and only one, desire: to be an old, very old man and able to travel to a place where there were only men. Scoundrels, cads, cowards, dunces, why not – but men. Yes, and then, at most, a few old women, women so old and withered that their wickedness only oozed out of them like hair on their facial warts – so old that they either had become human or were incapable of spinning intrigues about anything but their parson and eternal salvation.

And then perhaps a number of servant girls, as ugly as sin, dirty and sluttish, with all the defects and flaws of their sex, stupid, lazy, false, mendacious, girls you could entrust with the coarsest jobs of all and kick in the rear when they couldn't manage even that.

The following day Vera called.

They had dinner together and talked a little. No, not about anything special. She had asked him not to.

They didn't touch each other. It was as though they had become a couple of distant, quite good friends.

She didn't tell him she'd been fired.

His thoughts raced back and forth for quite some time afterwards.

He might be able to get her back now.

If he told her: I want to get divorced, I'm willing to do anything – to stay here with you, if you like, go to South America with you and begin a new life as a physician, if you like –

Begin a new life, well. *Could* he do that? Or was he too much bound by too many things?

Agnete –

She didn't bind him. He knew they'd had much together that was good. And it was only too obvious that she needed his help now. And he might be able to give it to her if...

Nevertheless he knew that there he was free. He could leave her, his peace of mind unruffled, if that was necessary. And he could meet her again later, when she was married, perhaps: Oh, Agnete, my dear, is it you?

One's lifelong habits –

They ran deep, he was tied to them, but he could let them go.

Work –

That was worse. Much of his self-respect, and much of what was decent in him, was bound up with his work. But *that* he would go on with, after all.

The children –

That was the worst. Agnete out of balance, given to religious hysteria. And the two children in her charge. A divorce would mean that she kept them.

It was a real hurdle. And he knew: that hurdle had been there all along. And he knew more: that hurdle he would never be able to clear.

One evening at this time he walked through the first floor of the Theatre Café. It was full of people as always, and he walked through the café from one end to the other without finding a vacant table. He was already on his way out again when it struck him: Didn't the lady sitting at the table over there remind him of something? He turned and went back.

There she sat, the lady he'd met on Drammensveien. He recognized her at once – the hat, the dress, the silver fox, the face with the dark eyes, there could be no doubt. But how he could have thought, for a single moment, that she was Helga, that was a riddle to him. There was a faint external likeness, that was all.

She was flirting with some fellow. She couldn't be even thirty years old.

That matter of age, by the way, he would have been clearly aware of already that first evening if he'd really thought it over.

He turned around again and walked out. The whole thing hadn't made any impression on him worth mentioning. In fact, he had known it for a long time.

Come to think of it – didn't he know something else too? Something dawned on him about a notice of a forthcoming marriage in some paper – Håkenrud and Helga – and wasn't it the case that Håkenrud lived in suburban Bærum, supporting himself by gardening, besides being a legal consultant and manager of the large tinsmith's business which his father had co-owned?

He must have heard all this ever so many years ago – or perhaps he'd dreamed it one of these nights. He didn't know for certain. For that matter, it was of no vital importance.

He met Vera a few more times. They chatted and felt at ease together. But there was a hurdle between them. Lately it was not only at night that the children called him. It seemed to him he could hear them in broad daylight.

During the last of these meetings she told him she would be changing jobs. An old friend of hers had provided her with an office job.

She sat a moment. 'You've seen him. You saw him at the Ingierstrand beach that first Sunday.'

She sat a moment again. 'His name is Andreas. He was the one my father was so angry with.'

Another pause. There was something which was difficult to say. At long last it came. 'He wants to marry me. Well, he has always wanted to, but... Oh, I don't know. I don't know, don't know... But...

'I know I need to feel secure. That's how weak I am.'

He hadn't said anything. She looked at him. 'Do you know – I despise myself. I feel I'm deep, deep down. All others – *all*, you understand – are very, very much higher up. But in a way – can you understand? – it's *good* to despise yourself, to be deep, deep down. Do you know, I can feel almost happy there. And at the same time it's almost unbearable. Sometimes I wish I could die.'

Afterwards he recalled something she said a little later: 'It has been very painful, much of this.

'But I don't know. I have a feeling I take it differently – than you. I'm more superficial, perhaps. I don't know.

'There's one thing I can never forget – that we're only a small part of something else which is much larger, and which takes its course, and much of what happens to many others is so much worse than what is happening to us.

'Even I have seen so much that's far worse.

'So I somehow can't get altogether absorbed by the thought of how badly off I am. Because, actually, I'm not at all badly off. But I'm superficial, I know.'

They said a quiet goodbye – two friends, each about to set out on a journey apart from the other.

So much for that.

When he was by himself again, he noticed it was quite difficult all the same.

If she had gone to Ramstad, he knew it wouldn't have been the end of the matter. He would've had to wait – if only so he could tell her sooner or later, go to hell!

Now it was different. Sometime in the future they could meet perhaps and talk together, smile a bit together. A pale friendship.

That, he felt, was an intolerable thought, worse than anything.

He told himself, it will pass. You've experienced such things before.

He had not experienced such things before. And if he knew it would pass, that was no comfort. No, because at the same time he knew one thing, one sole thing: this, even this pain, had been *life*. And that it would pass, that even the pain would pass, that was death.

Oh, it would pass all right.

The next morning he went down to his broker and asked for a final settlement. It had just occurred to him. But he might as well get it done.

The broker looked at him, not knowing what to think.

To quit now, when everything was going so nicely? Goodness gracious, the world was going straight to hell, after all. And now that Holland would have to abandon the gold standard fairly soon...

He had earned slightly above twelve thousand kroner in these couple of years, without lifting a finger.

He deposited the last portion of the sum in his account. He didn't know what to do with this money – he only knew it was not his property.

So much for that.

Afterwards he went to pack and to tidy up his place. When he was through, he stopped to look out upon the street, without seeing anything. Oh yes, it was raining. It had apparently been raining for several days already.

He happened to glance at a little spot on the windowsill. It was a dead mosquito. It lay on its back, with its legs extended at symmetrical angles. It looked like a solved problem in geometry.

*

He walked down the street in the autumn rain.

Was he through now?

Was he finished with it?

He didn't know.

Had he found any values on this expedition?

Oh...

Had any of his previous values passed the test?

Not many, as far as he could see.

Was he through with *her*?

He didn't know.

Didn't know, didn't know...

He knew only one thing: being grand was over for a while. It didn't work. For some reason or other it didn't work.

He felt completely empty. Empty and light, like a blown

egg. He knew that this emptiness would give way to other things – severe reactions would come, he could already feel their pulse in his mind. But now he was just empty and light. And he felt this emptiness like something clean – after his sojourn in a world of slime and blood, screams and moans.

Empty and clean.

He looked forward to dry, hard work.

He probably ought to put a notice in the paper:

> Dr Knut Holmen
> *ear, nose and throat*
> has resumed his practice.

That suited him fine. In a few days the hunting season would begin, and he could stand in for Strand. He himself had already had his vacation, of course.

And then it remained to return home. He could picture it to himself. It would all go quite nicely to start with. Later, well...

No. It was and always would be a mistake when old anxiety neurotics thought they could snatch a new happiness, a new confidence, a new youth, a new mission in life. New wine in old bottles...

The type of people who were inoculated with fear from childhood on wanted to, and had to, live behind their constrictive fences if they were to feel relatively safe. If such people were by accident let out into the open, there was no end to their misery and fear, and no peace to be had until they had managed to get back behind that safe fence again at full gallop.

The best thing was to stay in one's stall.

Who could otherwise foresee the consequences?

Oh I'm free – help, help!

Yes, he had known, during these days, what it would mean for someone like him to be a free man.

Arms stretched out of the dark for him from all sides. Hands reached him and clung to him.

He could wriggle a bit, he could squirm. To that extent he was a free man.

Would there ever be a chance of creating a new race, one that was not plagued by nightmarish fear?

Per and Eva.

There was no fear in them yet – that much he'd seen in their eyes when they came running toward him. He remembered himself as far back as three years old, and knew that *he* also had run to meet his parents – when he thought they wanted him to, perhaps also because he couldn't help it; but never without fear. He hadn't seen his own eyes then, of course, but he knew how they must've looked, he could picture the glint of fear, of *flight*, in the corner of his eye, even at the moment, or rather precisely at the moment when he came rushing toward his father or mother. It was worse, to be sure, where his mother was concerned, though – his father was often so melancholy and mustn't be disturbed. Per didn't yet have that glint, and Eva not at all. And he felt it was his duty, almost his only duty, to protect the two of them from that fear. They were small and defenceless and left in his charge. Otherwise, in all other matters, he felt open to blame. That is, he couldn't know in advance, of course, but if someone came to him and said, egoist, swindler, charlatan, he would quietly examine the accusation; perhaps he wouldn't even need to. On this one point he knew he was all right. He knew of a quite definite thing he himself had suffered under, an early emotional split between hope and fear, love and hate, and he thought: there he could offer these children a better start than he himself had had. He knew that, in this one feeling, he was authentic, without an eye to his own advantage. Accordingly, it was probably there his egoism and vanity were hiding. In time, most likely, it was precisely this authentic and unselfish aspect that would slowly and imperceptibly change into smugness, tyranny and coercion. Well. If only the right person would then come and knock him down!

And what if he succeeded in making the two of them into

free, courageous individuals? And Per turned twenty and had to take up the battle in a society that, in the meantime, had perhaps become even worse? Where freedom was prohibited and thinking punishable, and where you ended up in a concentration camp if you loved a woman who was unable to present a baptismal certificate for all her grandparents?

He knew there were still many things he wasn't clear about, he was still walking in the dark in more ways than one. His thoughts came like nocturnal puffs of wind, some cold, others milder, but he didn't know where they came from, or where they were going.

It was raining hard, he was soaking wet. His legs carried him home mechanically.

When he got home...

Per would come rushing at him, he knew that much.

'Oh, Daddy, where have you been all this time?'

'I have been on a journey. A long journey.'

'And where did you go on your journey?'

'In circles, I suppose. Yes, in a large circle, I believe.'

No, not only in circles, he thought.

CAMILLA COLLETT

The District Governor's Daughters

(translated by Kirsten Seaver)

Written in 1854-55 and translated after 140 years into English, this is the one and only novel written by a daughter of one of Norway's best-known literary families. Camilla Collett had felt her creativity stifled and her literary ambitions thwarted by society's conventional expectations of what a woman could properly achieve; it was not until she was a widow of 42 that she could finally finish her novel, which she called 'my life's long-suppressed scream'.

In an intricate study of relationships, the novel creates a bourgeois society reminiscent of Jane Austen, in which marriage is the only respectable career for a woman. Sophie, the youngest of four daughters of a cynical and disappointed mother, struggles against society's precepts and her own conditioning to be allowed to make an independent choice; but all her surroundings can offer her by way of models are disillusioned wives, lonely spinsters or crazed old maids.

'One does not know which to admire more, the strength and variety of her characterization, the picture of provincial life in a small and remote community, the descriptions of nature with the sudden seasonal changes or the economical power of the narration .... Most powerful is the portrait of Sophie herself, a character worthy to stand beside Cathy Earnshaw in *Wuthering Heights*, published seven years before *The District Governor's Daughters*.' *London Magazine*

ISBN 978 1 870041 17 1
UK £10.95
(paperback, 312 pages)

AMALIE SKRAM

Lucie

(translated by Judith Hanson and Katherine Messick)

This ground-breaking novel from 1888 tells the story of the misalliance between Lucie, a viviacious and beautiful dancing girl from Tivoli, and Theodor Gerner, a respectable lawyer from the strait-laced middle-class society of nineteenth-century Norway. Having first kept her as a mistress, Gerner is so captivated by Lucie's charms that he marries her, only to discover that his project to turn her into a proper and demure housewife is continually frustrated by her irrepressible sensuality and lack of fine breeding. What made her alluring as a mistress makes her unacceptable as a wife. His attempts to govern Lucie's behaviour develop gradually into a harsh tyranny against which she rebels in a manner which brings misery and despair to both.

Amalie Skram, a contemporary of Ibsen, expresses the same criticism of repressive social mores and hypocrisy here as he does in plays like *A Doll's House* and *Ghosts*, although in a deeply personal way. In this novel, as in her other work, she makes an impassioned statement on the double standard, contributing to the great debate about sexual morality which engaged many Scandinavian writers in the late nineteenth century. She also presents a closely-observed realistic depiction of a lively cross-section of Kristiania society from the turn of the century, ranging from high-society fancy-dress parties and country cottages to dark and dingy tenements reeking of poverty

ISBN 978 1 870041 48 5
UK £8.95
(paperback, 168 pages)

ARNE GARBORG

The Making of Daniel Braut

(translated by Marie Wells)

Daniel Braut, the protagonist of Arne Garborg's ground-breaking 1883 novel, is an impressionable boy whose one ambition is to rise above the poverty of his farming background in western Norway. Regarded by others as gifted, he sees education as the path to becoming part of the establishment. However, his long struggle is not only hampered by his desperate poverty, his unrealistic dreams and his provincialism, but takes a terrible toll on his personality. He is a mirror of his age, of a Norway slowly emerging from a predominantly peasant society into a modern urban culture, and of the religious, political and social upheavals of the late nineteenth century.

Marked by a puritanical childhood in Jæren, a district and a mindset from which he early distanced himself, Arne Garborg (1851-1924) was a writer who was left rootless and in conflict with himself, always searching. His writing reflects his personal crises, but also the linguistic and intellectual development of a country struggling to free itself of foreign influence and religious bigotry, and assert its independence.

ISBN 978 1 870041 81 2
UK £9.95
(paperback, 245 pages)

KJELL ASKILDSEN

A Sudden Liberating Thought

(translated by Sverre Lyngstad)

Kjell Askildsen is widely regarded as the finest short-story writer in Norway today. His reputation, based primarily on his Kafkaesque accounts of alienated individuals in a hostile environment , has grown steadily since he made his debut in the 1950s, when his first book had the dubious honour of being publicly burned by his father, who objected to its frank presentation of sexuality. One translation into French invited comparisons with Beckett (whom Askildsen has translated into Norwegian).

This collection of stories brings together works from all stages of Kjell Askildsen's career. It includes an early experimental novella, *Surroundings* (1969), about the developing tensions between four people cut off on a small island, as well as short stories from various collections, such as *Stage Settings* (1966) and the highly acclaimed *Thomas F's Last Notes for the General Public* (1983). The stories relate the struggles of ordinary people with the trivialities and absurdities of everyday life, where loneliness and despair are held at bay by grim determination and flashes of biting black humour. A few words can have a vital significance, and what is not said can be full of meaning.

'one of the few European writers who are of truly major stature'
Paul Binding, *Babel Guide: Scandinavian Fiction*

ISBN 978 1 870041 84 3
UK £9.95
(paperback, 240 pages)

JOHAN BORGEN

The Scapegoat

(translated by Elixabeth Rokkan)

Johan Borgen (1902-79) was one of the most productive and committed of twentieth-century Norwegian authors; his work spans fifty years, and as well as being an acclaimed novelist and essayist, he was active throughout his life as a journalist, literary critic and cultural personality. His style was always elegant, his wit sometimes caustic; but behind the lightness of tone lies a serious preoccupation with mankind's struggles to discover its true identity.

His novel from 1959, *The Scapegoat*, takes as its central character a figure familiar from earlier works: the splintered personality, a man in search of his own authentic self. Matias Roos is literally split in two, into an observing 'I' and an experiencing 'he'; he embarks on a journey at the beginning of the novel which takes him back into his childhood, forward into the future, and into a strange limbo of parallel time. He is a man obsessed with frontiers, the borders between countries, between war and peace, present and past, self and other; a man guilty of an unspecified crime, searching for a way to atone. Reality and fantasy merge as the novel explores with hallucinatory power his struggles to derive meaning from experience.

ISBN 978 1 870041 21 8
UK £8.95
(paperback, 187 pages)

HANS BØRLI

We Own the Forests
and Other Poems

Parallel English and Norwegian text
(translated by Louis Muinzer)

Hans Børli (1918-89) was born and lived in the wooded county of
Hedmark in south-eastern Norway. His days seem to have been
divided into two separate parts: by day, he lived the physically
demanding life of a lumberjack, but by night he turned poet and spent
the still, dark hours writing. His days, however, were an enactment of
his poetry. Børli's verse is alive with his experiences of the Norwegian
forests – with the moods of sky and water, with the creatures that
moved in air and woodland, and with the trees themselves.

In a series of books beginning in 1945, he wrote more than eleven
hundred poems. They form a poetic record of a life reminiscent in
spirit, if not in form, of Walt Whitman's *Leaves of Grass*. This
collection can only suggest the scope and richness of the poet's life-in-
verse, but it includes many of his most admired poems. Sometimes
lonely or even mystical, the finest of these poems bit deep like the
blow of an axe.

ISBN 978 1 870041 61 5
UK £9.95
(paperback, 160 pages)

JENS BJØRNEBOE

Moment of Freedom
Powderhouse
The Silence

(translated by Esther Greenleaf Mürer)

The three volumes of Jens Bjørneboe's personal odyssey of investigation into the inhumanity of man range through the whole gamut of human destructiveness, from religious persecution to wars to colonial exploitation, in an effort to find an answer to the problem of the evil of mankind – and, equally unfathomable, the problem of goodness in mankind.

The trilogy marks the high point of outspokenness and originality of one of Norway's most controversial modern writers. Jens Bjørneboe was an author and polemicist of fierce energy and deep conviction, who throughout his career provoked and upset the establishment with his unrelenting attacks on some of its most sacred cows: a repressive school system, a hypocritical Christianity, an inhumane prison system, power-seeking politicians, corrupt police and depraved moral guardians. With these three books, Bjørneboe turned his attention to a more general problem: the evil inherent in the human race itself. Why, his narrators ask dispairingly, does man behave so callously to his fellow creatures?

Moment of Freedom: 217 pages, ISBN 978 1 870041 41 6,
Powderhouse: 201 pages, ISBN 978 1 870041 42 3
The Silence: 201 pages, ISBN 978 1 870041 45 4
UK £10.95 each (paperback)

ARNE GARBORG

The Making of Daniel Braut

(translated and with an introduction by Marie Wells)

Daniel Braut, the protagonist of Arne Garborg's ground-breaking 1883 novel, is an impressionable boy whose one ambition is to rise above the poverty of his farming background in western Norway. Regarded by others as gifted, he sees education as the path to becoming part of the establishment. However, his long struggle is not only hampered by his desperate poverty, his unrealistic dreams and his provincialism, but takes a terrible toll on his personality. He is a mirror of his age, of a Norway slowly emerging from a predominantly peasant society into a modern urban culture, and of the religious, political and social upheavals of the late nineteenth century.

Marked by a puritanical childhood in Jæren, a district and a mindset from which he early distanced himself, Arne Garborg (1851-1924) was a writer who was left rootless and in conflict with himself, always searching. His writing reflects his personal crises, but also the linguistic and intellectual development of a country struggling to free itself of foreign influence and religious bigotry, and assert its independence.

ISBN 978 1 870041 81 20
UK £9.95
(paperback, 256 pages)

Norvik Press
Classics of Norwegian Literature

A Fortnight Before the Frost is the second book in Norvik Press's distinct series of English translations of classics of Norwegian literature (following Arne Garborg's *The Making of Daniel Braut*, translated by Marie Wells), published within its long-running 'Series B: English translations of Scandinavian literature'. This new initiative, made possible by the support of NORLA (Norwegian Literature Abroad) and the Fritt Ord foundation in Norway, will facilitate the regular publication of translations of classic works which have been unjustly overlooked in the English-speaking world, often simply as a result of the lack of a reliable and accessible translation.

Future publications in the series will include:

> Jonas Lie: *The Family at Gilje* (1883, translated by Marie Wells), to be published in 2011.
> Ragnhild Jølsen: *Rikka Gan* (1904, translated by Katherine Hanson and Judith Messick), to be published in 2012.

Works by Johan Borgen and Alexander Kielland are under consideration for future publication. Some books already published by Norvik Press, including Camilla Collett's *The District Governor's Daughters* (translated by Kirsten Seaver) and Amalie Skram's *Lucie* (translated by Katherine Hanson and Judith Messick), will be incorporated into the series as it progresses.

For further information, or to inquire about subscriptions to this series, please contact:
Norvik Press, Department of Scandinavian Studies, University College London, Gower Street, London WC1E 6BT, England
or visit our website at www.norvikpress.com